THE VOYAGE TO PARNASSUS,

THE SIEGE OF NUMANTIA,

and

THE TREATY OF ALGIERS

By MIGUEL DE CERVANTES

Translated by GORDON WILLOUGHBY JAMES GYLL

A Digireads.com Book
Digireads.com Publishing

The Voyage to Parnassus, The Siege of Numantia, and The Treaty of Algiers
By Miguel de Cervantes
Translated by Gordon Willoughby James Gyll
ISBN 10: 1-4209-4972-1
ISBN 13: 978-1-4209-4972-8

Please visit *www.digireads.com*

CONTENTS

PREFACE.

The latest works of Cervantes were the genuine continuation and completion of Don Quixote; the Journey to Parnassus, which was published in 1614; and finally, the Romance of Persiles and Sigismunda, for which a few days previously to his death he wrote a dedication to the Conde de Lemos.

Cervantes displayed in his Voyage to Parnassus a peculiar talent, a work which cannot properly be ranked in any particular class of literary composition, but which, next to Don Quixote, is the most singular production of its extraordinary author. The chief object of the poem is to satirize false pretenders to the honour of the Spanish Parnassus who lived in Cervantes' age. A happy effusion of sportive humour, but so composed that it is difficult to say whether the bards cited are the subjects of ridicule or praise. To characterize true poetry according to his own poetic feelings, to manifest in a decided way his enthusiasm for the art even in his old age, and to hold up a mirror for the conviction of those who were only capable of making rhymes and inventing extravagances, seem to have been the objects which he had in view when he composed this satirical poem. It is divided into eight chapters, and the versification is in tercets, but which the translator has given in heroic blank verse, as most suitable to the subject. It is half comic and half serious. Mercury appears to Cervantes, who is represented as travelling to Parnassus in the most miserable condition, and the god salutes him with the title of the "Adam of poets." Mercury, after addressing to him many flattering compliments, conducts him to a ship entirely built of different kinds of verse, and which is intended to convey a cargo of Spanish poets to the kingdom of Apollo.

The description of the ship is an admirable comic allegory. Mercury shows him a list of the poets with whom Apollo wishes to become acquainted; and this list, owing to the problematical nature of its half-ironical and half-serious praise, has proved a stumbling block to commentators.

In the midst of the reading Cervantes suddenly drops the list. The poets are now described as crowding on board the ship in numbers as countless as drops of rain in a shower, or grains of sand on the sea-coast; and such a tumult ensues that, to save the ship from sinking by their pressure, the Syrens raise a furious storm. The storm subsides, and is succeeded by a shower of poets who fall from the skies.

One of the first who descends on the ship is Lope de Vega, on whom Cervantes seizes the opportunity of pronouncing an emphatic eulogium. One of the most beautiful pieces of verse written by Cervantes is his description of the goddess Poetry, whom he sees in all her glory in the kingdom of Apollo, and to this picture is added that of the goddess Vain-glory, who appears to the author in the form of a dream.

There is a description of a second storm, in which Neptune vainly endeavours to plunge poetasters to the bottom of the deep. Venus prevents them from sinking by changing them into gourds and leather flasks. At length a formal battle is fought between the real poets and one of the poetasters.

It is a poem *per se*, and it has no prototype. There is added to the poem a supplement in prose, in which it is thought that the poet indulged too freely in self-praise. But who will not pardon the proud feeling of conscious superiority which sustains genius from sinking beneath the pressure of misfortune? His country denied him recompense, and he appropriated to himself that glory which he truly merited.

It has been the object of the translator to render as literally as the language would allow the verses of this poem. Parts of it are dark and mysterious, and the translator has done his best to unravel the sense and infuse it into blank verse, without the aid of any literary person, and has tried to make it a mirror of the original. He hopes that the three pieces in this Volume may be found to be characterized by fidelity and grace.

The entire Works of Cervantes have now been given in an English dress, and have appeared for the first time in any translation, with the Galatea by the same Translator.

THE VOYAGE TO PARNASSUS.

The "Voyage to Parnassus," composed by Miguel de Cervantes Saavedra, dedicated to A. D. Rodrigo de Tapia, Knight of the Order of St. James, Son of Senior Don Pedro de Tapia, Judge of the Royal Council, Adviser to the Holy Office of the Supreme Inquisition.

I address to your Worship this Voyage made to Parnassus, which gainsays neither your flourishing age nor your laudable studious exercises. If your Worship accords it the acknowledgment which I anticipate from your noble condition, it will remain famous in the world, and my desires will be satisfied.

Miguel de Cervantes Saavedra.

PROLOGUE TO THE READER.

If perchance, trusty reader, thou art a poet, and I should transfer to thy hands (albeit sinful ones) this Voyage, and shouldst thou find thyself in the composition, and signalized amongst sterling poets, render thanks to Apollo for the favour I have conferred on thee.

Shouldst thou not recognise thyself there, still thou mayest give thanks, and may God have thee in His holy keeping.

THE VOYAGE TO PARNASSUS.

CHAPTER I.

A certain Corporal out of Italy,
A native of Perugia, as I learn,
With Grecian wit and Roman valour too,
Impelled by a most reverend caprice
To visit Mount Parnassus had desire;
To escape the sundry noises of a court,
On foot, and all alone, and gradually,
He reached a spot, and bought an ancient mule
Of a grey colour, and a stumbling pace.
This antique brute did seem to have no fear,
Adapted not the less for any charge;
Large in the bones, though somewhat weak in power,—
Eyesight indifferent, though his tail was large;
About the flanks contracted, but in the skin
Harder much than any shield could be,—
With instinct he was perfectly possessed,
And nothing whatsoever came amiss;
As he was in April, so in February.
The valiant poetaster on the mule

Came to Parnassus, and was of Apollo bright,
Made much of also; with a serene front
He told when back the poet came alone
Moneyless to his country, that which in flight
His fame transported from this to th' other pole.
I who toil ever and o'erwatch myself,
To make appearance that of a poet I boast
The grace which heaven has yet not deigned to give;
I had desired to the Estafette to send
My soul, or through the air deposit it
Upon the summit of Æta renowned,
Descrying from that place the beauteous
Stream of Aganippe, that by a leap
Moisten I might in its current my lips;
And of the liquor sweet and rich remain
Full to the utmost, and from thence start forth
Poet illustrious, or at least superb.
Then, more than a thousand inconveniences
Themselves presented, and desire remained
In the blossom—weak and very ignorant;
For in the stone which on my back I find
Fortune has heavily o'erweighted me,
I also read my ill-acquired hopes—
The many leagues of the eventful day
Demonstrate clearly to me how they can
The well-affectioned free-will distort,
If in that very instant not arrives
The smoke of due fame succour to supply,
Both short and easy the hard way to make.
To myself I said, if I should come to see
Myself upon the difficult height of the mount,
And on my brow a laurel's garland set
I should not envy Oponte's good word
Nor of the dead Galarza the sharp wit,
Mild in his hand with Rhadamanthus' tongue.
But as in error always one begins
Trusting to my desire to the road I gave
My feet, because I gave to the winds my head.
In fine upon the hips of destiny
Mounting to the Election, in the seat
I was determined the great voyage to achieve,
If this equitation should astound
Know who does not yet know, that this is done
Throughout the globe, not in Castile alone.
No one retains it, or excuse can give
For not oppressing the loins of the great beast,
Nor mortal traveller can its use refuse—
The beast sometimes is wont to go as light

As through the air an arrow or eagle flies,
Yet sometimes doth it wend with feet of lead.
Light ever, any beast in truth the charge
But of a poet for the carriage due
May bear, although of portmanteau bereft
A fact infallible that although a bard
Is heir to riches, when they are in his power,
No increase knows, to lose them he is sure.
To be the cause of this truth I contend
That thou, Apollo, mighty father, dost
In their designs thy own desire infuse,
And as thou neither mix them nor confound
Mean things with those of great activity,—
Or sink them in the sea of profit vile,
Whether they be in earnest or in jest,
Without profitable aspirations
Upon the convex system of the spheres.
Displaying in the hardy wrestling-place
The actions bold of Mars, or amidst flowers
Of Venus the more soft and amorous acts.
Deploring wars, or singing about love,
Life glides away as if in a sweet dream,
Or as time is wont with jugglers to pass.
Poets are fashioned similar to dough,
Sweet, pleasant, soft as leather pliable—
A friend to revelling in strange residences,
A poet more discreet governs himself
By his idle fancy, ever over-nice
Of lasting ignorance and contrivance full,
Absorbed in his chimeras, and admired
For his very actions, yet he ne'er succeeds
To attain a rich or honourable estate.
Readers continue in the literature
As shows the uneven, common, and coarse style,
That I am a poet of this awkward stamp,
In grey hairs a swan, in voice a rough
Black raven, without time, being competent
To polish of my genius the hard trunk.
When on the summit of my changeful wheel,
One moment there I ne'er can find myself,
For when I strive to mount I stand stock-still.
But then to ascertain if a lofty thought
Can promise also some happy success
With slow and measured pace I follow it.
Some wheaten bread with eight morsels of cheese
I lodge in my pockets,—my repository,
On the road serviceable, and the burden light
To the gods I said unto my humble cot,

To the gods, Madrid, to the gods, ye meads and fonts
Which nectar do distil, ambrosia rain—
To the gods, sufficient conversation
To entertain a breast pregnant with care
And numberless pretenders out of grace,
To the gods, a sight deceitful, yet pleasant,
Where were a brace of giants quite consumed
By lightning from the incensed Jupiter—
To the gods, the public theatres, esteemed
For the crass ignorance, I exalted see,
In a hundred thousand quoted nonsenses.
To the gods, St. Philip's spacious promenade,
Where the Turk's gallows is wont to fall or rise,
As I do read in Venice's gazette.
To the gods, the subtle hunger of some knight,
Who not to see me stand before thy gates
This day from my country, from myself I spring.
So by degrees the harbour I did reach,
To which the name of Carthage is affixed,
Sealed against winds and in security
To whose clear and significant renown,
Prostrate themselves, all harbours the sea bathes,
The sun discovers, and man navigates.
Upon the country then I bent my view
Smooth as the sea, which to my memory brought
Of the hero, Don John, the heroic deed
Whence with the exalted soldier's renown,
I with my valour and enflamed breast,
Humbly the victory did participate—
There with vexation and mortal despite
The haughty Ottoman his bravery saw
Trampled to pieces and reduced to nought—
With hopes encompassed, and quite bereft
Of fear. Immediately I a vessel sought
To put in practice my lofty intent,
When on the liquid azure-coloured main
I observed a vessel fitted with sail and oar,
Advance to take its station in the port.
No ship more gallant, takeable to sight,
Of all which Neptune's shoulders and broad back
Have e'er oppressed, nothing superior—
Such stately vessel never witnessed
The ocean stream, not in the Armada famed,
Which the revengeful Juno hurled below.
Nor was at the day of Vellocino famed
Argos, so well constructed and so proud,
With so much riches gaudily adorned.
When it into harbour sailed, the beauteous

Aurora through the portals of the East
In soft and amorous braids did sally forth.
Suddenly, a noise was wide diffused,
The royal galley salvos issuing,
Which did awaken, and stirred up the world.
The sounds of clarions did the bank so wide
Completely fill with luscious harmony,
And eke the pleased and cheerful populace.
The early hours did enter into day,
By whose light a distinction more clear
All saw the strange contents of the vast ship.
It heaved out anchors, mooring in the port,
A spacious skiff cut furrows on the sea
With melody, and cries and jocund sounds.
The mariners employ their proper art,
Covering the stern with carpeting, all such
As is of gold, the warp and weft of silk
The very thresholds on the shore abut.
From out the skiff emerged a cavalier,
Borne on the shoulders of four principals.
In whose bold carriage and gesture severe
Mercury's figure to the life I saw.
Messenger to the mythologic gods,
In whose quick figure and composedness,
With winged feet and the Caduceus,
Symbol of prudence and discretion,
I say,—I viewed the being—identical;
Who bore in charge deceitful embassies
From the high Colosseum to the Earth.
I saw him, and scarce he set his neatly wing'd
Feet on the sands, most truly fortunate
To find themselves traversed by steps divine.
Then I, revolving multitudes of things
In my imagination, quick fell down
Before those feet, beauteous for ornament.
The talking God did order me to rise;
And in some measured and resounding verse
In this wise to address me did commence:—
O Adam of the bards, Cervantes, O,—
What wallets and what garb is this, my friend?
Indicating ignorant discourses, too.
I, to his demand replying, said,
My lord, Parnassus-wise I go, and poor,
And with this neatness prosecute my way,
Then he to me—Mortality above
Cyllenian spirit art thou elevated,
Be all abundance, all honour on thee.
Thou provest thyself to be a son of Mars,

Veteran and valiant, as is indicated
By the hand you carry, crippled still, and maimed.
Well do I know that in the naval fight
Thou lost the movement of thy valorous left
Hand, for greater glory of the right—
This superhuman instinct I do know,
Thy breast conceals a rare inventor's prize,
Which Father Apollo not in vain imparts—
Thy works the very corners of the earth,
On Rosinante's crupper hoisted up,
Discover, and with envy move to war.
Pass on, inventor rare, further advance
With thy subtle design, and aid supply
To Delian Apollo, of vast weight—
Or ere the vulgar squadron comes to call
E'en more than twenty thousand seven months' old
Poets, whom so to be are much in doubt
The very roads and avenues are full
Of these *canaille*, who towards the mountain wend,
Unworthy quite to come within its shade.
Thyself with thy verses quickly arm, and set
Thyself in trim to follow out this path
With me, giving up thyself to the great works,
With me be sure a passage certain quite
You will enjoy without disturbance—nor
Procure what some provision are wont to call,
That you may realize the fact, I say,—
Enter now into my galley, and behold
Things that may astonish and reassure.
I who thought all a mere delusion,
Advanced quick into the beauteous ship,
And witnessed what caused admiration.
From keel to the round top, O extraordinary!
The ship with verse was wholly fabricated,
Without admission of a line of prose.
The decks were plastered o'er on every side
With glosses, all made at the wedding time
Of her who Malmaridada bears the name.
There was the rabble of romances all,
A race audacious, yet most necessary,
Adjusting themselves to every action.
The stern, material most extraordinary,
Unnatural, and of verse legitimate—
Of foreign labour, still most various.
Of infinite power appeared there two tercets,
With strips of writing on the left and right,
Perfect, yet giving ample room to row.
The gangway entire was made, as seemed to me,

Of a long melancholy elegy,
Which not for singing but for weeping was—
By this I understand when one should say
That which is wont to be said unto a wretch
When he does ill, the gauntlet passes too—
The mast ascending to the very skies,
Prolix enough in difficult metre too,
Was tarred all o'er with songs of six fingers;
And the yard of the ship by which a cross was formed—
Of difficult additions, with the wood
Clearly displaying of what they were made.
What holds the yard to the mast, a talking thing,
Of *redondillas* wholly was composed,
Whereby more light it showed itself to be.
Verses in couplets the rigging appeared,
Of a thousand times ten thousand nonsenses,
Such as is wont to tickle up the soul,
Convenient spots most firm and honest too;
Of stanzas powerful tables also were,
Which bore a poem and more on its back,
'Twas something strange to witness undulate.
The flags which trembled in the yielding air,
Of sundry rhymes were a little warm composed.
The common sailors who crossed to and fro
Appeared enchained in verses interwove.
As books are worked by authors diligent,
All these dead compositions e'en were framed
Of verses loose or stanzas of six lines,
Making the galley lively more and more.
In fine with manners bland and most polite
Mercury observing that I all had seen
Of the ship, 'tis reason, reader, that you praise:
To him I felt united, and his voice sent
To my auditory faculties reason clear,
Replete with harmony angelical,
Announcing amongst matters which are rare,
Both new and foreign to the living world.
You will detect, if in it you observe,
How that it is a vessel worthy most
Of admiration, which I caused to be
A fear to realms adjacent and remote.
Machines of enchantment none construct,
Only the genius of Phoebus divine,
Who can, who wills, reaches and to such mounts—
He formed them; O new destiny, alone
That I should raise thereby as many bards
As well from Tagus to Pactolus' stream.
From Malta the grand master, to whom spies

A secret notice give that in the East
Barbarous weapons, arrows show themselves;
He fears and sends the nations to convoke,
Which seals the white cross on the receiving breast,
For by its strength is fortitude increased:
After whose imitation Phœbus hath
Arranged that to Parnassus famous bards
Should reach, who struggle with adversity.
I, condoling with the sad event,
In the light skull-cap already informed
In what I have to do, urge on the pace.
The bright banks of Italia have I swept,
Of France the shores I saw, but touched them not;
To come to Spain, my true direction,
And there with sweet and happy behaviour,
I do believe that I an end shall make,
And so right easily completion find:
Thou, though in age I see your slothfulness,
Shalt be of my undertaking the great God,
And of my wishes the solicitor.
Take leave, thyself not a moment detain,
And to all those inscribed in this list
Wilt tell Apollo how ready I am;—
A paper from his pocket he drew on which
Numberless names of poets I saw, 'mongst whom
Zangueses were, Coritos, and from Biscay,
Some others too from Andalusia;
A certain set born in the two Castiles,
In whom the gravity of poesy dwelt.
Mercury said, I wish you would declare
Of this genteel crowd, for you surely know
The loftiness of their wit, the very names.
So, I replied, of all who are most grave
I tell you what I know, thee quick to stir,
That you may praise before Apollo's face.
He held his peace. Their lot will I recount.

CHAPTER II.

What from my ancient mouth, intent to hear
The God loquacious stood, then quite mute fell,
As one who listens and would silence keep;
When on a sudden a loud sneeze I gave;
Blessing myself for this sad augury,
At the great Mercury's acute command,
I scanned the list, and saw amongst the first
The Licentiate Juan de Ochoa, friend
To the poet, and a Christian true.

Of this youth in his praise I do allege
He can accelerate, and death impose
Upon an enemy by his discourse;
And should he not divert or dissipate
His genius on the Spanish grammar's rules,
His lot will be to Phœbus equivalent,
For by his poetry only to the world,
Given, he trusts, to set the base on the head
Of the inconstant wheel or variable bowl;
He who of comedians is the luminary,
Of Poyo the licentiate, bears the name.
No cloud hath he his clear sun to obscure,
But being continually entertained
In schemes, chimeras, and inventions,
No help requires for martial noises.
The name of him who third stands on the list,
Hippolito Vergara he is styled,
Should you be bent to raise him to the mount,
Remember that in him you raise a shaft,
An arrow, arquebuse, and a bright flash,
Brandished against the eyes of ignorance—
That wight, who like the golden month of May,
A genius hath, and even now begins
To make an effort with his comedies
Godinez is; that other enamouring
Sensitive souls by his well-balanced verse
When of love's tenderness he sings or wails,
Is one equivalent to a thousand troops,
When for the rare and scarce seen enterprise,
Chosen they were and honourably called.
I say 'tis Don Francesco, professor
Of arms and letters with the selfsame name,
Whom for his equal Phœbus doth confess,
Calatayud his patronymic is:—
This has been said all whatsoever things
To say I am able, envy foul to scare.
Who follows next a sacred poet is,
I say illustrious, Miguel Cid is styled,
Imparting fear e'en to the Muses' quire.
That other whose verses justly are extolled
Above Calisto's very choicest bards
So celebrated by the trump of fame,
Is this agreeable, this beloved soul,
So sharp in wit, sonorous yet so grave,
Above all bards whom Phœbus' self has seen—
Who hold the key of composition,
With grace and subtlety in such excess,
Perhaps the world his equal cannot find.

This Don Luis de Gongora, whom I fear
By my short praises to deteriorate,
Though he doth mount unto the highest grade.
O thou spirit divine, who dost attain
To the well-merited guerdon of thy desires,
And to the hopes so justly estimated.
Already in thy new vocation
Divine Herrera thou thy mind appliest—
In inspiration towards heaven's trophies.
Now by thy beauteous light, so clear and rich,
In gorgeous splendour seest thou secure
That which thy heavenly soul beatifies.
Thy ivy leaning on the resistless wall
Of immortality, dost not calculate on
Delay in the shades of this dark world and wide.
And thou, Don Juan de Jauregui, who
The learned course of pen so much aspires,
That 'bove the spheres are elevated quite;
Although through thy voice Lucan's self doth breathe
Quit him a little, and with piteous eyes
Look to Apollo's much necessities;
Thee a thousand spoils in expectation stand
From a thousand inconsiderate, seeming to be
Plains fertile, yet being nought but stubble sheer.
And thou for whom the Muses do assure
A contract, Don Felix Arias, perceivest
That for their gracefulness they thee conjure;
Beseeching thee to defend from this bad race,
Impure, their comeliness, and of Aganippe,
And Hippocrene too the never-failing stream.
To be thereto participator thou wilt
Consent,—a poet of the sweetest strain
Verses to make with greatest difficulty,
Thou wilt agree not, for thy vein discreet,
Rich and abundant never will permit
Aught bearing shadow of imperfection.
My lord, he who comes here abandon quite,
I said to Mercury 'tis a natural
Who jokes and biting satires much affects—
This is one whom you well may estimate,
Alonzo de Salas Barbadillo,
Towards whom I do incline and value much.
The man who here comes I must declare to you
No reason is for him to embark, and thus you may
Eject him—the god said, to hear it I'm pleased.
He is a rapacious one who Ganymede
Would imitate, while dressing like a Goth.
And thus I counsel thee to let him pass.

But with this next you must not so arrange,
The great Luis Cabrera, in stature low,
Yet all accomplished, for all he knows,
The master recognised in history,
And in discreet discourses, so discreet
That Tacitus you will see, if I instruct—
A gallant soul is he who comes, subject
To changeful fortune's sharp vicissitudes,
The hard time's pressure and mutation.
At one time opulent in falling wealth,
But now in the firmest and most constant state
Most rich, at thy command still hold him firm.
The lofty rocks ever immoveable
Are laved by the ocean wave but not displaced
By billows in their variable course;
Not less the earth doth blustering Boreas
The lofty cedars drag, when high incensed,
He would the stoutest trees deracinate.
This man who as a living example has set
In truth of such philosophy is named
Don Lorenzo Ramirez de Prado.
The worthy who in succession comes, I say,
Is Don Antonio de Monroi, I see
In him is courtesy and genius.
Satisfaction to most high desire
Science and valour heroic doth impart.
In him I find a thousand virtues, and think
A cavalier is this of a presence,
Truly agreeable, who from Torquato gets
A soul without much recognised difference.
I treat of Don Antonio de Paredes,
To whom his friends, the sacred Nine, did give
In tender years old wit and management;
He whom to elevate you fatigue yourself,
Is Don Antonio de Mendoza, I see
In raising him Apollo you oblige.
This man is the Muses' recreation,
The grace, the liveliness, discretion;
By which discretion trophies he doth deserve,
Is Pedro de Morales, proper stamp
Of well-bred courtesy, the asylum is,
Where my good fortune truly takes its stand.
The next though savouring of sharp Zoilus,
Is the great Espinel, who on the guitar
Is numbered 'mongst the first in style and touch.
This worthy who with force can hurl the bar,
Leaving behind the tops of Pindus' heights,
Who swears, vociferates, and rends and boasts,

Is characterized more by a bard than fop,
Jusepe de Vargas styled, whose sharp
Wit and uncommon status I describe.
The next to whom contribute just renown,
Gayness and wit which may indubitably
To the Muses proffer fruit and flowers mature,
Is the much-famed Andres de Balsameda.
With whose intelligence both grave and sweet
The great Apollo satisfied remains.
Inciso comes, glory and ornament
Of Tagus. Manzanares honour bright,
Who with such offspring his content augments.
He who is chosen millions amongst
De Guevara Luis Velez the brave is,
Who may be styled sorrow's diverter eke.
A giant poet in whom I recognise
A humorous verse, a foreign wit as though
A Gnatho or a Davus did describe.
The next Don Juan de Espana who worthy is
Of human and celestial renown,
For in his lines divinity appears.
This man for whom, of Lugo, mettlesome are
The Muses, is Silveira the renowned,
Whom to remove with reason you afflict,
The next in our succession is the strange
Great Pedro de Herrera, recognised
For lofty wit in honourable points;
He who from out oblivion's prison doors
Extorted Proserpine the beautiful,
With whom he Spain and Douro has enriched.
In the contentions rigorous you will observe
What fears and hopes surround him in our times.
The fault of our less fortunate age, the effect
Of his approved worth to demonstrate.
What, further yet? Is this the celebrated
And grave Don Francisco de Farias?
This same, of whom I ever the oracle was,
Apollo of Granada, devoted.
Also of this our clime, and far remote,
Is Pedro Rodriguez. This is Tejada,
Of lofty sounding verses, resonant,
Upraised in every kind of majesty.
He who buds verses through the very pores,
Friends and a country finding where he lists,
Possessing treasures in another soil,
Is Medinilla who the foremost was,
To sing romances over th' obscure tomb,
In rank among arranged cypresses.

Now he who hastens in his noontide years,
And flies to the sacred laurel, is the Don
Fernando Bermudez, where wisdom dwells;
The very memorable singing bard,
Who, by the subtlety of his mother wit,
Of Eriphile treated in the woods.
He who commences in the new column,
With the other twain, his fit associates.
Enumerate them, although I deem it low.
Miguel Cejudo and Miguel Sancho come
United here, equalled unequally.
In these the Muses boast a powerful shield;
For in the current of well-turnèd verse,
With wit and erudition rare replete,
Ready will be to encounter matters grave.
The mighty cavalier, so well inclined
To the salutary reading of good bards,
And to the sacred mount with light doth wend,
Is Don Francisco de Silva—glorious name!
At most, what now shall be? O age mature!
In his green years, of edification full,
Don Gabriel Gomez come. Secure,
He, with Apollo, doth the victory hold.
Ignorant of, and to the vulgar harsh.
For honour of his genius, for glory
Of his flourishing age, and that we may admire;
From age to age, his worthy memory,
From this vast subject let us now recede,
The hope abridging of the noble deed,
Apollo looking on the grand Valdez.
In him we see a lively, learned breast,
A subtle genius in exaltedness;
Wherewith we can and do stand satisfied.
The other learned Figueroa is,
Who Amarillis' constancy sweet sung,
In dulcet prose and a well-measured verse.
Four others approach in distances minute,
With mighty letters all inscribed in gold,
Whose tenor signifies importance high—
Of the four ages infinite, forsooth,
The memory shall endure, duly sustained
With gravity, in their compositions.
Should bright Apollo's royal residence
Happen to topple from its exalted height,
By these four bards shall it be quite restored.
In them doth Nature set her impressive stamp
Throughout all parts; so that they worthy are
Loftiness to enjoy, all height beyond.

This verity, great Count de Salinas,
Thy rare works practical credence offers too,
Which in their end and aim divine appear.
Thou, of Esquilache, Prince, who boasts
Of mighty credit every hour and day,
Thyself exceeding art superior,
The bulwark strong shall be to the mighty ill,
Which fears Apollo from such Vantages,
No such deceitful force anticipating.
Thou, Conde de Saldaña, who, with feet
So tender, presseth lofty Pindus' top,
By the wings of wit thyself high elevating.
The torch of light unextinguishable must be
Which to the sacred mount conducts, wishing
To find a place there, ere the light be quenched.
Thou, he of Villamediana, most
'Midst Greek and Latin authors celebrated
Who ever reached the adventurous laurel boughs.
Thou wilt, by paths and ways, traverse the track
Conducting to the mountain; though more sure,
The simple pilgrims thereto reach in time;
On whose appearance these four very walls
Of famed Parnassus arrogance will drop
From the young men, or fools in ignorance bound.
Oh, how many circumstances, and how grave,
Shall I relate of the four, who happily
Will surely reap Apollo's 'vantages.
And more thereto, if Alcañices' name
We add, renowned Marquis (for there be
No more than one), will five Phœnixes make.
Each one a column to itself shall be,
Basing the edifice and supporting too
Of Phœbus, 'bove the circle of the moon.
This man (assisting at the office grave,
His business) laurel and palm elevating
Which Phœbus gives for honour and benefit.
In this science a marvel new starts forth,
Unique and rare in jurisprudence' laws,
Known as Don Francisco de la Cueva.
To Homer him I justly do compare,
The great Don Rodrigo de Herrera hight,
For letters and for virtues far renowned.
The worthy following next is Don Juan
De Vera, who, for union of sword and pen,
They honour in the fifth and fourth circuit.
This one, although his soul and body are crushed.
Giving no sign of being Christian,
His works no time will ever eat away.

The list slipped from my hand unwittingly
In this same moment; and the God said, "What
You have referred to makes the business clear.
Cause that, with feet and cogitations quick,
They all come here, that I may contemplate
The vigour of such strong suggestions."
"Francisco de Quevedo scarce can come,"
Said I, in swift rejoinder. He then said,
"From hence without him I cannot depart;
Of Apollo he is the son, the son
Of Calliope the Muse; impossible
It is to go without him. I am fixed.
The scourge is he of the poets themselves,
And from Parnassus with his foot will hurl
The unworthy ones whom we expect and dread."
"O Lord! "rejoined I; "short indeed his pace;
He will not compass it in an age entire!"
"Of this," said Mercury, "I no cognizance take;
The poet, who a very knight would be,
Upon a cloud hovering 'twixt grey and clear
Will come, a cavalier to every taste."
"Should he say No," I ask, "what will prepare
Apollo? what carriages, and e'en what clouds?
What dromedary? what spirited steed of pace?"
"Much," he replied, "and much do you advance
In your requests. Be silent, and obey!"
"Yes, I will do it; what you suggest's not wrong,"
To him did I respond; and he did seem
Something disturbed with me. In a moment's space
The sea uprose, and angry winds burst forth.
My visage then, as 'twere of one defunct,
Did so arrange itself, and so convert,
That I conjecture it was charged with dread.
I saw the night blending itself with day,
The sands of the deep ocean raise themselves
To the region of the air, despite the cold.
I saw the elements in direful rage,—
The earth, the sea, the air, and e'en the fire
I witnessed terrify the shattered clouds.
And in the midst of this vast restlessness,
The clouds, replete with poets, scattered them
Upon the bark, which nearly was submerged,
Had not a thousand syrens—and yet more—
Assisted to give check to the vast storm,
Which caused boundings through the very yards.
One, whom I thought Juana la Chasca was,
With body dilated, and outstretched neck,—
To a hobgoblin very similar,—

Made up to me, and said, "By a single hair
Hung this devoted bark, all void of hope
That any friend would come to succour it,
Let's drag it into safety and no joke,
Carelessly attentive the meanwhile
To the discourses of Sancho Panza.
With this the hurricane becalmed itself.
The sea was tranquil, and serene the sky,
The zephyr chasing away the rumbling sounds.
My view I turned, and in a light flight saw
A cloud transpierce the clear air, whose colours
Reflected were, as if of frost congealed—
O wonder new! O rarest accident!
I saw, and must describe it, though in doubt
Of the fact, which I for a mark declare
What I could well discern, what came within
Clear observation, was that a cloud in two
Parts was divided to assist in rain.
Whoe'er has seen the earth preoccupied,
With such a disposition, that when
It rains, a fact it is well recognised
That from each drop minute in a brief space
Of dust there rises either toad or frog,
Which with a jump or despatch moveth on.
Such could imagination form, sovereign
Virtue, that from each drop of the moist cloud
A form arises, endued with human shape.
Not to give credence to this fact I tried
A thousand times, but my sight it confirmed,
Which clear I saw bereft of ligaments.
The selfsame forms were of the very list
Of poets, to which reference has been made
Whose vigour no one knoweth to resist.
Some men were recognised for very good,
Others for knaves and fools,—as Christ is God,
Of very little value, and ill-dressed.
These men among I fancied to have seen
Antonio de Galarza, styled the brave,
A follower of Apollo and well loved.
The vessel filled itself from stem to stern,
And its capacity,—no one denies
A spacious seat, the most that I commend.
Another cloud rained Lope de Vega down,
Poet illustrious, whose verse and whose prose
No one exceeds,—yea, no one reaches it.
A very marvellous thing to see it was
Of poets—the very closely packed swarm,
Recite their long lays, honey-sweet with zeal,

This dead of thirst, of hunger that dead too.
I said, observing how they strained the voice,—
Mercy on us! what poetasters rise
In such excesses, recognised a fault,
Mercury's self, and trying it to mend
Into the centre of the boat light leaped,
And with a colander, which opportunely there
Was found, whether of old or modern make,
With a scarlet cloth he seized a thousand bards,—
Those "of the cloak and sword" he cast not off—
Infinite times he applied the colander,
Till nought but cockle did the harvest prove.
The good and righteous through a sieve did pass,
The husk remaining on the surface, which
Showed poetry to be more harsh than songs.
And without proffering the reasons why
They fell in his displeasure,—quickly gave
Mercury, to the sea these bards in heaps.
Among the rejected a blind poet was heard
Who 'midst the breakers went on murmuring
With blasphemy, and a piece of Apollo's coin,
A tailor (though he strived with lazy feet
Opening a gangway with his puissant arms),
Said, Beastly is Apollo, hence I live.
Another, who apparently, pettish moved,
Being a cobbler of a first rate name,
Two thousand times said, not this madness alone.
A cloth-cutter now works, perspires, impels
Himself to be conducted to the shore,
Yet more his life than honour did esteem.
The floating squadron virtually reduced
Unto the troop marine, to the galley turns
Its face, with signs of being offended too,
And one for all being spokesman said, I would
This Phœbus' harsh ambassador in his line,
Treated us well, and not in this fashion.
But what he said, they hear,—I am so bold,
The greatness of this mountain to profane,
With new productions and a novel style.
Mercury held his peace, and then began
His chambers with curiosity to arrange,
Giving a feast with grace illustrious;
Anon resounded the sweet clarions' breath.
And Mercury filled with satisfaction,
The dolphins showing no sad augury,
Oars to the water gave, sails to the wind.

CHAPTER III.

Of this royal Galley were the oars
Of dactyles formed, and so impelled by them
That o'er the sea's surface did it lightly glide.
The sail extended to the topmost height.
Of very delicate ideas constituted,
Woven of various webs of love compact—
Gales sweet and amorous blew directly on
The stern of the vessel, all demonstrating
Attention upon the great voyage set.
Like spinning-wheels the syrens danced around,
Imparting pushes to the wanton ship,
By whose assistance its career dashed on.
The water of the white sea was likened
To bed quilts turned about, and formed
A blue appearance on the deep green main.
The boat's crew fully entertained themselves,
Some glossing over authors' passages hard,
Some sung their verses, others them composed—
Among them many who for rare were held
Sonnets indited, oft illustrated
By different accidents of love's history.
Others all kindness and dissolved quite
In purest sugar with intonations bland,
And satisfactory mellifluence,
In melting tones both grave and peacable
To pastoral eclogues recitation gave;
Disporting wit, wisdom, and gaiety.
Others their lady-loves were celebrating
In dulcet rhymes and from the enamoured mouth
Cast for them the *pabulum* they required.
To him it happened who on love's thought dwelt,
To praise the amorous conflicts of his Dame,
With taste excessive and much elegance.
One chanted how that a sheer amorous flame,
In midst of a liquid element burnt it up,
And roared like unto bulls fretted with darts.
In this wise floated poesy from one
To the other, making this bard to announce
His love in Latin, that in Arabic.
This way doth the Galley go along,
The ocean furrowing with such levity,
That e'en the winds consent it passed not on.
Anon the magnitude displays itself
Of the open area of Valencia's shore,
By art and nature beauteous equally.

Quickly the presence acceptable came
Of the great Don Luis Ferrer, his breast
With honour marked, his soul divinely touched.
The God debarked, going directly forth
To give the man embraces infinite,
With his appearance and aid satisfied,
He turned his visage and the wiles of Don
Guillen de Castro did reiterate, who
Desirous came to find himself thus clasped.
Christoval de Virues followed him,
With Pedro de Aguilar, joint band,
Noble creation of Turia's banks.
It was not possible that a more valorous
Squadron should Mercury meet, nor did desire
The God one greater or more honourable.
Immediately upon the coast was seen
A troop of worthies from Valencia—
Who came to inspect the unrivalled Galley's form.
The hands of all were charged with instruments,
In style peculiar pamphlets memorable,
With genius fantastic, mettlesome,
Burning to find themselves 'midst victory.
Which sure and certain they did hold to be
In what relates to this world's dross and dregs.
However, Mercury closed to the door.
I say, consent he would not that they embarked,
But why he so said I will not avow.
Away he went fearing they would rise up,
Being so many, and such candidates,
On Parnassus' empire new to found.
And hereupon one saw with fiery pace
Andro Rey de Artieda come—
By age nor weakened nor attenuated.
A very spacious circle did all make,
And closing him in the midst, did him embark
In valour richer than in current coin.
In th' instant did they raise the anchors up,
The sails were fastened to the mainmast's height,
The meanest sailors doing speediest work,
Through the fresh air the clarion resounds
Its deep-drawn music, and anon returns
Each Syren sitting to the wonted work.
Athwart the clouds Phœbus beheld the bark
And said in accents easy to be heard,
Here am I satisfied and my hope is raised.
Impelled by strength of oars and syren's hands,
The galley quickening left the winds behind,
The speed being prosperous and marvellous.

One read contentment in the very face
Of all the passengers who were on board,
Lasting, natural, nothing violent
Some on account of heat in skins were cased,
Some not in gaudy Gothic to appear,
In homely hermit's clothes did dress themselves.
Now did the saline waters wide expand
For the galley's passage, as it cleft the air,
As with extended pinions flies the crane.
In fine, we came unto the sea's limits,
Where it outstretching forms the Narbonne Gulf,
Defenceless quite against the power of winds.
The perfect person of God Mercury,
Sitting on paper of six reams, appeared,
With a crown garnished, and sceptre too.
When suddenly a cloud which pregnant seemed,
Produced four poets on the gangway pass,
Or rained them down by pre-ordained concert.
One of these was he to whom god Phœbus gave
His honour, Juan Luis de Casanate,
Poet renowned of sterling weight and worth.
Apollo's self his genius entertains,
Him praises giving, rewards, benevolences,
So simple I should be in lauding him.
At the second shower, nor Cato of Utica
Could be a parallel, nor doth Phœbus boast
One whom he so admires, or on whom thinks.
Of th' auditor Gaspar de Barrionuevo,
My weakly spirit is unable quite
To extol his merit as I ought to do.
The wide vacuity of the boat was filled
By the great Francisco de Rioja,
At the point where he fell from the clouds therein.
Christoval de Mesa there I viewed,
Down at the feet of Mercury, yielding fame
Unto Apollo's self, the God's image.
At the mast's summit a sailor seats himself,
Loudly proclaiming that the city shows
Its appellation Genoa, Janus means.
The city leave a little to the left,
Said Mercury, let the vessel also sail,
Its route pursuing on the starboard side.
Towards Tiber steering, a white line we perceive,
The sea within, having quite traversed through
The narrow and the perilous Roman beach.
At a distance sees one all the air condensed
With smoke, which Stromboli vomits from his jaws
Of sulphur, fire, and horror constituted.

They fly the hideous isle, soliciting
The milder west, so that the passage which
Doth shorten it, levels and easy makes.
We come now to the offings of that point,
Caieta, where the pious Æneas' nurse
Her forced, last, and fearful passage made.
At a short distance hence the far-famed mount
We saw which girdleth in our hemisphere,
The ashes of Tityrus and Sincerus too
Repose therein, and thence on this account
'Mongst mountains it may hold an honoured place.
Quickly is disclosed wherein repose
The remnants of its friendly, natural power,
A composition to form for many more.
The grievous sorrow without fatigue we saw
Of beauteous Parthenope, situate
At the sea's brink, her feet in fetters linked,
With castles and with turrets proudly crowned;
For strength and beauty in equal degrees
Held, recognised by all, and wide esteemed.
He of the light-winged feet commanded me
That I should hasten, and on the firm-set earth
Step, and to the Luperci mandate give—
In which, account should of the war be given
So dreadful, yet inducing them to come
To the hard and fierce assault at the soldiers' cry.
Sir, replied I, if there should be by chance
Another who the embassy might bear,
More grateful far 'twould to the two brothers be
Than it could be to me. I know full well
It could be better managed; Mercury said,—
I understand not,—Go, do it, ere time fly.
I stand in fear that they should hear me not,
Rejoined I, though I have no care to go;
Yet in obedience am I ever prompt.
Who tells me I know not, or who exhorts,
For me they entertain as I do think,
The will, albeit the sight is rather short.
If this were not the case, this very road
No such poor drawing-room could have, nor in
Extravagance so profound could be plunged.
Should any of the promises be fulfilled,
Of the very many on the parting made,
May the God aid to raise me to the ship.
Much did I hope, and much they promised me,
Yet it may be that occupations new
Will force them to forget what they have said
Many, my Lord, into the ship you hoist,

Who from the dirt will make you raise your foot,
Away, excuses make for further proofs.
None, said he, have me questioned in this guise;
Should I but disembark and capture them,
I vow to God I'll seize the Count and all.
To these two great men I an enemy grew,
Who having raised themselves to poetry,
The point attaining, which one can discern,
They do desire with a slothful tyranny
Themselves to raise up by the very hand
Of science, which conducts to ends divine.
By the Sovereign Apollo's throne
I swear; no more I add, burning in rage
That one and the other all expense shall pay (echo a las barbas)
He further continued, saying, Doctor Mira
I'll lay a wager, if the Count order not,
That he also within his point retire.
Let the gallant Lord appear, why hide himself?
But him to capture, if he likes it not,
Be there no seeking, watching, or rounds kept.
In this perhaps so unjust enterprise,
Can they disdain to find in it as much
As conscience limited and honest be?
Is heaven in want of fiery-souled bards?
Since at each step the fertile earth buds forth
Poets, who many and so various are?
No sacred hymns above do they not hear?
Does not sweet David's harp its sounds emit?
Engendering comfort accidental, new?
Daintiness ceases, and the yard-arm is still,
Which reaches to the top, obedience swift,
Good upon good, the effort of the crew (fue de la chusma).
A short time intervened, when a loud noise
Was heard, that paralyzed the auditories.
It was the sharp yelping of the canine race.
It disconcerted Mercury; and the crowd
At the sad sound stood still, and in each breast
The heart's firm nerves in trepidation shook.
Suddenly the narrow strait disclosed
Itself, the Scylla and Charybdis dire,
More fearful by its furiousness yet made—
The breakers how presumptuous observe,
Continually aspiring to the clouds,
Wishing to sweep the vaulty heaven itself.
The prudent wanderer did them overcome,
The lover of Calypso, what time he
Traversed this watery path—Mercurius said,
We, his prudence closely imitating,

Will cast ourselves into the sea we pass,
The vessel meanwhile flying glibly on—
Meanwhile the pitiless waves champ, gnaw, and suck
The wretched caitiff to its mercies given,
I stand secure until the pass be free.
Let them detect if in our galley there be
A bard sufficiently unfortunate
Himself to give to the sea's ravening maw.
They sought him, and one Lofraso they found,
A military man, Sardinian bard,
Who in a corner lay dismayed, and withered—
He to his twice five books of fortune went,
Adding another ten, choosing his time,
Which rather unoccupied appeared to be.
The whole crew cried aloud, To the sea he goes.
Lofraso view, without assistance go—
How? will there appear no charge on conscience,
So much poetry pitched to the absorbing waves
And its inclemency quite sink us all?
Let Lofraso live, while gives unto the day
Apollo light; meanwhile the band of men
Observed discreet and lightsome fantasy.
Lofraso, true renown to thee belongs,
Sincere epithets, and pointed too—
I joy that you my boatswain I can call.
This said Mercurius to the cavalier,
Who in the gangway settled down his foot,
With lash in hand, ferocious, pitiless—
I think it was composed of his own verse.
I know not how it was, in a moment's space
Either did Lofraso so, or heaven disposed
We issued from the strait to safety quick,
Without hurling the poet in the main,
Although the bard Sardinian merited it.
New dangers quick, another importunate
Dread threatened all, had not a hollow yell
From Mercury come, such as no mortal yells.
To the helmsman crying,—a vast fish—Stop the boat,
Strike sail at a blow, and then immediately
The deed was done, and danger was removed.
Those mountains you behold so closely joined,
Of Acrocerania bear the classic name,
With infamy associated, I ween.
The vessel's oars are honourably composed,
The tender, sweetly-flowing Gothic too,
And those adapted to the long-necked vase
The cold and fresh are well adapted too;
The heated also well adjusted are,

And where the hose is vast and voluminous—
At the impending danger quite alarmed,
All thrust themselves into the vessel's sides,
With arms both weak and powerful to act
Below the vessel's keel in divings plunged
The syrens, who no separation sought,
And e'en themselves outdid in feats of strength.
In a brief space the floating mass arrived,
At sight of fair Corfu, and on the right
They quitted too the isle impregnable,
Shaping the galley's course unto the left,
They swept the coasts of famous Græcia—
Where heaven its beauty proudly shows itself.
The flattering breakers here displayed themselves,
Impelling sweetly the brave bark along,—
As if she smiled at the agreeable plains—
And quickly touching on the Orient dawn,
The golden sun dashing the horizon—
With rays discoloured as threads from his face
A sailor cried aloud—a mountain, lo!
A mountain is discovered, wherein is kept
That excellent steed, yclept Bellerophon.
We land upon the mountain, and on foot
Apollo comes to receive us, I believe
Lofraso said, and goes to Hippocrene.
From hence I do discern, I see, I prove
That 'midst the bushes joyously partake
The Muses nine of recreation sweet,
Some old, others in their novitiate;
With hasty steps and measured as it beseems,
Five glide on foot, and four do creep along.
If thou this time, said Mercury, O bard
Sardinian, that they my ears do lop,
Or hold these beings for illegitimate;
Tell me why you do not yourself remove
From ignorance, my poor fellow, and take care
Your strains they do recite in their complaints?
Why now prevent us with your fables false
From proffering to Apollo what's his due
For having your destiny ameliorated?
And now by a wind which was by no means slight,
The bright Apollo lowered to the strand
His foot, for in his car no rashness is—
He shook the rays off from his face divine,
Appeared in shoes and good habiliments
Determined satisfaction all to give—
Him following behind a very numerous
Squadron of maidens, aptest in the dance,

Though small of stature, still of gesture quick.
'Twas after known by me that these maidens,
The truest most, the lesser ill observed,
No other were than th' hours of sun and time.
The smaller ones were broken in the midst,
The sound ones happiest, and so thereby
All were in all most expeditious.
With cheerful gesture quick Apollo then
Embraced the soldiers, who did fondly wait
The great event which he proposed to them,
Nor in the selfsame way affectionately
All did he treat, portraying difference
Towards those to whom he chiefly preference gave—
To some of nobleness and excellence
Embraces fresh he offered and reasons eke,
Decorum and pre-eminence guarding too—
Others among, Juan de Arguijo he clasped,
I know not in what, or how, or when he made
A voyage so sharp and so extended too.
With him in his desire was satisfied
Apollo, and confirmed in his idea,
Ordered, forbade, abandoned, made, unmade.
This reception finished unparalleled—
Don Luis de Barahona found himself
For his great merit duly elevated.
Apollo, ever verdant, gives a crown
Of laurel branches, liberally, a vase
From Helicon's waters and Castalia's spring.
With pace majestic quickly he returns,
And well-considered squadrons, suddenly,
And follows him to famed Parnassus' skirts,
And at Castalia's font at last arrives;
On sight of which multitudes were cast down,
And seat themselves by side of the crystal stream;
Many not only did content themselves,
But did their legs and arms and members too,
And parts concealed of bodies, plunged therein.
Some persons, more discreet, the savoury
Waters did gradually sip, allowing long
Space to the taste, dainty pauses between,
Health drinking, and unworthy jests repudiating;
With the mouth downward drinking, not with sips,
The luscious liquor freely did they quaff.
In both their hands others the twisted vase
Did hold, while some, from the mouth to the stream,
Did fear to find endless impediments.
Gradually the fountain passes off,
And finds its way to the recipients,

The forge not being satisfied from thirst.
Further Apollo said, "Those other fonts
Aganippe and Hippocrene are styled.
Both are savoury and both excellent,
Sweet and perennial is the liquor of both;
All much improved in quality and mass,
By the lofty geniuses who come to taste.
They drink, and rise to the mountain's towering top,
Amidst the palms' and cedars' lofty height,
And e'en these peaceful olive trees among."
Replete with taste, and of all anguish void,
Following Apollo, the bright squadron moved,
Some to a football, some to saltations went.
Sitting, I saw, at the foot of an old oak,
Alonso de Ledesma, composing
A canticle angelic and divine.
I knew him, and he, running, came to me
With arms outstretched, as to an ancient friend.
But nothing moved by reason of the noise,
"Dost thou not see," Apollo to me said,
"That not with himself is Ledesma? seest not
He is beside himself, and with me stands?"
Within a myrtle's shade in a green retreat,
Geronimo de Castro took his place,—
A youth of genius, strange and unusual,—
A very peculiar kind of song warbling,
As I conjecture, with sweet voice. I stood
In admiration; for in Madrid he had been.
Apollo understood, and said, "A soldier
Like this—it is not profitable that he
Should buried be midway 'twixt ease and sleep.
Him did I drag along, and I know how
That power, none other, can my power obstruct."
And now arrived the hour opportune
Which strength should well supply, in my idea,
To a poor appetite with fasting faint.
This did not pass for mere opinion
That the army led by Delius' command
Should satisfy a miserable hungry wight.
First he did lead us to a garden rich,
Where nature's self her power doth manifest,
And that of industry more exerts and glows;
The very Hesperides less beauty showed;
The hanging gardens did not equal it
In grandeur, beauty, or situation;
In its comparison, Alcinous'
Gardens were nothing; in whose ample praise
Most subtle wits have occupied their minds;

Not subject to the mutability
Of time; for every spring produces, sure,
Fruits in possession, not in hope alone.
Nature and art do prodigally appear
To strive in competition, and doubtful stand
As to which of the twain is victor, which excels.
A stuttering and dumb demonstration,
If the tongue the most expert essays to praise
In adulation and devoid of guile.
United to a garden an orchard was,
A wood, a thicket, a meadow, pleasant vale,
Which well agreed in all these attributes.
Replete with so much loveliness and grace
That it would seem as 'twere of heaven a part,
A soil most beauteous, and most plenteous.
Apollo sat himself upon a height
And gave injunctions to the world that all
Should there be seated after mid-hour of day,
And that the banks should truly indicate
The genius and the value of each one,
And none to other be embarrassment,
That in despite of importunity,
Or of desire ambitious seats be placed
In the most opportune, pleasantest sites.
A thousand laurels or more adjusted were,
Within whose shade and mass were resting, too,
Some of that number in contentment blest;
A few there were who occupied the palms—
By myrtles, ivy, and the gnarled oaks,
Diverse poets did ensconce themselves.
Humble though the company, for the nobles were
Seats elevated high as thrones could be,
For thou, O Envy, here doublest thy rage,
In fine were occupied in first estate
The trunks of that expansive circuit's round,
In honour dedicated to sublimest bards.
Ere I in congregated numbers blent
Could find a situation, so on foot,
Choleric, withered in vexation stood;
I said unto myself, Is't possible
That angry fortune should in extremes pursue?
Who many offends is he in dread of none?
And turning towards Apollo, with a tongue
Disturbed, I said, 'Twill pleasant be to taste
What's heard. The third part is accomplished;
The fourth part of this enterprise ensues.

CHAPTER IV.

Verses to make doth indignation move,
Should th' indignant wight be somewhat wild,
The verses will partake of the perverse.
Of myself know I no more but that I am prompt
And equal find myself to indite in rhyme
That which ne'er wrote the Pontus-banished bard.
This did I to Phœbus say, No estimate make,
My lord, of the vain vulgar who pursue
Thee, and against the sacred laurel lean.
Envy and ignorance closely follow him,
So envied thus and persecuted too,
The good he hopes is never consequent.
The structure by my genius did I make,
By which to the world the Galatea fair
Did sally forth, safe from oblivion.
And I am he through whom "The Confused One,"
Unhandsome never, did on the stage appear.
If justice to the work be rendered,
I, who in style and judgment equally
Comedies have composed, which in their time
Were deemed both grave and affable on the stage:
In my Don Quixote I entertainment gave
To the most peevish, melancholy breast,
At every hour, in every season's change.
A way I opened in my novels too,
Whereby the Spanish dialect should display
Due propriety blent with extravagance;
I am the man who in invention's power
Many excel; who in this essential fails
A consequence is in fame will likewise fail;
But from my tenderest years I ever loved
The sweet art of enchanting poesy,
And in it did I essay to gratify all.
My pen albeit humble ne'er did fly
To subjects deemed satirical, low means
To base rewards leading and sheer disgrace.
The sonnet I composed which thus began,
Principal honour of my known writings,—
"A vow to God whose greatness terrifies."
Romances numberless have I also writ,
That one "Of Zealots" chiefly do I prize
'Midst others which I do hold for condemned.
Therefore am I in anguish and pity
To find myself on foot without a tree
To me conceded on whose strength to lean.

Here am I too, as they say, upon the point
To give to type "Persiles" excellent,
Whereby my name and works I multiply.
In cogitations subtle and modest
Disposed in sonnets of twelve verses each;
Honour gave I to these known subjects,
To Phillis equal did Filena too
Reverberate through the woods, which listened more
To one and th' other cheerful canticle.
In sweet and variable rhyme raised up
My hopes expectant the light flying gales,
Which in them and the sands were thickly sown.
I held, I hold, and ever shall hold thoughts,
To heaven be thanks for these my tendencies,
Ever exempt and free from flattery,
Nor will I ever set foot on the road
Which towards untruth, deceit, or fraud conducts,
Total ruin to all sanctity.
'Gainst my contracted fortune I rage not,
Though on the ground I be as I discern,
And in such state my disadvantage weigh.
With little am I content though I desire
Much. By these reasons inflamed with bland remarks
Did Timbrean Apollo answer give.
Malignant fortunes ever are in the rear,
And the broad current from a distance take,
They are much feared but never are excused.
Good comes to some by sudden movements, yet
To others moves it on by slow advance,
And evil keeps no different degree,
The good which is acquired, preserve it eke
With cunning, diligence, discretion,
No greater virtue is than to enjoy
Thyself hast wrought thy own good luck, and I
Have thee perceived in unison with it.
For with th' imprudent very little obtains,
But if you from your quarrel would emerge,
Cheerful and not embarrassed, but consoled,
Double your cloak and on it seat yourself.
Sometimes a fortunate event ensues
When without reason lot itself denies,
Honour more merited is than e'er attained.
It well appears, my lord, without remark,
Did I rejoin, that I possess no cloak.
He said, though it be so, to see it I'm glad,
Virtue's a cloak wherewith one stops a gap,
And narrowness may cover nakedness,
Which free and exempt from envy it escapes.

My head to this deep counsel I inclined,
And on my feet I rested, no good seat,
Where favour doth not work or opulence.
Some uttered murmurs, seeing me deprived
Of that same honour which was due to me
Of virtue full and of the planet of light.
It now appeared that a new splendour did
O'ercover day, whilst the surrounding air
Was smit with sounds of dulcet melody:
And there on one side of the site was found
A bevy rare of nymphs quite beautiful,
With whom the ruddy god made infinite sport.
One came the last, as if bringing up the rear
Abounding in brightness, like unto the sun
In his procession 'midst the luminous stars.
The greatest beauty did vanish away
Before her quite, for she did shine alone,
Surpassing all, joyful and satisfying.
She did in truth resemble, when she showed
Herself, pearls liquid and roses between;
Aurora when she rises at first dawn,
The vesture rich, the very precious goods,
The jewels which adorned her marvellous styled,
Came into hopeless competition.
The nymphs whose wishes were her to assist
In beauteous aspect and demeanour pure
Did show, as if they were the liberal arts.
All with a loving, tender affection,
With science clear and choice unitedly,
The holiest respect towards her observed;
They showed in serving her themselves were served.
And from th' event, by every nation too,
Were held in greater veneration.
To ebb and flow the currents infinite,
The ocean and the depths demonstrated,
Father to be of rivers and of fonts.
The herbs their virtues did present, with them
The trees their fruits, and eke all fragrant flowers,
The very stones the virtues they enclosed,
All sacred love its chaste prerogatives,
The exquisite tranquillity of sweet peace,
And bitter war its horrors did evince.
To demonstration appeared the spacious
Clear way, whereby the sun continually
Its natural yet forced career pursues.
The inclination, O force of destiny,
Whereof the stars are composed and exist,
How it doth influence this star or that sign.

All this she knows, all this disposes too,
The sanctified and ever-beauteous maid,
Joy and admiration in command.
Of the speaker I demanded if in the fair
Nymph any deity did lay concealed,
And if 'twere right homage to proffer her—
For in the rich adornments that she showed
And gallant bearing she displayed in full,
She seemed of heavenly not of earthly mould.
Thou showest thy ignorance, did he reply,
After an intimacy of many years
Discoverest not that she is Poetry.
Her ever have I seen in mean clothes wrapped,
Did I rejoin,—never saw her attired
With ornaments both rich and copious.
It seems as in disorder her I saw,
In vestments of the colour of primy spring—
On working days or days of festival.
That which is poetry in reality,
The grave, the modest, and the elegant,
Said Mercury, the lofty, the sincere,
Ever is in vesture the most pertinent
For any acts which it imports to do;
When 'tis to business indispensable—
No inclination to soothe or serve the mob
Versifier, malignant, impudent,
Least silent in what most 'tis ignorant.
Another there is, false, grief-full, and base,
And old, a friend to drums and instruments,
Which benches never doth or taverns quits,
Nor rises two or one inch from the ground.
Great friend of marriage and of baptisms,
With hands extensive but with little brain—
Momentarily falling into paroxysms,
No certainty in declaring, yet declares,
Things absurd enacts, and solecisms.
Bacchus whence it exists, its taste declares,
In couples scatters pennyroyal herb,
Wild mint and gentian and plants of rare kind (compa y vereda, y el
    mastranzo y juncia).
This that thou observest the decorum is,
Of earth the gala, and the heavens too,
Wherein the Muses do their meetings hold.
She secrets does lay bare, and closes too,
Touches and indicates of all sciences
The superficies, what is best conceals.
Look on her presence with more eagerness,
On it you see stamped in abundance full

Whatever excellence can be contained.
There rest in her in the same dwelling-place
Moral philosophy and the divine,
The purest style and chastest elegance.
Depict she can in midst of clearest day
The night, and in the night howe'er obscure
The lovely dawn which pearls of dew creates.
The course of rivers she doth hasten on,
And it she does detain; to fury the breast
Incites, and quick to softness can reduce.
By a powerful medium she can herself insert
'Twixt shining arms in opposite array,
Victory gives and victory takes away.
Let observation mark how the woods lend
Their shades, the shepherds their bland canticles—
Woe lends her lute, Pleasure her festivals.'
From Syria pearls, Sabæa praises lends,
Tiber its gold, Hybla its honeyed sweets,
Gayness from Milan, intense love from Spain.
In fine, she is the cipher whence is drained
The profitable, honest, delectable—
Whereby the parts enhance the venture self.
'Tis from so admirable, so quick genius
Which sometimes touches to points in suspense,
To hold I know not what inscrutable—
The good are praised and offence ensues
To th' evil by her voice, and of such sorts,
Some her adore, others not understand.
Immortal all are her works heroical,
Her lyrics sweet indeed, in such a strain
That mortal things turn to the contrary.
And if sometimes sweet adulation appears,
It is inserted with such artfulness
That honour awaits, not reprobation—
Glory for virtue, punishment for vice,
Are suitable actions furnishing the world,
Of lofty genius and goodness a proof.
In this condition stood I, when through the neat
Windows with jasmine and roses bedight,
Did love himself present as I understand.
Religious persons, six did I perceive
Endued with honourable and grave aspects,
With lengthened togas, clean and stately too;—
Of Mercury I inquired for what purpose
These beings were wrapped up and not appeared,
And yet seemed creatures of profound respect.
To which response he lent—Themselves show not
To observe decorum and the lofty state

Which they do hold, and so conceal the face.
Who are they, I rejoined, if so to speak
Is given? He replied, for certain not
Because Apollo hath so ordered it.
Are they not poets? Yea, I am not assured
To think for what cause they refuse to pass
With their bright genius into th' open plain;
Wherefore themselves demean and play the fool,
The talent hiding which gracious heaven gives
To those who will know how to appreciate it.
Then said the King, Who is that? I suspect
Zeal hinders them from making themselves known
Without anxiety the vile mob before.
Can no science whate'er be brought to compare
Unto this universal poesy?
What limits exist wherein it to confine?
This being truth, he wished to ascertain
Amongst those on the card, how one applies
This fear, hypocrisy, or squeamishness;
My Lord makes verses and refuses then
They should be known, and yet to many them
Communicates; the strange tongue doth accuse.
The more for being good, and multiplies
Fame's self its valour, and to the lord doth sing
With voice of glory in commendation rich,
What further now? Save if one raises up
Testimony unto a Pontiff bard,
They do declare what 'tis—the god alarms—
By the life of Lanfusa the discreet,
Should you not tell me who these worthies are
In bonnets and a rochet close encased.
With features and with gesture discomposed,
I try to bring into a noisy crowd
These so quieted and so composed.
By god, said Mercury, and by my faith,
I scarce can say it, and yet I declare
To your contention I the blame refer—
I said, my lord, hence I on myself impose,
Never to say but what thou bidd'st me say,
I say so on the base of friendship's faith—
He said, Let them not push us to a joke,
Hand it to me—I'll tell it to the ear,
For I believe there are more than thou saw'st.
He whom thou didst observe with neck erect,
Wanton, with robe of state and figure tall,
In honesty and valour vested too,—
Is Doctor Don Francisco Sanchez, yield
All the praise Apollo owes to him,—

Such as can raise him to the empyrean height,
And all the more his famous wit extends;
Yet in the green leaf of his latter days
A hope survives of consecrated fruit.
He who in elevated fantasy,
In ecstasies relishing, himself regales.
And imitates my aspirations close,
Is Master Orense hight, whose sprightliness
Expands itself into rare eloquence,
Such as in Athens' halls is signalized.
His native genius unto science knit,
And sciences expanded raises him
To rank which is acknowledged excellence.
He with a paleness holy which destroys,
And that branch covers with a laurel leaf,
A plant both leafy and in cup-like shape,
Fray Juan Baptista Capitaz is named,
Unshod and poor—yet attired very well
With the rich ornaments that fame supplies.
He who in proud rigour of forgetfulness
His name doth proffer with eternal joy.
And is of Apollo and the Muses loved,
Ancient in wisdom and no more a boy—
Professor of Humanity is, as I think,
Doctor Andres del Pozo the renowned,
Of wit unmeasured, a Licentiate
Is he, although of Mercy's order, Friar;
Recognised as the Muses' tributary.
His appellation is Raman, help sure,
Whereby is Mercury strengthened and restored,
Sees obstinate forces to their contraries turned.
The other whose temples thou seest circumscribed
In honoured triumph with gay Daphne's arras,
His glories sculptured are in Alcalá—
In its renowned victorious theatre,
The swan doth chant him in no sorrowful strain—
As being first in mark and likelihood
To his witty sayings all the rest is hurled
With due propriety into his learned cap.
For them composed is or discomposed.
Those some six persons to whom I referred,
Who in positions sacred were arranged,
And for religious purpose constituted.
Hold praises all for irksome benefits
Which are to poets imparted, and rejoice
To bear the praise without all nominal aid.
Why then, my lord, asked I, do such contend,
In writing and due notice proffer eke

Their rhymes concerning stop they and create.
However genius hath its covetousness,
And praise itself will ne'er depreciate
What justice owes to its acknowledged rights,
That which the bard cannot appreciate,
Why then doth he verses indite and speak?
Why then disdain that which he more extols?
Contented ne'er was I nor satisfied
With honeyed hypocrisies. Plainly did I seek
Praises above for what I praiseworthy did—
With this Apollo requires that this same band
Religious here in secrecy should come—
Thus said the God who holds by eloquence.
Suddenly was heard a cornet's sound,
And voices crying out, Give way, aside,
There comes a poet of most lively stamp.
I turned myself to see, and on the side
Of a mountain a postillion and knight saw,
Running as one may say upon the wind—
More as a crier the postillion served
Than as a guide, at whose impelling voice
The undivided squadron fell on their knees.
Mercury asked me then, Dost thou not know
Who is this sprightly, this gay gentleman?
I do surmise that thou his presence dost know.
Well, I rejoined, it is that famous man,
The great Don Sancho de Leiva, whose sword
And pen have been to Apollo profitable,
This very day will he triumphant be,
With similar succour, and at the same time
A thing which seemed only imaginary.
Other favours not less important too,
For the dreaded events are now most manifest made
To wit, and force, and valour a supplement.
A modern troop upon the left-hand side
Of the mountain showed itself; O heavens!
What proofs you give us of your providence!
Juan de Basconcelos, the discreet,
Forward advanced upon a bay steed, zeal
Imparting to the Lusitanian Muse.
Behind him Captain Pedro Tamayo
Straight followed, and although with gout infirm,
Alarmed he was at the enemy and swooned,
And found himself in flight and then in rout,
Who in the doubtful thrusts of heady fight,
Admires his genius and his valour notes.
Also arrived upon the fertile earth,
Adjusted underneath a signal white

Upon the right of the Sierra broad.
Others of whom a quick review the God
Apollo made. Amongst the foremost men
Was the young Don Ferdinand de Lodena,
A bard of primest order nevertheless,
Upon whose genius God Apollo rests,
His glories waiting for the time to come.
With royal majesty and unheard-of pomp
He marched along, and at the mountain's base
The properties of the mount solicited.
Juan de Vergara the Licentiate, was
Who then came up, with whom the illustrious crowd
In midst of neighbours quickly made a stand
Of Phœbus' and Esculapius'. glory and lustre,
But let the saints well favoured it announce,
His fame herself doth illustrate.
With him and with applause was a reception
To Juan Antonio de Herrera given,
Who on the line, division unequal set
O who, with tongue in nothing flattering
But with affection pure in great excess,
To two who arrived might praise extended be,
But no such weight befits my shoulders broad.
The two who did arrive were the famous
Masters, Don Calvo and Valdivieso.
Quickly there was discerned on the fluid
Surface of old ocean a small bark
Hastily by oars of bulk impelled;
It came to shore, and on the point debarked
Don Juan de Argote y de Gamboa
In company with Don Diego Abarca,
Subjects worthy of incessant praise;
And Don Diego Ximenes y de Enciso
Ventured a leap from the high prow to earth.
In these three were assurance and gaiety,
Impressed how much taste was therein contained,
A notice giving of their wit and works.
With Juan Lopez de Valle other two
United came, Pamones one of them,
'Gainst whom the Muses prejudice entertain.
For why? Because he set his foot whereon
None other ventured, and with fancy new
Is more importunate than agreeable.
From a far soil through ways uncultivated
Did come the Irishman, Don Juan Bateo,
A Xerxes new in our day's memory.
My organ of vision now I turn, and see
Mantuano, who for Maecenas Velasco holds,

Whose occupation was very prudent.
These two will leave throughout the foreign lands
Their names extended on their own soil as well,
As thou, Apollo, truly hast ordained,
Between a pair of fruitful bearing hills
(Who will create although he understands)
Whose coronation is of laurels and palms.
Th' aspect solemn of Abed Maluenda
Did show itself, imparting glory and light
To the mount, and triumph in hope's wide contest
But what of enemies the victory
Will not a genius so flourishing reach?
A goodness worthy of such memory.
Don Antonio Gentil de Vargas, I
Crave space to see you, who duly arrived
With art and briskness and in valour clothed,
And though thou beest of Genoa hast shown
Thyself to be imbued with the Spanish Muse,
So that the squadron entire hath thee admired.
From the remotest India, separate world,
Has my friend Montesdoca newly come,
Who knitted up Arauco's broken knot
Apollo said to the two: Both it behoves
Your rich possessions stoutly to defend
From the crude mob, who little shame affect,
Who armed with error and blind arrogance
Would canonize ye and deathless fame impart,
And ignorance which for divine would pass,
So far affection can, that one indeed
May hold it for himself in ignorance,
And for a genuine poet would pretend.
In this especial miracle, a vast
Prodigy is within the marine disclosed,
Which in some modest verses I recite:—
A ship adjacent to the firm-set earth
Arrived, and from the locality it holds
One plainly sees the cargo and decides
More than four thousand sacks did it exceed (salmas)
Which are as tons by salesmen recognised;
The body broad and stature to correspond;
Thus as the vessels charged with their freight
From the Eastern Indies do at Lisbon touch,
The greater they are, the higher estimated.
The very same vessel came from stem to stern
Well packed with poets, lawful merchandise.
Duty in Calicut and Goa paid,
The ruddy God into convulsions fell
At sight of such superfluous impudence,

Which to the mountain came succour to crave,
And all in silence prayed devotedly
That in a moment shipwreck entire should make,
The God who wields the trident o'er moist seas.
One of the number of the famished crew
Planted himself upon the broad ship's side
As if of humour out, and right peevish,
And in a tone which neither was sweet nor soft,
Holding a piece of money, issued a cry
(Indicating grave and choleric)
What the impatient said; I hearing marked,
Because for arrows I his reasons took
Which far advanced towards cleaving heart and soul.
O thou traitor, he said, that poets hast
Canonized freely in extended list,
By indirection implying cause and ways.
Whence holdest thou Megances, the sharp sight
Of thy low ingenuity, that thus blind,
Thou art so false an historiographer?
I thee confess, O barbarous, and not
Deny that some of the many whom thou hast
Selected, forced by prayer and speech
Into the place which is their due, hast put;
For on the *residuum* without a doubt
Prodigious praises have been heaped up
To heaven's height the fortune has been raised,
Of many who in dark oblivion's heart,
Without a sight of sun, or moon, or stars,
Projected lay. Nor called, nor chosen was
The great Iberian shepherd, Don Bernardo,
Who by appellative is Vega styled.
Envious thou wert, careless and tardy eke,
Both to Henares' nymphs and shepherds too,
As through thy enemies the dart was sent
While poets thou entertainest worse by far
Than those that in thy flock are. I suppose
Perspire they must, if they would better be.
Should this aggression not my mind disturb
From this time seven versicles I divide
Which are accustomed whirlwinds to be called.
With whom discretion, gaiety, advice,
Have little else to see, and thou dost place
Them two leagues further e'en than paradise;
These late chimeras, thy inventions these,
One day may sally forth to open show,
If thou dost moderate not, or be composed.
This threat and also this discourtesy
My quick-impressed heart hast filled with dread,

And pushed athwart all my known patience.
To Apollo turning, with a diffidence more
Than from my years might well expected be,
With voice disturbed, with gesture, I approach,
And said, with obvious ingenuousness,
"I find out that to serve, purchase I must
All present fears at price of future ills.
Procure, O sir, that in public there be read
The list which Mercury from Spain did bring;
Therein 'tis seen that small blame rests on me.
Should thy Divinity be in choice deceived,
And only I approve what he said to me,
Why should this simple one against me rage?
With a good cause and reason I afflict
Myself, to witness how these wretches incline
In fear to hold me harsh and keep me long.
Some, for I did cite them, me abhor;
Others, because I failed to enter them,
Have been determined me to aggravate.
I know not how with them I shall arrange
Those entered there, and those who are not in the list
Cry out aloud. I tremble between both.
O thou Lord, who art God, face those placed there
That they demand their wits! Call both, and name
Those who more subtle and more ready were.
And why this muddy fear which scares me quite?
Not finishing me quite, though the fight is done.
Cover me with your mantle and your shade,
A signal on me set, that all may know
That of your house and workmanship I am,
And no one then will dare to give me offence."
"Turn your eyes round, and witness what doth pass,"
Comes the reply from Phœbus infuriated,
Who, burning in his ire, consumes his heart
Again I turned, and seeing the most joyful feast,
The most unfortunate yet compassionate
The world e'er saw or ever yet will see—
Oh, do not hope I shall describe it here,
But in the Fifth Part; where I truly trust
With intonation and quick voice to chant,
That all shall think I am a dying swan.

CHAPTER V.

The monarch of the trident moist now heard
The prayers of Apollo, listening
With tender soul and heart to mildness tuned.
His eye he cast about, his feet to the waves

He gave; and ere him the poets descried,
In a moment upward raised to heaven his eyes.
He now, through passages hidden and occult,
Below the ship's level did cower down,
And traitorous trick played he to his heart's content.
With his trident struck he right into the hole
Of the hollow vessel, and the *vacuum* fills
With th' acrid rill of a most copious stream.
Admonished of the danger, th' air sends forth
A noise confused, from whence resulted eke
Thousands of others which form fears and pains.
By slow degrees the unfortunate vessel is
In the deep bowels of the azure main
Concealed, which buries so many souls at once.
The cries mount up through the divisible air,
Of those unfortunate souls, who heavily pant,
To witness their inevitable end.
They vault and mount to the rigging, and spy out
Which in the vessel is the highest place;
And there do many cling and quick retire;
Confusion, fear, surprise! The sensitive,
Greatly disturbed, guessing intuitively
That from this world to the other the leap is short,
Conjecturing nor art nor remedy,
But each believing his own fate to stay,
Instinctively resolve to swim for it.
In this way many plunge into the sea,
Where from the puddle of the bank leap frogs,
When fear or any noise notice implies.
The white waves, cleft asunder, gape outright;
Stroke after stroke follows, both legs and arms;
And though they weak are, and incompetent,
And in the midst of such embarrassments,
Their eyesights settle on the bank beloved,
Embraces infinite wishing to give.
And well I know the fatal company,
Rather than here, would joy to find themselves
Keep time in Seville's pleasant city erst.
They have no preference for suffocation;
Discreet enough in this they do appear;
Yet here do little their efforts avail.
The father of the waters now displayed
More of his rigour. Himself in his car
With furious countenance and a gesture sad
Four dolphins, each of variegated play
Of hue, with cords composed of woven works,
With arrogance and with fury him impelled.
The nymphs concealed in their moist alcoves

His anger felt, O vengeful deity,
Who steal'st the natural ruby from their cheeks.
The swimming bard who in presumption
To reach the bank where 'tis prohibited,
Loses his footing, and wastes his obstinacy.
His brief career effectively is stopped,
By the sharp points of the great God's trident,
Then a cruel, bitter homicide.
Whoe'er a diligent youth hath witnessed
Surpassing quite himself in daintiness,
For no comparison is more exact
Pecking in his hat the husks of grape,
Which reward or imposition there had placed,
With a pin's point or needle finely shaped.
Yet with no less appetite or haste
The infuriated god the poets strung
With infamous taste and with a dubious smile.
The crystal car at length to anchor came;
The beard was long with shellfish sprinkled o'er,
And eke with two enormous lampreys crowned—
Two sheepfolds strong (aprisco firme) they of this beard did make
A muscle, a morsillon, polypus, crab,
Such as are found within a rock or cleft,
An aspect very venerable and old
Of green with azure, silver-plated o'er,
Strong to appearance and with iron points.
Although as one enraged quite darkened o'er
In countenance he seemed when rage's force
Disturbs the feeling and the complexion too;
But most in rage he was against all those
Who swam the most. Forth sallying at the pass,
They judging for glory a so recreant deed.
In this, O new and wonderful event
Worthy to be related bit by bit,
With verses in Torquato Tasso's vein
Up to this point I have not called, but now
Your favour I invoke, O Muses apt
For the high strain I do aspire to reach—
The locks break open of your rich cupboards,
Giving me the breath which such a case requires;
Not humble, mean, not low, nor ordinary—
Let the air cleave the clouds, measure and press
The Alcidalian Venus, and descend
From heaven that no one make obstruction—
With greyish streaks invested was there used
A long vast robe adapted to its end,
Which one might say was square containing all
Such mourning as is for Adonis worn,

Immediately the tusk of the boar pig
Across his groin was fearfully disposed,
In faith, as if the boy had Maco been,
And would his face defend from tushes huge.
Aimed at his life, and beauty would destroy.
O valiant youth, more than judicious,
How hast thou been advised? Thou dost not well
Engaging in such cruel, horrible fights—
In this the softest doves, those innocents,
Divinity's own car are wont to draw
Over the level waters and stiff hills
On one side and the other did they run,
Till they encountered watery Neptune's face,
Which was precisely what they sought to see.
To the gods they met they very respectful were
After Moorish fashions making salaams—
Rejoicing to find themselves in union.
A grave decorum too they all observed,
And Cipriania at that point procured
To show the great wealth of her comeliness.
The farthingale was lengthened to a point,
Which came with certain pushes of the foot—
Kicks for the god who saw them and lay dead.
A poet rejoicing in Quincoces' name,
Did half alive advance into the salt
Waves, groans emitting—yet did he not cry—
But with all this in ill-articulated
Words, O my lady, thou of Paphos born,
And of those other two islands also named,
Be moved with compassion me to see
Benumbed both hand and foot, already drowned
In other streams than that of Garrafo.
Here, here shall be my pyre, my funeral pile;
Here also shall Quincoces be interred,
Who a pedagogue was by education.
Thus spoke the wretched wight, and he was heard
By the divinity with such complaisance
That round she turned to settle the farthingale.
Now quick on foot and piteous she arose
Fixing her orbits on the poor old man,
Her voice from her throat as from a funnel drew
With superciliousness and with disdain,
Between the incensed and grave, sweetly she spake
What gave perplexity to the watery god,
And though the reasoning savoured not of the prolix,
Yet not the less it was to memory brought
Whose brother he was, and eke of whom the son,
Representing how the glory was small

To take from those who miserable were indeed,
Th' inglorious triumph and sad victory.
He spake, If fate's decree immutable
Had not the fatal sentence uttered,
These ever had in ignorance remained.
A chip, no more, in your presence am I,
As I perceive, O lady beauteous,
My resistance is superfluous,
And yet this cannot be; for already is come
The moment when thy soft and gentle hand
Will evidence give of its hard and conquering power.
But this proceeding ever inhuman is,
A thousand times recited in his verse,
Lashing the waters of the pellucid sea.
Nor old nor lasting dost thou appear to me,
Venus replied, and he her an answer gave.
You melt me not, though I am enamoured of you
In such a way,—the really fatal star
Hath influence o'er these wretches. I cannot
A happy issue to your quarrel give.
From the decree of fate a finger's point
Can I not deviate, and that thou well knowest,
Accomplished all must be, and I yield to fate.
Thou must accomplish all thou shouldst effect,
Replied the goddess, for thou dost retain
Of such volition, both the door and keys.
Although ferocious fate doth death ordain,
The method may not be acceptable
Which in it are comprised many deaths;
Where on the liquid element up rose
The storm awakened up its dormant force,
The winds blew eager and more hastily,
The famished company, but not thirsty yet
To the fresh hurricane is delivered up,
And not to suffer further, dies content.
O rare example! such as ne'er was heard,
Was never seen, contrivance admirable,
In the vast kingdom of Gnidus observed
Instantly the Sea of Calabashes
Became congealed, and some most powerful
Exceeding two and even fathoms three,
Skins full of wind, and in construction firm,
Without dispersing the white foam of the sea,
In different sizes floated on all sides,—
This transmutation principally was made
By Venus, for the very languid bards
To sink them down Poseidon presumed not
Who asked of Phœbus for his arrows sure,

Whose arms thrown down and duly set apart
Might defraud Venus of her artful tricks.
Apollo these denied, and see you now
The old man with his trident quite enraged,
Thinking a pass to make from side to side.
But down he glided and did not perceive
The wound, and making a certain motion slipped,
Impatient there remaining in a rage.
Whereon old Boreas did wake up his wrath,
And drives his storm incontinently on.
Which by a hog's bristle is so symbolized.
The affectionate deity then solicited
That certain poets (zarabandos) should live on harmlessly,
Of those selected from the starched sect,—
Of those white, tender, soft, and complaisant,—
Of those who momentarily divide themselves
Into strange sects, and to opposite bands.
The opposing winds mildly compose themselves
To satisfy the sweet petitioner,
And with a sole gust the sea moderate,
Carrying off the grunting herd of swine
In Calabashes, and transformed skins
Unto the kingdoms of the drooping west.
The sweet seed widely was diffused about
In Spain—truth certain does so superabound
That for this quality it is esteemed and known,
That though in arms and letters fruitful 'tis
More than in many provinces it abounds,
It is well sown in a capricious soil.
After the change which heaven's self has made,
O Venus, or who it can be, having no care
To observe as I do, punctuality,—
No Calabash I see, nor long nor short,
And of a poet, no imagination,
Who here doth stretch, encumber, shrink, curtail.
But when I see a hide, O indiscreet
And foolish fantasy, so deceived indeed,
To what frivolity art thou subject?
I think that the foot of the skin to the mouth attached
Is a visage of a poet quite transformed
Into that figure which so inflated is
I say, firm poet, and available.
O man well-clothed and with shoes well-shaped,
Immediately I figure to myself
A hide, a calabash, and in this sort
Betwixt opinions contrary I expire,
I do not know whether I hit or miss,
In what to calabash or hide relates,

And in one way with poets I converse have.
Kestrills who prey upon the lizard tribe
Can never hope pre-eminence to enjoy;
Such as do hawks who pay no country dues (no pecheros),
Settled in peace are now the differences
Of Phœbus and the bards duly transformed
Into such hollow vain appearances.
The winds and seas assuaged, the mighty God,
Poseidon's self submerges discontent
In his deep palaces of crystal framed.
Doves, softest natives of the air, do fly
Clean through the winds, and the fair Cyprian is
Safely delivered to her own dear realm,
And as if of triumphs signal, brisk she was.
The petticoat from mourning being exempt
In hide remaining so fair and so brisk,
'Twas known that Mars did after visit her,
That day entire, and the two sequent ones.
Though all that precious time the squadron stayed,
The fatal ruin fixedly looking on,
Which the *Canaille* had caused to be transformed,
And seeing the shore cleared of the populace,
Apollo proffering succour ill-applied
Resolves at length the great affair to end.
Just at this instant a tremendous noise
Was heard, so that the crowd did stir-themselves—
Alertness using and quick hearing too.
A beauteous carriage, obvious to sight,
Rich, upon whose seat there was arranged
Don Lorenzo de Mendoza, the grave—
And to his happy genius was attached,
With his much valour and rare courtesy,
Jewels inestimable as ornaments.
Pedro Juan de Rejaule came,
In another carriage great Valencian,
Mighty defender of all poesy
Sitting on his right hand did also come.
Juan de Solis, specimen of youth,
Of genius rare and white in his green years,
And Juan de Carvajal, doctor renowned,
Made up the third, and not to be annoyed
They left him to pursue his hasty course
For the divinity at the upraised
Valour of these three, which the coach contained,
Nor mount nor hill could be obstruction.
They traverse in flight the elevated crest,
The clouds they touch, the empyrean almost reach,
And joyfully they press the renowned earth

With this most honoured and most steady zeal.
Bartolomé de Mola and Gabriel Laso
Arriving, lighted on the hallowed mount,
The high top of Parnassus honoureth
Don Diego, who De Silva is styled,
His pace stretching over the summit's height.
To whose vast genius and unequalled renown,
All sciences in full obedience bend,
And elevate him beyond mortality.
Shadows expand, and eke diminishes
The day, and the black covering of the night
Furnished with stars in revolution comes,
The squadron which on expectation's foot
Stood, to lazy sleep itself yields up,
Hunger and thirst, and mortal despair,
Apollo then less luminous in aspect,
Fetching a leap towards the Antipodes
Followed his accidental powerful course,
But first he liberty gave unto the five
Poets, entitled to his request, that they
With earnestness, extraordinary, should ask
To show them laughter, joke, and playfulness,
And enterprises similar—Phœbus thus
Did quickly to their wishes condescend.
The sole unique gallant of Daphne is he
Who uses courtesies upon such acts
Discovering our pole, and the opposite
From the dark place of frights unspeakable,
The languid Morpheus forth his hyssop draws,
Wherewith he many has drugged and quite subdued.
The liquor that they say from Lethe is,
Which from the fountain of oblivion flows,
And bathed the eyelids of all successively,
It puts to sleep those with hunger pressed,
Two things in opposition, hunger and sleep.
Unto poets conceited privilege—
I still remained in sleep, senseless as wood,
My fancy floating on a thousand thoughts
That to recount them I engage my word,
However difficult in themselves they be.

CHAPTER VI.

Of one of causes three which those in sleep
Do cause, or dreams which for appellatives
Do they give who are roasters of good speech.
First of those things concerning which a man
Does treat of more than commonly; the second

Demands the medicine that is nominated,
For the humour which in us fully abounds.
The third bears reference to revelations
Which more than th' other two to our good redounds.
I slept and dreamed, and the dreams to the third
Cause did sufficient principle awake
To mix a surfeit and teeth set on edge,
The sick man dreams whose entrails doth consume
The burning fever, and even in the mouth
A spirit of fire does there predominate.
The lip doth touch the fugitive crystal glass,
The sleeper's comfort all imaginary,
Increases the desire nor slakes the thirst.
The valiant soldier fighteth in his sleep,
Almost as restless when to his open eyes
He sees before him his antagonist.
The tender lover his contract fulfils,
And in his dreams doth ideas realize,
That without storm his haven dear attains.
The covetous man his heart delivers up
To his accumulated wealth in dreams,
Which no time hath his soul repudiated.
I who at all times have decorum used,
Both in my sleeping and my waking hours,
Who am no Troglodyte or Moor by birth;
My soul I gave unto the open doors,
Letting sleep enter by the eyes' inlets.
With taste and glorious anticipations,
Four thousand spoils did I in sleep enjoy,
And these I reckoned up, failing in none,
Realized in accumulations,
The time, occasion, opportunity,
The place all corresponding to effect,
United were, each for the other made.
Two hours was I in sleep discreetly too,
Without imagination or vapours
In any way disturbing my poor brain,
A loosened fancy thousand flowers among
Me to a mead transported, where were exhaled
Panchaian and Sabean odours too.
The pleasure situation raised
Within itself a view whilst sleeping, lives
Much more than when awake itself displays,
I palpably saw, but in description weak.
For what relates to impossibilities
My pen has ever shown itself but coy.
What makes of possibles a glimmering,
Of sweet, of soft, of certain consequence,

All my obliterations do explain.
To no disparity opens the way,
My cramped genius, and it ever finds
The door stand open to consistency,
How can any extravagance delight,
If it be not appropriately made,
Its grace displaying in its very course?
Then indeed untruth not satisfies,
When truth appeareth, written with very grace
Grateful to all simple and discreet.
I say, returning to the account, that I
Saw many persons wander o'er the plain,
With pleasing battle shout and with loud cries.
In-decent vesture and due courtesy,
Some to whom hypocrisy did give
A poor attire, yet simple, neat, and clean.
Others the colours which the day doth boast,
When first the morning manifests itself,
Cold 'midst the braids of fair Aurora's hair..
The spring in its diversity proffers
Of gaudy colours a superfluity,
At sight of which the taste is high enhanced.
Superfetation and exorbitance
Revel united o'er the verdant meads.
With sprightliness displaying simplicity
Upon a throne from earth high elevated,
Where wit and nature are in conjunction,
In gold and marble full elaborated
A female I saw, who from the sole of her foot
Quite to her head was in adornment set;
To see her and hear her sing, enchantment quite.
She seemed as if majestically throned,
Her stature of gigantic size; although
Her bulk was large, yet just in proportions.
Her beauty more eminent did appear to be
When at a distance seen—and not so much
The composition was if too close viewed—
Replete with admiration, at top of fear
My eyes on her I laid, and in her marked
That which in my delirious verse I chant.
I could not quite affirm if maid she were,
Though I have so averred, for in such case
The sharpest vision may stumble and ill guess.
Always divested are the greatest parts
Of reason with judgments fraught with malignity,
Pronouncing vessels broke which are entire.
Her hawk's eyes amorous in intensity,
Betrayed a certain meekness, which made them

Beauteous in lustre and expression.
Whether 'twere artifice or custom's rule,
Augmented were sometimes the rays of light,
And sometimes issued forth a subdued beam.
Two nymphs assisting at her side there were
Of such a gesture sprightly and polite
That wondering souls were rapt into suspense.
In the full presence of a lofty throne,
Their lips in reasons did they quite unfold,
In sweetness rich—of science destitute.
Their boastfulness unto the skies they raised,
Which in reality were small or none
Written in blottings of oblivion.
At the sweet murmuring and the opportune
Reasoning of the two, she of the position,
For nothing yet in beauty equalled her,
Quick on her feet she set, and in a point
Of time to me appeared to raise her head
The clouds beyond, I speak the very truth—
Yet lost she not for this, her comeliness,
Quite contrary, even more grand, showing
Perfection equal to her grandeur too.
To such a length extended were her arms
That from the spot where day doth rise and die,
The opposite extremes were compassed quite.
The infirmity which is the dropsy styled,
The body so wide expands, that it would seem
The ocean self might therein be comprised.
After this manner the composition did
Of all these parts enlarge, yet not for this,
Such said I, did her beauty disappear.
Astonied stood I, wishing to witness eke
The rest of this vast prodigy, and I would
A finger readily give the truth to solve.
Some one, I know not who, quite clear and still
Unto my hearing spoke, saying, Await,
And I will what you wish to learn declare.
That which thou sawest, which grows in this wise,
Which space alone can scarce within contain,
Aspiring in her greatness to be first,
That which through the clouds ascends and springs,
Till it arrive at the moon's circled orb
(Although the mode of rising is unknown)
Is she, confiding in her fortune, who thinks
To seize and hold fast of th' inconstant wheel
The very axle, and this without change.
This same doth find no ill in what succeeds,
Haughty and arrogant who fears it not,

In excess ever, venturesome and gay,
Is she who with extravagant design
Continued by degrees so to increase
As to attain the stature vast you saw.
She does not cease to grow, for not daring
To undertake most notable emprise,
Whence all can see excess and extremity.
Hast thou not heard tell of the memorable
Arches and amphitheatres, temples, baths,
Both hot and cold, porticos, strong walls
Which in despite and disrespect of years,
In remnants still remain, or entirely so,
Having deceived both time and hungry death.
I replying for myself, no piece
Of these of which thou speakest, cease to hold,
Clenched and riveted in my very brain.
I hold the sepulchre of the widow fair,
Colossus vast which unto Rhodes is joined—
The lantern eke serving for a bright star;
But come now, let us go to the very point
Of that which I desire—Be it quickly done.
To me replied a voice in emission low,
And so pursued, saying, Not to be blind
Thou mightest see who the great lady was.
At length you have a lay brother's sharp wit,
This same figure unto the clouds is raised,
By the winds impregnated, not knowing how.
The daughter is of desire and fame likewise,
She was th' occasion and the instrument,
Where'er extended is the world's wide length,
Not seven wonders to see, but a hundred sights.
A small count is a hundred, though one says
A hundred thousand and more millions, yet
One does not imagine how the sum exceeds.
She thus conducts memorable ends unto,
Edifices seated on the earth,
Touching the confines of the lofty clouds.
She is it who ofttimes the war has raised,
Where peace reposed sweetly, nor could she
Confine herself within her straitened bands.
When in the flame she died there was consumed
The bold, the strong, the cruel arm of fight,
She cooled the horrible waste incendiary.
Thus she who hurled the Roman cavalier
Th' abyss into of a fire-devouring cave,
Armed all in proof, and with the shining steel,
This same creation with a wonder new
Raised from ambitious condition,

Of impossibility makes proof.
From burning Libia to the frozen spot,
Scythia in memory elevates her fame,
Expanded o'er in works of vast emprise.
In fine, she is lofty in vain-gloriousness,
Interposing in these large exploits
Victory arrogating from age to age.
Herself she promises to herself,
Triumphs and assays without holding fast
To the bald occasion by the firm forelock.
Her natural sustentation, her drink too,
Is air, and doth in an instant increase
So much, that medium none is found therein—
Those twain endowed with placid visages,
Whose place is at her two sides, are those who
The apparatus of Atlas do serve
Her delicate voice, her lucid orbs of light
Appearances of humility and reasons
Wanton, which love itself stamps on the face,
Rendering them less human than divine—
And are (with peace and patience sentinel)
Sisters of adulation and untruth.
These in her presence stand continually,
Words unto the ear administering,
Which of serene prudence have the guise.
And she who of better feeling is deprived
Sees not the flowers of pleasantness amidst
That there a poisonous serpent is concealed;
And so impelled by an unjust desire
The crystal vase she tries, and forthwith drinks
The mortal poison, destitute of fear,—
Who amidst the cautious would more presume
Ceasing from adulation, soon will see
How glory fleeteth like the wanton winds.
He listened,—and in listening did this same,
In glory vain such a report send forth
That to my sleep it gave a troublous end.
And now did the next day disclose itself,
Dew turning into pearls, flowers scattering,
Wanton in sight, wanton in virtue eke.
The very sweet young brood of nightingales,
With songs not learned declared their nature too,
To be enamoured of a thousand loves.
Goldfinches also did their tunes repeat,
The ready larks the music did entune,
Reiterating what they all composed.
Some of the squadron put themselves in haste,
Not to permit the God of day to find

Them all engaged in the forced act they were.
Quickly now the lady did look out,
With a countenance of reddish German tinge,
Through the balcony of the frigid morn—
Part in front were stout, part loose and weak,
As he who dreads the expected circumstance
Who sees himself overcome if he desires.
In Spain's tongue, and Toledo dialect
Courteously salutation proffered he
And quickly for the event himself prepared
And placed on summit of a rock in front
Of a squadron's force, with voice sonorous, grave,
This very speech did utter suddenly,—
Oh happy spirits wherein is contained
The joy of speaking and the subtlety
Of that same learned science, known by all.
Whence in its own natural comeliness
Beauteous poesy assists, and is
From top to base in its perfection
Thou wilt not for thy life or mine consent
(See with what plainness to you Phœbus speaks)
That this low race defiant should triumph—
This scum, I say, which doth bedevil itself,
This multitude which unto heat impels,
Even its ruin and ours sets on foot
Ye of my eyes the glory and the light,
Lanthorns where my light doth residence' find,
Either by nature or by habit's law,
Will you consent that this embassadress,
A hypocritical mob, which so saucy is,
Of such puerilities be the inventress?
Indicate famous, memorable proof
Of your great valour in this very act
Which to their chastisement and your glory leans.
With indignation just arm thou the breast,
The mob with intrepidity assault.
Vagabond, lazy, and eke profitless.
I know not if I nothing give, or e'en
A mite (money of Barbary vile and low)
To this same mob, which now our peace disturbs—
The noise of more than one attempered drum,
The wry-necked fife and trumpet loud of sound,
Which rage enkindleth and sour phlegm subdues.
Thus ye to secret virtue I incite
That ye the sleeping souls will waken up
In the same fashion as now presses us.
Already resound, already touches mine ears
Of the opposing squadron the loud noise

Of cries confused fully constituted.
Yes, it is right not asking or in demand,
That each, such as an expert warrior,
Letting no caprice disorder him,
Preserving order and tact military,
So execute his acts as a valiant man,
There to remain victor or amongst the slain.
Upon these words on the western side appeared
A squadron almost numberless of tribes
Barbarian, struck with poverty and blind
Our partisans at the same moment raised
A cheerful cry,—not timorous—they cry, Arm,
And through the district space resounded, Arm—
And though they died, to arms all wished to fly.

CHAPTER VII.

O Muse belligerent, thou who dost possess
A voice of brass, and metal be thy tongue,
When to resound the fame of Mars thou com'st,
Thou, through whom diminished and destroyed
Is the human race; thou who art competent
To snatch my pen from ignorance, and defect—
Thou broken hand and yet full of rewards,
In doing it I say one thing I ask,
That thou in doing it not less rich remain'st—
Pride and blown wickedness and the audacious
Intent of a noble nation ill observed,
With mortal noise itself discovereth—
Grant me a voice all suited to the fact,
A subtle pen, yet with a sharpened point
By passion nor affection prejudiced,
That may readily a summary give
With novel sentiment and in purest style;
With truth resplendent in its entirety;
The contrariety and unequal aim
Of one or the other squadron, all on fire
Its bands dissolving in the wayward wind.
That of the Catholic band which views the false
And great at the mountain's foot, so firmly placed
That it aspires to mount the lofty top—
With passage large, yet in symmetrical
Order it crowns the mountain, self-exposed
To the fury which madly the rest rejects.
Th' advantages they weigh, and well dispose
Their valiant spirit to the dread assault,
Wherein they set their glory and revenge.
Replete with rage, and lacking patience,

Apollo his standard, beauteous to behold,
Orders immediately its erection high.
Upraises it a marquis, who Mars himself
His fiery presence wholly represents;
Naturally, sans art or industry.
A bard most celebrated, and of account;
For whom and in whom great Apollo, lord,
His glory, taste, and fortitude augments.
The ensign was a white and elegant swan
Painted to the life, that one would say
Its cheerful voice takes leave of the vain air.
His colours follow on the standard close,
By a cheerful body of pipers borne,
Respected, e'en though a lack of entirety.
The sweet recorders, blowing martially,
Turn quickly to the soldiers' tardy step,
With metal instruments accompanied.
Geronimo de Mora here is found,
A poet excellent and a painter too—
Virgil and Apelles both in one,
And with the authority of a marshal's staff,
Which gives a name to a soldier's highest rank,
Assists the business, and the crowd repels.
The more the commotion was, the greater fright,
Into the enemy, unequal and fierce,
In fused Biedma, of immortal fame,
And with him Gaspar de Avila, first
Follower of Apollo, whose verse and pen
Would envy in Iciar raise, dread in Sincero.
Juan de Metanza came, figure and sum
Of erudition vast, lively and brisk,
Obnoxious not to death or senility.
Apollo him from Guatemala snatched,
And, for his aid, enlisted him against
Th' evils consequent on acts of the *canaille*.
Miracles to work in dangerous times
Cepeda thought, and Megia followed him,—
Of boundless praises poets worthy both.
Of Andalusia clearest luminary,
And of La Mancha, without peer Galindo,
Arrived, with dignity and playfulness.
From the high top of Pindus, so renowned,
Descended three strange sons of Portugal,
To whom I render my sincerest praise.
With rapid step, and arms for valour framed,
Fernando Correa de la Cerda with,
Pressed Rodriguez de Lomo, mount and plain,
And for it is that Phœbus reason hath,

The great Antonio de Ataide came,
With noisy fury and right implements,
The opposing forces measures and adjusts
With his Apollo lord, determining
Battle to give, and battle thence exacts.
The rough, hoarse sound of cornets more than one,
Of venery and of war the instrument,
Phœbus' auditories quick invade;
Beneath all feet trembles the earth itself,
Oppressed by poets numberless, who gave
Assault and battery to the holy mount.
The general fierce of this intrepid race,
Which bears a stag on its broad standard's front,
Is Arbolanches hight—a snout for a life!
There were they standing on the lower part
And on the mountain's brow, each fronting each,
On which same plains did tremble Mars himself,
When one band, in appearance goodly souls
Of the Catholic sort, unto the enemy passed,
In numbers a good twenty by just count.
I with my eye do follow his career,
And coming to the halting-place of his
Intent, with voice perturbed to Phœbus say,
What prodigy is this? what portent vast?
Or rather should I say what augury ill,
Which thus cuts off my briskness and my breath?
That renegade who went away the first,
Not only for a poet was he held,
But also for a very prating churl.
That individual light who ran behind,
Have I seen at Madrid in knots of men,
Glibly squandering his poesy.
That third person who parted hence so gay,
For satirist, ignorant, and for a heavy man,
I know he was so recognised by all,
Conceive I cannot how Mercurius hath
Admitted such shabby poets to his list.
'Twas I Apollo said who was deceived,
Who of his genius on the first aspect
Discovered proofs, that they would be excellent,
This same conquest to facilitate,
My lord, I then rejoined, I thought indeed
That no deceit imposed on deities.
I say in nothing more or less can be
Prudence, which is the offspring of long years,
Having experience for his preceptor.
The Deity is who notifies these ills,
Apollo answered, On my conscience

I understand thee not, somewhat disturbed,
To mark the insolence of these twenty men,
Thou, soldier Lofraso from Sardinia,
Wert one of those channels all barbarous,
Who did the sum of th' adverse ones enlarge.
Yet not for this reduction ever feared
The valiant of the squadron Catholic;
Bards notable well versed in wisdom's lore,
Contrary quite such courage they conceived
Against the fugitive scouts, that they
Made havoc on them and did slaughter them.
O false and cursed troubadours who pass
For poets well versed in their profession,
Being nought else but worse than very dross,
Between the tongue, the palate and the lips,
Your poetry continually moves on
Assaulting virtue with a thousand wounds.
Poets of impudent hypocrisy
Hope also that for your completion quite
The fearful day already has full dawned,
The music of your voices so confused,
Resounded through the air likewise confused.
Thick clouds condensing in the wayward wind,
Upon the mountain's lap creeping like cats,
A troop poetic crawled, aspiring eke
To the topmost round, which strongly guarded stood,
They fixed their feet securely now and then.
With slings of awful noise and strong cross-bones
Freely discharging ruthlessly they moved—
Not of inflamed lead the horrid balls
Composed were, yet equally murderous,
Nor could more quickly the discharges be.
A book much harder than a solid stone
Struck on the temples Jusepe de Vargas,
Terror, grimaces, awe awakening.
He cried aloud, and to a sonnet said,
Thou now who comest, shot by satiric plume,
Why dost not thou thy infamous course divert?
And that dog there with pebbles irritated,
Who him avoids who throws, and lags behind.
And if he were the cause of the contumely,
Between the fingers of his beauteous hands,
The lofty sonnets into pieces tear,
Threatening the sun and moon and twinkling stars.
Then Mercury said to him, O living ray,
Whence this just indignation emanates,
Superlative in valour and degree.
The sword do brandish in thy dreaded hand,

And cast it valiant, e'en temerariously
Through that same part where danger's self doth guide,
Whereon a breviary of enormous bulk,
A book indeed, came whirling through the air,
Of verse and prose which th' opponent hurled.
Of verse and prose the sheer madness did
Indicate that of Arbolanches were
The greedy works continually weighed down.
Some rhymes were brought, which virtually would
A Christian squadron rout and overwhelm,
If a second time perchance they were impressed
To Mercury, into his right hand he gave
A satire antique and licentious,
In style acute, of sound sense destitute.
Of prose badly composed and intricate,
A subject all awry, sans sap or wit.
Four novels did Pedrosa heavy launch,
Whistling anew, and rending forcibly
The air, four books of rhymes alone sent forth,
Fabricated 'twould seem of negligence.
Phœbus observed, and said as he them saw,
Heaven the author,—pardon, I did await
For other rhymes, for Spanish poesy.
Pastor de Iberia next came on, though late,
Demolishing fourteen of our author's books,
Making a muster strong of wit and force.
However, two masters, and both valorous,
Two luminaries of Apollo, soldiers two,
In language one, and in assertion sharp,
On opposite sides of the mountain located,
Oppressively upon the crowd they told,
Forcing the populace to regurgitate.
It is Gregorio de Angulo who
Buries the *canaille* with Pedro de Soto,
Of mighty genius and a cultured vein.
A doctor this, th' other unique and styled
Licentiate, of Phœbus followers both,
Combining rarest works with souls devout
The two opponents makest thou to fight
Measuring unworthy swords, which they stout grasp
Hard and persistent in their obstinacy.
They bite hard with their teeth and closely gripe
With claws, quite imitating the wild beasts,
All pity, all remorse abandoning.
Dragging his skirts, advancing, he th' author
La Picara Justina, perspiring,
Legitimate chaplain of the opposing band,
As if he were a Culverin, he discharged

His monstrous tome from out his hands, which was
The ruin total of our camp and men.
Tomas Gracian, he of an arm bereft,
Medinillas' grinders fairly he wrenched out,
And of the thigh a portion carried off.
At this, one of our sentinels awaked
And bellowed out, All of ye, stoop your heads,
The adverse faction more novels discharge.
Two warriors fought for a protracted space,
One on the other with mad frenzy fell,
Awful strokes dealing with dexterity.
Six Spanish couplets thrust him on the mouth,
Wherewith it made him vomit up his soul,
Which sallied forth free from its narrow cell,
All fury's ardour, and bright Phœbus' calm,
Confined in doubt in both the adversaries,
For the pretended and victorious palm
In this, the dusky standard of the stag
To the white cygnet yields, falling on earth,
Smitten quite through and through to the heart's core.
His ensign who was from Andulasia,
A troubadour repentant who did mount
Far heaven beyond, smit with obdurate pride.
His very blood congealed in his veins,
And died outright when he perceived the crowd
Most pertinacious, and in defiance stiff.
Though absent was the great Lupercio,
With one sonnet alone, his proper work,
Enacted what was hoped from his known fame.
He fairly quartered, joints broke he and undid
Quite fourteen ranks of squadrons full opposed.
Two circles slew and wounded a Meztise.
From his jokes sapid and his verities
The great Cordoves a stitched copy-book
Shot forth, and down came four bands in the mire,—
Signs sure of laxness and of weariness.
The spirit of the barbarous mob did yield,
More weakly fighting and more leisurely,
The fatal battle stoutly was renewed,
One on the other falling, all pell-mell;
No armour did avail, nor coat of mail.
Five sons of song, mounted on five male colts,
Arrived, and made assaults upon our flanks,
And cleanly carried off five of our band.
Each fell like unto a Moor, decked finely out
With letters and ciphers, more than a mandate
Of an enemy prince, all circumspect and close.
A string of Moorish novels were produced,

The very same as if they were chain shot;
He hurls with fury and *malice prepense*,
And that two squadrons should not be advised
Of ours about the recent firing, prompt.
'Twas necessary that a rout ensue.
Phœbus, indignant, wished to avail himself
Of all his power and sole sufficiency,
And deal the enemy the last sad blow.
A sacred canticle, there to purify
His wit, his sprightliness, and gallantry,
Bartolome Leonarda de Argensola,
As if Apollo's self a petard sent
Where the obstinacy is most tight,
Most hard and furious the defiance too.
"When did I stop to contemplate my state?"
The canticle began, which Phœbus puts
Into a place most noble and high raised.
All look at it, all so arranging it
With eyes of Argos, order, quit, and see
Itself opposing to all stratagem.
So mingled all, that none exists who can
Discern what evil is, or what is good,
Which Garcilasista is, Timoneda which?
But a youth remote from ignorance,
Great scrutinizer of all history,
Flash in his pen and thunder in his voice,
Arrived; his soul so rich in memory,
Of a sound will and robust intelligence,
Apollo's glory and the Muses' friend.
With this man was achieved the victory,
For he knew how to say, "This man deserves
Glory, but that man only punishment!"
And as now with distinction do appear
The just and unjust in contention,
The taste increasing to the pass of pain,
Thou, Pedro Mantuano, excellent,
Wert he who in the fight confused did see
Which was the recreant, which the valiant man.
Julian de Almendaiz refuse not
Immediately on his arrival, though late,
To succour the red Apollo with his Muse,
For the white hair I comb, and swiftly run
To see the comedies bedevilled set up,
For quite divine, in the thick knot of folks,
And all despite of the clear and polished
Of comic works, best of Hesperia,—
Wish them to be paid for and acknowledged,
However little in this market is gained;

For discreet is the Common of the Court,
Although on common misery it trench;
For plain one gives it not—to the Court gives it
Polypheme stanzas to the poet, who not
For guide would take us or his north pole star.
Inimitable ye are; and to the wise
Sprightliness in secret discovering
All elegance may truly subjected be.
With these munitions our condition
In such a way was so ameliorated,
That th' opposing party was vanquished.
Now was abased haughty presumption,
Thrown from the mountain low, as many were
Who had presumed to ascend the side so steep.
The voice prolix, with canticles all hoarse,
The bad success with rigour it converts
To sorrowful uninterrupted plaints.
This happens too, that falling, he resolves
Upon a briar to sit, or an old weed,
And in this plaint, like Ovid to dissolve.
Four heaped themselves in mass on an old oak,
As though they all were as bees on a hive,
And they esteemed them for their laurel friend.
Another gang, virgin as to the sword,
In tongue adulterous, gave certain care
To the feet, by reason of their starched life.
Bartolome, also De Segura styled,
The touchstone was of secured victory,
Such is his wit, and such his amiableness.
In this resounded through the wanton winds
The voice of victory reiterated
The chosen number, in accent clear and strong.
The miserable—the very fatal fall
Of the Muses from the clean aristocrat (*tagerete*),
With grief for many ages was bewailed.
On the side of woe (ah me!) is surely set
Zapardiel, famous for his fishery,
Without of rest an instant, interposed.
The voice of victory freshens itself,
Victory sounds here, there; victory
By our brave military sons acquired,
Who, joyous, chant of glory perfected.

CHAPTER VIII.

Upon the falling of the vast machine
Of the poetic host so arrogant,
Which in its unseen might strives powerfully,

A bard, a youth, a student only yet,
Spake, "Patience have, and in a future day
It shall be ours, wrought by my valorous hand.
I will anew my sword's blade deftly whet,—
I mean my pen—and with it so will cut,
That excellence new to constancy it give.
Comedy yields, if one due notice takes,
A large field to the genius, whence it may
Its name from death deliver and decay.
Juan de Timoneda was an example
Who by his printing did eternal make
The comedies of Lope de Rueda.
Five overturnings in Tartarus will I give,
For having recited one which I possess,
El Gran Bastardo de Salerno hight,
Apollo looks, and sees dealt out below
The fiercest blow from the most sprightly hand
That ever time hath witnessed in its course.
On this the clear sound of one ignobly born,
Set wings upon the feet of these subdued
People, tardiest, laziest in the world.
All hope of glorious victory being lost,
No one is there but waits not with light step,
If not for honour yet his life to keep,
From summit of Parnassus' altitude.
At one bound he on Guadarama leapt,
A new unseen and still undoubted fact.
By the same passage, Fame, the talkative,
The news of victory extended wide,
From clear Cayster's stream to Jarama,
Turbid Esgueva victory bewailed.
Pisuerga laughed, and Tagus eke did smile,
That sand instead he raised up grains of gold.
From dust, from weariness, and from exercise,
Thymbrean Apollo's ruddy sunbeams stopped,
As if the colour were turned to deep gold.
Seeing accomplished his desire in full,
At sound of so-called Mercury's guitar,
He made a passage to the Spanish dance.
In the fresh current of Castalia
His visage did he lave; shining remained
Like to the steel of Turkish battle-axe;
Quickly he polished it, its front adorned
With majesty and sweetness all combined
Clear indications of the joy he felt.
The very queens of mortal loveliness
Did sally forth from their sequestered spots
Pending the hardy trial of the fight,

Crowned with the leaves of the tree evergreen,
In midst of which was divine Poesy,
Embellished all with decorations fresh.
Melpomene, Thalia, Terpsichore,
Polyhymnia, Urania, Erato,
Euterpe, Clio, and Calliope,
Mettlesome briskness demonstrating,
Weaving a dance all new, all intricate,
To the dulcet melody of my instrument
Mine, true I said not well, after the use
Of him who others' verse for his own recites,
I falsified, more worthy praise they are.
The meadows ample and th' adjacent fields
Stand full of squadrons who had victors been,
Ever increasing, never on the wane,
Awaiting from improvements soon to see
Of guerdons merited the realization.
From six hours' pressure and labour intense,
All the elect themselves thought they were called,
For all aspired to prizes of great weight,
Rating themselves far higher than their worth.
Neither at qualities nor at wealth look they,
Each holding to his proper genius,
And if but four succeed, the rest run mad.
But Phœbus who ne'er wished that any one
Of him should have complaint, to Aurora sent
That she should go, and in a propitious hour
Cull from the leafy folds of Flora four
Curious baskets of red roses, mixed
With six of pearls, such as a goddess weeps.
And of the Nine being beauteous in extreme,
Chaplets he asked, and for the donative
In nothing lazy did they show themselves,
Three of them to my fancy beauteous most,
I knew they sent them to Parthenope,
And Mercury it was who with them weak.
Three subjects did the others crown anon,
There strangers to the very mountain where
Their name and country were eternized.
Three Spain reserved, and three poets divine
Adorned the head, worthy the glorious act.
But envy, a monster form to mortal man
Accursed, and worm-eating, burning eke
In wrath, to murmur at the gift begins.
He said, Shall it be possible that in Spain
There be nine bards with laureated crowns?
Apollo lofty is, simple the deed,
Defrauded is the residue of the crowd

Of the expected guerdon, and repeat
The hymns of envy in a degraded strain.
All hold themselves for laureated bards
In their imagination before
The trial, sending plaints to heaven of wrongs.
But certain poets of romantic vein
Hope to attain the generous reward
Despite of Phœbus in his quickest reach.
Others of Latin origin despair
To touch so much as a single laurel leaf,
Although they forfeit life in the demand.
Who most enrages, the least vengeance hath,
And some their hands pass over forehead and face,
Longing to be crowned with the sacred leaf.
Yet each impertinent desire full sure
Apollo doth repress, rewarding bards
Who in the valorous squadron were enrolled.
Of roses, jessamines, and amaranths
Flora herself presented baskets five,
Aurora also gives as many pearls.
These were, dear reader, the bright donatives
Which Phœbus scattered with munificent hand
Amongst the poets, youths of undoubted fame;
Leaving each satisfied and quite mettlesome.
With pearls and roses many in their hands,
Rating the prize at superhuman price.
And that more wonderful the feast should be,
And the rejoicings which followed in train,
For a victory, prodigious in renown,
The good and the important Poesy
Sent out to bring the feast in, whose large paw
Opened the fountain of Castalia cold.
Covered with scarlet of the finest woof,
A lackey instantly did him introduce,
Champing a bit of burnished steel i' the mouth,
Rosinante might have envied him.
To mighty Pegasus the bold presence,
And Billadoro of Aglante, Lord,
With wings, I know not how many, adorned
Both hands and feet, manifestation sure
That in velocity he the winds outran,
And to give evidence how agile he
And quick was, raised himself four pikes in height,
With boldness and with gesture well arranged.
Thou, who to me lend'st ear, if ear thou dost
Apply, to the sweet history of the voyage,
Things novel in rich taste shall apprehend.
Of the good trotting-horse the ironwork

Was all of metal e'en as diamonds hard;
No hurt receiving from a pressure extreme
Of the dove colour known as columbine.
Smooth in a case his tail secure he keeps,
Which free from tangles trails along the ground.
Of carmine colour and the poppy hue
Were the dense hairs of the mane and thick tail—
Mane and tail both without parallel.
Now went he on in haste, and now quite slow,
Flying sometimes, and making high curvets too,
As though he wished to neigh, then quickly ceased.
For bards acknowledged a new felicity,
And his superfluities gathered up,
Into two pouches great, of leather stiff;
I asked for what cause they had all this done?
Mercury answered, in a waggish style
With glimmerings of irony, hard to say,
Tobacco is it that which they collect,
Salutary for vertigo in the head,
Afflicting the weak brains of any bard.
Urania in such wise arranges it,
That to the nostrils of the patient placed
Doth health recover and soundness restores.
Upon this fact my forehead I wrinkled up,
Having a great distaste for this so strange
Remedy remote from ordinary.
Apollo said, My friend, you are deceived,
The thought did teach me, surely this remedy,
Vertigo cures and qualifies the ill.
This horse eats not that which in a dire siege
Hard and beset with ills the soldiers eat,
Who stand midway famine and death between;
This beast consumes daintily treated thought,
Amber and musk 'twixt cotton interposed,
And doth imbibe dew from the meadow's breast;
Sometimes we give him of starch a basketful,
And with the carob tree hunger satisfy.
This no restraint imposes, nor for it he goes.
Let it be so, said I, in time precise,
Tough in the brain I do continue still,
No giddiness of head doth cause me pain.
On this our lady universal styled,
I mean the truthful divine Poesy,
Who with the Muses and Apollo dwells,
Light in habiliments encased too;
The mountain traverses and embraces all,
Beyond all usage beauteous and benign.
Oh the victorious blood of the old Goths,

He said, From henceforth to be treated well,
With sweet and discreet practice, handsomely
I hope to be, and in respect be held,
By the ignorant vulgar, which does not attain
To know though I am poor, honoured I am.
Riches I do bequeath you in sure hope,
But in possession not. Secure the reward
Which to the kingdom of great joy aspires.
But by the comeliness of this mount I swear
That I would wish at least to deliver up
A privilege of infinite use to you;
Not the least is mineral, in this valley,
Water it produces good, salutiferous,
And monkeys which in likeness are to swans.
Look round and see, O friend, the countless sands
Of the gold-carrying Tagus, quite in peace
Secure in its sweet hours, its current runs.
This deed unheard of you in fact assures
A name, which shall not die, while Phœbus gives
Breath to this mundane globe with light serene.
O wonder new, O novel accident,
Admiration worthy, causing dread,
Whose strangeness wonder new in thee excites,
Morpheus, the god of sleep, enchantment through
Did here appear whose crown was fabricated
Of branches of the henbane's sacred root (beteño),
Torpid in his appearance and his life,
Accompanied by a base laziness,
Which leaves him not at Vespers or at Nones,
On his right side does he to silence draw,
The careless to the left; his vestment was
Of a soft wool entirely fabricated.
Of the sad waters of oblivion styled,
A vessel vast he dragged, of hyssop too,
Coming exactly by anticipation
He seized the poets, stiffly by the tuft,
And though the accident did their faces turn,
Enflamed in colour to *piropo* like,
He bathed us with cold water, whose effect
Did in us cause a somnolence so deep
That we at least two days profound did sleep.
Such is the potency of the fluid, such
The power of these same waters, that they can
In competition stand with death itself.
Wit has he quite enough that very truths
Divested of all credit do remain,
To show how they contingencies exceed.
Or waking from a sleep so forcible

No mount saw I, no reckoning, no goddess,
Nor god, nor any poet visible.
Of a truth a thing extraordinary, ne'er seen,
I cleared my sight and it appeared to me
As if I in a town's centre found myself.
The fact invested me with pure affright,
And wonder eke, I turned to see for fear,
Or dark delusion stole away my mind,
Repeating to myself, I am not deceived.
This city sure is Naples the renowned,
Its streets I traversed a whole year or more,
Glory of Italy, light of the world.
Though many cities it environs too,
None are but say that Naples radiates all,
Sedate in peace, constant in heavy war,
Parent of all abundance and *noblesse*.
Elysian fields it boasts, sierras too;
If in my brain I am not versatile
It seems to be as if 'twere changed in part
Of its site, yet in its beauty still increased.
What theatre is that which doth divide
With it all which in beauty is comprised—
Grandeur and gayness, industry and art?
Upon my eyelids surely sleep doth reign,
For 'tis an edifice imagined quite
In symmetry surpassing each structure.
At this same juncture all unknown to me
Arrived a friend, styled Promontorio,
A youth in days gone by, a martial wight.
Wonder augmented on a notorious view
And palpable eke that he in Naples stood,
An accessory dread to wayfarers,
My friend did me most tenderly embrace,
And holding me in his arms cried out aloud,
I held in doubt extreme that I were here.
Father he called me, I, him son did call,
And truth exactly stood in its verity.
That here one could declare a fixed point,
Promontorio said to me, Father, I guess
That some great accident to your white hairs
Drags them so far, yourself being half defunct.
In my youth's hours so fresh and temperate
This very soil I dwelt on, son, said I,
In vigour brisk and wantonness of heart;
But will, which subjects most things to its sway,
I say the decrees from heaven, it has me drawn
Aside, which fact delights more than afflicts.
I would say more but that a powerful noise

Of footsteps, clarions, and ear-piercing drums
My soul do terrify, but mine ear delight
At the sound, I turned round, and the vastest saw
Of festal apparatus e'en by Rome
Seen, in its happiest time of pre-eminence.
My friend then said to me, Him whom you see
Looking on that misshapen mountain, whose
Gaiety doth oppress e'en Mars himself,
A lofty subject is, who holds subdued
E'en envy's self in her rage, because he treads
In rectitudes most straitest, path direct—
So smooth in gravity and condition,
That in an instant augments and suspends,
And with advice opinions rectifies.
I would require ere further you proceed
You look attentively at what you see,
And judgment give equivalent to the act.
Juan de Tasis shall be of my account
The principal, for memorable it may be,
And my words reach to my intent full sure,
This youth so noted for his liberal views
Who took his countship from an humble town,
Yet was he king, in his works admirable.
This same who never his possessions hides,
These always he divides, and scatters those,
One who already knows whence, and yet knows not
He who the threads of fame securely holds
Elevated high his honoured name,
That liberal and prodigal e'en is styled,
Here would he prodigal be, and covetous there.
The principal support of a tourney
Which I compare to superhuman feasts—
His greatness corresponds to the desire
Which shows itself in cheerfulness, noting
The royal marriage betwixt Spain and France.
That to which your attention give, though hard,
The cheerfully sounding sign of the tournament is,
Stupendous, in its admiration rich.
Great Archimedes would ashamed be
To see this marvellous theatre reduce
His genius, and designs quite overpass.
I saw now that the generous youth, who here
In silver and vermilion too, transcends
The airy course of fixed mortality,
The Count of Lemos is, who by his works
His fame diffuses through the world's expanse,
And so reach heaven, the earth traversing.
Although he issues first, the second is

Of those who are supporters, and on this fact
I found and qualify advantage true.
The Duke de Nocera, both light and guide
In military art, the third support,
An agent good in this day's festival.
The fourth, who may eventually be first,
Is of Saint Elmo powerful chatelain,
Whom I prefer e'en to the god of war.
The fifth, another Æneas of Troy,
Arrociolo, who through valorous might.
What's healthful gets by operative hand.
The concourse vast and numbers of the race
A hindrance made to a farther advance,
In the prudent relation so commenced;
On this account I asked that he would place
Me, where no great impediment interposed,
To view the progress of the stately feast,
For soon as in my contemplation 'twas,
It to celebrate in my numerous verse,
Favoured by Phœbus' inspiration,
The deed I did, and now do see what I
Had dared nor think nor say—hence is abridged
A voice and genius the most operative.
Important is it in silence to pretermit,
That admiration may the defect supply,
The magnitude of the case thereto exhorts.
After that I conscious was of a high
Elegance, magnificent and wonderful,
Which neither was above nor below point.
The memorable Juan de Oquina in prose
Composed it, and glory to th' impression gave,
A fact most fortunate for the living age;
For neither in fiction, nor in truthful writ
Is found, that other festivals have been,
Nor e'en can be more worthy memory.
From this moment I know not how I was
Betrayed when I great Duke Pastrana saw;
A thousand welcomes to the comer give.
And fame herself in all truth satisfied,
Recounted how in his presence she was joyed,
And with his courtesy beyond compare,
An Alexander new in his excellence,
In giving that which went to satisfy
All that true magnificence can boast
With admiration struck, with fear replete,
Into Madrid I went in pilgrim's suit,
Which for sanctification is true gain—
From afar his bonnet he veiled for me

The famous Alcevedo, and said, "To god
Welcome art thou, my cavalier and friend,
I know full well Genoese and Tuscan speech."
And I rejoined, Your Highness truly is
Right welcome here, thanks to your patronage.
Luis Vellez I met, a shining light,
A very courtier in discretion,
Him in the street in mid-day I embraced,
The breast, the heart, the soul, and dexter hand
To Pedro de Morales eke I gave.
Justiniano did I glad receive.
While turning round a corner I perceived
An arm my neck embracing, wondering whose.
The embarrassment did cause me more than joy,
For to be one of those (I refuse not
To say so) who went the contrary way, and were
Diverted from their intent dishonourable.
The other two to Layo themselves joined,
And with the rabbit's smile of falsity,
With gratulation much held me in discourse.
I, an arch wag, a poetaster old,
Returned their salutation courteously,
Without denoting pride or an evil will.
Thou doubtest not, dear Reader, doubtest not,
That simulation oft is accustomed
To other virtues increase to supply.
Sayest thou not to us, David, though thou
Dost seem a fool in Aquis' power, from thy
Mildness while feigning folly, greatness effects.
I left them hoping a coalition
And an occasion meet to offer them
A trial of their madness or their fear.
If any bard upon the way I met,
To thought I myself surrendered if they were
Of those who fled, and without speech passed on.
My hairs upon my head did stand erect,
Through fear I might encounter some poets
Of the many I could not as such recognise.
Who with a burnished dagger, or secret
Three-edged poniard might an inlet make,
Which by a way direct the heart would reach.
Though this be not the guerdon I await,
For fame which I from so many have acquired,
With grateful soul and heart of sincerity.
A certain youth of a stiffnecked race,
Professionally a poet, and in tone
Of manners known for a Goth a thousand leagues
Replete with courage and presumption too,

Said to me, Sure I know, Cervantes, who
May well a poet be, though but a page—
With poets ignorant art thou overcharged.
So leave me to myself who long to see
The stately fountains of Parnassus' height—
I think some doating you will have sans doubt.
I think I say not well, better 'twere said
This verity I touch and see it too.
Another which all silver did appear,
Of mother-of-pearl, of crystals, pearl and gold,
Composed were his verses infinite.
Bravo, said he to me, what a hunted bull—
I know not I why no one me hath placed,
In such a list with a so barbarous decency.
So had Apollo thus discreetly done
To these two worthies I said, of this deed
Of ignorance or malice I know nought;
With this I went straight off; full of despatch,
I sought my antique dismal inn, and then
All beaten threw me on my pallet mean,
At a too long day's work exhausted quite.

APPENDIX TO THE PARNASSUS.

I awaited some days to repair my strength after so extended a voyage, at the end of which I sallied forth to see and to be seen, and to receive gratulations from my friends and ugly looks from my enemies, for I do not think I can be without them, in accordance with the lot of humanity.

It fell out going one morning from the monastery of Atocha, that a youth joined me, seemingly about twenty-four years of age, less or more, neat, adorned and wrapped up in a suit of grogram, but with a neck so long and be starched that I verily believed it would require an Atlas to raise it up. The issue from this neck were two flat fists, which, starting from the wrist, mounted and jumped by the long bone of the arm upwards, and looked as though an assault on the beard was intended. Never did I see ivy so covetous of an ascent from the foot of the wall where it rests up to the battlements, as the desire which animated these fists to give some strokes with their extremities. Finally, the extravagance of the neck and fists was such that the very face was buried, and in the fists were lost the arms. I say then that this selfsame youth joined me, and with a grave and settled voice said, "Peradventure your worship is Don Miguel de Cervantes Saavedra, he who lately arrived from Parnassus?" At this question I believe certainly that my colour left me, for in a twinkling I imagined and said within myself, If this be one of the poets whom I have placed in my narrative, or should have put there, and he comes now to recompense me for the debt he deems due! However, extorting force from weakness, I rejoined, "I, sir, am the identical person of whom you speak; what would you of me?"

He on hearing this quickly opened his arms, and seized me by the neck, and had saluted me on the forehead, had not the largeness of the neck prevented it; and he said to me, "Señor Cervantes, esteem me your servant and friend, for I have been of a long season much devoted as well to your works as to the fame of your condition." On hearing this I breathed, and my spirits, which were somewhat dashed, calmed down again; and embracing him with reservedness so as not to discompose his neck, I said to him, "Your acquaintance I have not made, sir, save to serve you; by the proofs you seem to me to be a courteous and well-governed man, qualities which are estimable in all who can boast them." Whereupon we interchanged other courtesies, and offers of politeness uprose, so that he said, "Your worship Cervantes will know that by the grace of Apollo I am a poet, or at least desire so to be, and my name is Pancracio de Roncesvalles."

Cervantes.—I had never credited that, had not your mouth announced it

Pancracio.—And why not, my friend?

Cervantes.—Because poets, for a wonder, are as refined as yourself, and that is the reason they are so lofty and of so high flight. They even catch the spirit of things as well as the material part.

"I, sir," said he, "am a youth, am rich, and also am in love,—attributes which undo in me the sloth which poesy inspires. As for my youth, I am mettlesome, with wealth enough to display it, and with a love not appearing indifferent"

"The three parts of the road," said I to him, "you have reached to qualify for a poet."

Pancracio.—Which are they?

"That of riches and of love; for the productions of wit in a person rich and enamoured are the terrors of avarice and the stimulants of liberality, and in the needy poet the moiety of his divine creations and sentiments raise the careful to seek an ordinary flight. Now, friend, speak to me of your life, what sort of broth poetical do you taste, or what pleases most? "To which he replied,—

"I do not comprehend your meaning about broth."

Cervantes.—My meaning is, to what order of poetry are you inclined? to the lyric, heroic, or comic?

"I am dexterous at all," said he, "but what most occupies my mind is the comic."

Cervantes.—In this style have you composed many comedies?

Pancracio.—Many; but one only has been acted.

Cervantes.—Did it go off well?

Pancracio.—Not in the vulgar eyes.

Cervantes.—But in those of the competents?

Pancracio.—Neither.

Cervantes.—Why?

"The cause was that it was wide in the reasonings, not very pure in versification, and loose in invention.'

"Faults such as these," I said, "would show culpable in Plautus himself."

"And more," said he, "they could not judge of it, for they cried out so that they would tolerate no further hearing of it. With all this, the author kept it for another day—but obstinately to oppose—what opposition!—scarce five persons came."

"Believe me, sir," said I, "comedies have their days, like pretty women; and to hit that off well is as much in chance as in design. I saw a comedy fairly hissed (apedreada) in Madrid, which was crowned with laurels in Toledo. So not for this first disappointment do you cease from composition; and it may so be, when you least expected you may light on the happy conjuncture which realizes to you both credit and money."

"About money I am indifferent," replied he; "I had rather enjoy renown, whatsoever it be,—for it is a commodity of the rarest taste, and of not less importance to witness many who make exit from the comedy, all satisfied, the bard who composed it standing at the entrance of the theatre, receiving gratulations from all."

"Its deductions boast these joys," to him I said, "that sometimes the comedy is so intolerable, that not a soul raises his eyes to observe the bard, nor within four streets of the Colosseum, not one who recites raises his eyes, ashamed and out of countenance at being deceived, having taken the comedy for a good one."

"And, Señor Cervantes," said he, "are you given to caricature? Have you composed any comedy?"

"Yes," said I, "many; and were they not mine, they would seem to me to be worthily praised,—as they were praised. 'The Manners of Algiers,' 'Numantia,' 'The Great Turkish Affair,' 'The Naval Battle,' 'Jerusalem,' 'The Amaranth Flower, or that of May,' 'The Harbour of Love,' 'The Solitary and Bizarre Arsinda,' and many others whose names have slipped my memory. That which I most esteem and appreciate beyond others was and is styled 'The Confused Person,' which, with peace be it averred, of all the comedies, known as 'Cape and Sword,' represented to this very time, may be undoubtedly pronounced the very best"

Pancracio.—Do you retain any others?

Cervantes.—Six I have in reserve, with six admixtures.

Pancracio.—Why then not cause them to be acted?

Cervantes.—Because no authors seek me, nor I them.

Pancracio.—They do not know you have them?

Cervantes.—Yes, that they do. But as they retain poets in the house (paniaguados), and they get on well with them, they seek no better bread than is made of wheat. But I think to give them the go-by to press (darlas á la estampa), that they may see sadly what passes quickly, may dissemble, and not understand the representation, for comedies have their opportune seasons and conjunctures, even as do popular songs.

We had got thus far in our colloquy when Pancracio thrust his hand into his bosom and drew out a letter with its envelope, and kissing it, put it into my hand. I read the superscription, and saw that it ran after this fashion:—

"To Miguel de Cervantes Saavedra, in Garden Street, opposite the houses where the Prince of Morocco used to dwell, in Madrid. For the postage of a letter, half a real, I say, seventeen maravedis."

The postage money offended me, and the declaration about the half real, I say seventeen. And turning it about, I said to him, "Being in Valladolid, a letter was brought to my house for me, with a real for the carriage. My niece received it, and paid its transport, which she never paid to him. But there was exemption of blame, because many times she had heard me say that in three things money was well spent,—in alms, in paying a successful doctor, and in carriage of letters, either for friends or foes;—for those of friends counsel us, and those of our enemies can indicate thoughts. They gave it to me, and in it was a wicked sonnet, faint-hearted, without politeness or wit, speaking evil of Don Quixote; and what afflicted me more was that the real was paid. So I resolved henceforward to take in no letters with postage to pay. So that if you would take this you may return it, for I know that it cannot affect me so much as the half-real they demand of me."

"Observe, Señor Cervantes, that this very letter is from Apollo himself. He wrote it some twenty days past in Parnassus, and gave it to me that I should deliver it to you. Read it, sir, and I am assured that it will impart joy."

"This will I do," said I, "but I demand, ere I do read it, that you would inform me how, when, and by what means he came to Parnassus? "And he replied, "As I went, I went by sea, and in a frigate, so that I and some other ten poets were freighted in Barcelona. When I arrived, it was six days after the engagement which took place between the good and bad poets. Why I went, it was to find me bind myself to my profession." "Certainly," said I, "you were well received by Apollo?"

Pancracio.—Yes, we were, although we found him much engaged on it, and the ladies' Muses ploughing and sowing with salt that part of the field where the battle was fought. I asked him why he did so, and he answered me, "that in this wise Cadmus sowed the dragon's teeth, whence sprung armed men, and that from every head of the hydra which Hercules cut off arose seven others, and that from the drops of blood of Medusa's head all Libya was filled with serpents."

In like manner, from the tainted blood of bad poets who had died in this spot, there began to arise, of the size of rats, other rat-like poetasters, who filled the earth with noxious seed, and for this reason they ploughed up that place, and substituted salt, as if it were the house of traitors. On hearing this I quickly opened the letter, and I saw what it imported.

Delphic Apollo to Miguel de Cervantes Saavedra, Health.

The Señor Pancracio de Roncevalles, bearer of this letter, will recount to Signor Miguel de Cervantes in what he found me engaged on the day he came to see me with his friends, and I say that I am disconcerted at the want of courtesy that was exercised on his departure from this mountain of Parnassus without taking leave of me, or of my daughters, knowing how well affectioned I am to him, and the Muses also. But if any excuse there be that a desire animated him to see your Mæcenas, the great Count of Lemos, or the famous festivals in Naples, I accept the excuse and grant pardon.

After you quitted this spot, much misfortune befell me, and I found myself in considerable straits, especially in censuring and finishing the poets which were born of the blood of the evil ones, who died here, although, thanks to heaven and my perseverance, this evil was not without its remedy.

I know not if from the noise of battle or the vapour which was cast out on the earth moistened in the blood of enemies, gave me a giddiness in the head which almost made me foolish; I cannot attain to writing anything of taste or of profit, so, if you should see there any poets, albeit the most famous, write and compose impertinences and matters of insignificance; I blame them not, or hold them less, but I dissemble with them—for since I am the father and founder of poetry, I rave and seem out of my wits, hence it is not surprising they should seem so too.

I send to you, sir, some privileges, orders, and arrangements touching the poets, which you must guard and fulfil to the very letter, for I assign to you all my power as right requires.

Among the poets who came hither with Señor Pancracio de Roncevalles complaint was made that some were not in the list of those which Mercury brought from Spain, and that you did not cite them in your Voyage. I told them that mine was the blame and not yours, but that the cure for this ill was that they should be famous in their works, they would secure fame and bright renown, without going about soliciting foreign praise.

Should occasion for a messenger arise I will issue more privileges, and state what is passing in this mountain.

So do your worship, advertising me of your health and that of all friends. To the famous Vicente Espinel you will give my commendations, as being one of my oldest and truest friends.

Should Don Francisco de Quevedo be not departed for Sicily, where he is expected, shake his hand and tell him not to fail to come and see me, for we shall be neighbours. When he came there, by reason of his sudden departure, I had no opportunity of talking to him.

Should you encounter any fugitive of the twenty who crossed to the opposite faction, say nothing, afflict them not, for bad venture enough have they; they are like devils who bear woe and confusion with themselves, go where they may.

You will take care of your health, look to yourself, and look to me also, particularly in the dog days, for although I be your friend, in these times I look not to obligations or to friendships.

Keep the Señor Pancracio de Roncevalles for your friend, and have him in communion; for although he is rich, it is of no consequence that he is a bad poet. Keep yourself well, even as I desire. From Parnassus, this 22 nd of July, the day on which I put on my spurs to mount to the very dog-star, 1614.

Your Servant,
Bright Apollo.

On finishing the letter I found that I had written on a loose paper,—

PRIVILEGES, ORDERS, AND REGULATIONS,
WHICH APOLLO SENDS TO THE SPANISH POETS.

The first essential is, that poets be as well known for the slovenliness of their persons as for the fame of their verses.

Also, should any poet say he is poor, that he instantly be credited on his word, without any other oath or verification soever.

It is required that every poet be of a mild and becoming mental habit, and that one should not look at stitches, albeit they appear in his stocking.

Ditto, should any poet touch at the house of a friend or acquaintance, and should stay there for material sustenance, that although he swear that he has eaten, let it not be believed, save that he be made to eat by force, which in that case will be no great things.

Ditto, that the poorest bard in the world, though neither Adams nor Methusalems, may say that he is in love, though he be not so, and should give as the name of his lady, now styled Amaryllis, now Anarda, now Cloris, Phillis, or Filida, or Juana Tellez, or any other name at will, all may be done without asking reasons why.

Ditto, we ordain that every poet, of whatsoever quality or condition, be held for a son of some important somebody by reason of his noble profession, like as are esteemed for old Christians those children who are styled of the stones.

Also, that it be ruled that no poet dare write verses in praise of princes or lords, it is my intention and expressed will, that flattery and adulation never traverse the portals of my house.

Also, that every comic poet who may have successfully printed three comedies, enter gratis into the theatres, though there be no alms at the second door, should it so be, then he may enter without payment.

Also, take notice, should any poet wish to print any work he may have composed, that he dedicate it not to any monarch, if the composition be esteemed; if it be not good, that he will not botch up the address, though it be made even to the Prior of Guadalupe.

Also, take note, that no bard depreciate himself by saying what is, were it good it shall be worthy of praise, if bad, there will not fail of some one to laud it, that when the broom is found, &c.

Also, that each good poet may dispose of me, and what there be in heaven at his own good-will; and that it be recognised that the rays of my periwig may be transferred and applied to the hair of his enamoured one—he may make her two eyes, suns—that with me there shall be three, and hence the world shall walk more illumined, and that he may avail himself of stars, signs, and planets—so that when least he thinks of it, there may be for his use a perfect celestial sphere.

Also, that every poet whose verses are intelligible, esteem himself highly, holding the aphorism (refran), Ruin awaits him who keeps company with ruin.

Also, take notice, that no poet of gravity roam about in public, reciting his verses—those which are good in the halls of Athens may be recited, but in the public ways not.

Ditto, this is a precise injunction, should any mother have very small children, distorted and prone to cry, that they be threatened and frightened with a bugbear (coco), saying, Mind, little ones, for a certain poet is coming who will hurl you with his abominable verses into the abyss of Cabra or into the well of Airon.

Also, that fast days mean only those which the poet has broken that morning by biting his own nails during composition.

Also, should any poet say he is a ruffian, a bully, and a desperate man, let him surrender those attributes, and go the way which fame leads to attain excellence.

Again, notify that he be not held for a thief who would appropriate others' verses, and pass them off for his own, whether in conception or in part, in which case he is as much a thief as Cacus.

Also, that each good bard, though innocent of an heroic poem, or has enacted wonders in the stage, with howsoever little means he may yet reach the name of divine, as did reach Garcilasso de la Vega, Francisco de Figueroa, Captain Francis de Aldana, and Hernando de Herrera.

Again, we notify, should any poet be favoured by a prince that he be not the less visited, nothing be asked of him but that he follow the stream, and that he mind he keep his land vermin and his waterworm, and that he will help to sustain a poet, whatever sort of worm he may be himself.

In sum, these were the privileges, advices, and laws which Apollo sent to me, and which the Señor Pancracio de Roncevalles brought me, with whom I remain in amity, and the two we have united to despatch a proper reply to the Lord Apollo, with the news of this court.

Notice will be given of the day on which all interested may write.

THE SIEGE OF NUMANTIA.

PREFACE.

It has been deemed useful by the translator to add some remarks on these three works of Cervantes by Sismondi, and they are here appended.

The tragedy of *The Siege of Numantia*, and the comedy of *The Treaty of Algiers*," are the only two which have been preserved out of twenty or thirty dramas, written in 1582, soon after the author's release from captivity. Those which he published in 1615 were never represented. To be just to Cervantes, we must reject all our theatrical prepossessions, as he wrote on a different system, and with another object in view, than those who published the regular dramas. His are a series of pictures all connected by the chain of historical interest. In some he has endeavoured to excite the noblest sentiments of the heart; in his "Numantia," patriotism; in his "Algiers," zeal for the redemption of captives. Such are his only unities. In analyzing the models of antiquity we do not apply to all of them rules equally severe. We do not forget that Æschylus, like Cervantes, was in the van of his art. If we compared the "Numantia" with the Persians or Prometheus many points of resemblance would strike us, in the grandeur of the incidents, in the depth of feeling, in the nature and language of the allegorical personages, and lastly, in the patriotic sentiments of the compositions; in these he has approached nearer to the most ancient of the Greek tragedians than any voluntary imitation could have accomplished.

There is a strong feeling of patriotism manifested by Cervantes in his "Numantia." He has taken as the subject of his tragedy the destruction of a city which valiantly opposed the Romans, and whose inhabitants, rather than surrender themselves to the enemy, preferred perishing beneath the ruins of their homes, slaughtering one another, and precipitating themselves into the flames. It is not a tragedy for modern representation; it is too extensive, too public, and too little adapted to the display of individual passions, and of those motives which operate upon persons and not upon nations. It is an expiatory sacrifice offered up to the Manes of a great city.

The tragedy, written in octave stanzas, with the Spanish redondilla of four trochees, rhymed in quatrain, is employed. The translator has adopted the English iambic, and the redondilla is transfused into metrical lines, as better suited than rhyme for these dramas. Southey has used the same system in his "Thalaba." He says he felt that while it gave the poet a wider range of expression, it satisfied the ear of the reader. No two lines are employed in sequence which can be read into one. Two six-syllable lines compose an Alexandrine. It cannot be distorted into discord; he may read it prosaically, but its flow and fall will still be perceptible.

In the "Numantia" Scipio declares to Jugurtha the repugnance which he feels to continue a war which has already cost the Romans so much blood in contending against the obstinate valour of the enemy and the want of discipline which his own army betrays. Scipio, ascending a little rock upon the stage, gazes on the soldiery, and then addresses them in a speech of elevated feeling and martial eloquence. He directs various reforms, and orders the women to be removed, and nothing to be left productive of luxury or effeminacy, suggesting that then it will be easy to vanquish the handful of Spaniards enclosed within the walls of Numantia. Two Numantian ambassadors arrive, and declare it was to the severity, avarice, and injustice of the generals who had hitherto commanded in Spain that the revolt of Numantia was owing; that the arrival of Scipio had induced them to sue as ardently for peace as they had before courageously sustained the war. Scipio demands a higher satisfaction, and refuses all overtures of peace, and dismisses the ambassadors with an exhortation to look well to their defence. He then informs his brother that he had determined to surround Numantia with a deep fosse, and to reduce the place by famine, and orders circumvallation s to be commenced.

Spain is symbolized by a woman crowned with towers, bearing in her hand a castle, as derived from the name and arms of Castile. She invokes the mercy and favour of Heaven, and complains of perpetual bondage.

The circumvallation achieved, the Numantians contend against hunger without engaging the enemy. One side of the city is washed by the Douro; hence they address that river, beseeching him to favour the Numantians, and to swell the waters, to prevent the erection of towers and machines on its banks by the Romans.

The Douro, followed by three tributaries, advances upon the stage, and declares he has made the greatest efforts to remove the Romans from the walls of Numantia. That the fatal hour is arrived, and the only consolation left is derived from Proteus, who has revealed to him the future glories reserved for the Spaniards, and the humiliations to which the Romans are destined. He predicts the victories of Attila, and the conquests of the Goths, which are to renovate Spain, the title of "Most Catholic" which will be bestowed upon her kings; and lastly, the glory of Philip II., who will unite the territories of Portugal to the two kingdoms of Spain.

In the 2nd Act the Numantians assemble in council, and Theogenes inquires from his countrymen by what means they can escape the cruel vengeance of their enemies, who without daring to combat with them, have reduced them to perish by hunger.

Corabino proposes that an offer shall be made to the Romans to decide the fate of the two nations by a single combat, and that if this is refused they should try the effect of a sortie through the fosse, and attempt a passage through the enemy. They propose sacrifices to appease the gods, and auguries to ascertain their wishes. In this Act two Numantian soldiers, Morandro and Leoncio, appear; the former, the lover of Lira, a young damsel of Numantia, was on the eve of marriage, when the nuptials were deferred on account of the war and public misfortunes. Leoncio accuses him of forgetting in his passion for Lira the dangers of his country. This dialogue is interrupted by the arrival of the people and the priest, with the victim and the incense for the sacrifice to Jupiter. Presages now present themselves—torches will not light—smoke curls toward the west— and invocations have their responses in thunder—eagles fly in the air and pounce on vultures, tearing them—the victim is carried away by an infernal spirit just as it is about to be slain.

Marquino, a magician, endeavours by enchantment to discover heaven's will, and approaches a tomb where three hours previously a young Numantian had been buried who had died of hunger, and he invokes his spirit from the infernal regions; and the address is very poetical, speaking commandingly and contemptuously as magicians are wont who are not quite the slaves of Lucifer. The tomb opens, the dead rises, but moves not Marquino by fresh enchantment bestows animation and compels the body to speak. The corse announces that Numantia will neither be the conquered nor the conqueror, but that her citizens shall destroy one another. The corpse then sinks into the tomb, and Marquino, in despair, stabs himself and falls into the same grave.

The 3rd Act leads us into the Roman camp.

Scipio gratulates himself on having reduced Numantia to the last extremity, without finding it necessary to expose his soldiers. A trumpet is heard. Corabino appears with a white flag in his hand, and proposes to terminate the quarrel by single combat, conditionally that if the Numantian be vanquished the city gates shall be opened; if, on the contrary, the Roman champion is overcome, that the siege shall be raised. Scipio with *hauteur* rejects the proposal, which would place him on equal terms with the enemy when he is assured of conquest

Corabino vituperates the Romans, and he retires.

A council of war is assembled, and Theogenes stating the failure of the sacrifices, of the enchantments, and the challenge, proposes making a sally. The women, informed of the proposed *sortie*, crowd around the council-chamber with their infants in their arms, and each in feeling language demands to share the fortunes of her husband. Theogenes swears the women shall not be abandoned by their husbands, but be protected living or dying. He then proposed that in the middle of the great square of the city a pile should be raised on which all their riches should be cast; that to mitigate hunger the Roman prisoners should be slain and eaten by the soldiery—which resolution is adopted. A terrific love scene ensues. Lira, to the passionate exclamations of her lover, only answers that her brother had died of hunger the preceding day, and that on that very day her mother had perished, and that she herself was on the verge of death. Morandro determines to obtain food to prolong his mistress's life, Leoncio resolves to accompany him, and wait the obscurity of the night to make the attempt into the Roman camp.

The pile is lighted and the property is heaved within; a man declares when all their property is consumed that the women, children, and old men will all be massacred by the soldiery to save them from the conquerors. A terrible scene occurs of a mother and her child—a nameless mother nourishes her infants with blood instead of milk, struggling against the excess of suffering which human nature was not formed to support. At the commencement of the 4th Act an alarm is sounded in the Roman camp, and Scipio demands the cause. He learns that two Numantians had broken into the camp and had carried off some biscuit—one fled and the other was killed. Morandro enters wounded and bleeding, weeping over his friend's fate, for the biscuit he carried to Lira was moistened with his tears, which he lays before her and expires at her feet. She refuses to touch the food, while her little brother seeks refuge in her arms and in convulsions dies. A soldier appears pursuing a woman whom he tries to kill, according to the Numantian decree. He refuses to slay Lira, and bears away with him to the funeral pile the two bodies which lay before her.

The allegorical personages, War, Famine, and Sickness, appear, and dispute for the ruins of Numantia. Theogenes passes over the stage with his wife, two sons, and a daughter, conducting them to the pile where they are to die by his own hand.

Viriatus and Servius fly before the soldiers. Theogenes beseeches a citizen to put him to death. The Romans perceiving the stillness of the city, Caius Marius mounts upon the wall by a ladder, and is shocked to see the city one lake of blood and the streets choked with the dead.

Scipio fears the loss of a triumph—he wants one citizen to be chained to his car—they discover Viriatus, who had taken refuge on the summit of a tower, whom Scipio invites to surrender; he heaps curses on the Romans and precipitates himself from the tower and falls lifeless at the feet of Scipio.

Renown, with a trumpet in her hand, terminates the tragedy by promising eternal glory to the Numantians.

Ferocity reigns through the whole drama. The tragedy does not draw tears, but a shudderng horror, almost a punishment to the spectators. With all its imperfections it is a noble production, and like Don Quixote, is unparalleled in the class of literature to which it belongs; and he may be styled the Æschylus of Spain, for the conception is in the style of the boldest pathos, while the execution is vigorous and dignified, evincing a skill in gradually heightening the tragic interest to the close of the piece.

DRAMATIS PERSONAE.

SCIPIO.
JUGURTHA.
CAIUS MARIUS.
ROMAN SOLDIERS.
QUINTUS FABIUS.
MAXIMUS, *brother to Scipio.*
Two AMBASSADORS *of Numantia.*

ACT I.

SCENE I.

[SCIPIO *and* JUGURTHA *enter.*]

SCIPIO. This very difficult and heavy charge
    The Roman Senate has devolved on me,—
    So much fatigues, o'erweighs, and presses me,
    That it unhinges quite my diligence.
    War in its course so strange and yet so wide,
    And which so many Roman lives has cost;
    Will no one hesitate to suspend its course,
    Or no one dare its fury to renew?
JUGURTHA. Who, Scipio? who the fortune entertains,
    And valour yet unseen, which in thee lives?
    For in it and in thee securely dwells
    The victory and triumph in these wars.
SCIPIO. Force regulated with discretion
    Levels the loftiest mountains to their base,
    And the ferocious strength of the mad hand
    Distorted renders what was level before.
    Nothing presents this mischief to repress.
    The fury of the present armament
    Of fame and trophies quite oblivious
    Prostrate lies sunken in a burning lust
    This only I suggest, earnestly wish,
    With our people a new treaty to make,
    That first restoring what is in amity,
    I quickly shall our enemy subdue.
    Marius.

[CAIUS MARIUS *enters.*]

CAIUS MARIUS. Sir.
SCIPIO. Procure a notice to be given
    To all the soldiers at this very time,
    That no impediment be interposed,
    And that in the same spot they all appear,
    Because I would a brief harangue or word,
    Proffer to them all.
CAIUS MARIUS. I'll do it straight.
SCIPIO. Proceed, for it is good they all should know
    My new contrivances, and their old usage.

    [CAIUS MARIUS *exit*.]

JUGURTHA. I can aver, my lord, no soldier exists
    Who does not jointly love and fear thee too;
    And for this thy valour extreme in truth
    From the Antarctic to Calisto[1] spreads.
    Each soldier bold in his ferocious soul
    When the trump calls him to the occasion,
    Purposes in thy service quick to enact
    Deeds passing those of fabulous histories.
SCIPIO. First it is necessary that each one refrain
    From vices which 'mongst ail extended be.
    Should these not be abandoned, nothing can he boast
    In common with those who excellent fame have gained;
    Should this prevailing evil not be quenched,
    This ardent flame permitting to take root,
    Vice, only vice, 'gainst us establish will
    War, worse than enemies of this soil can do.

    [*This band goes within, having first sounded the drum.*]

    The general commands
    That the military all armed unite
    In the principal square immediately,
    That no one under penalty omit
    Upon the spot to be seen,
    Lest from the list he be erased forthwith.
JUGURTHA. My Lord, I doubt not but it well imports
    To govern the army with an iron hand.
    To the soldier if a loose rein once be given,
    Injustice only doth it precipitate.
    Military rigour is abridged
    When justice is deprived of due support.
    Although with multitudes the general may
    With painted ensigns and squadrons be found.

---

[1] *Calisto*, a constellation—the Bear.

[*At this juncture as many soldiers enter as can, and* CAIUS MARIUS, *armed in antique style without arquebuses; and* SCIPIO *mounts on an elevation on the platform, and surveying the soldiers, addresses them.*]

SCIPIO. Well, by your pride of nature, noble friends,
    And splendour of martial decorations,
    I recognise in you the sons of Rome,
    Yea, brave and valiant sons. But by your hands
    Fair and effeminate, by the glossy show
    Of your smooth faces, you should, I rather deem
    Of Britain be born or Belgium. You yourselves,
    By your neglect, your reckless disregard
    Of all your duties,—you yourselves have raised
    Your foe, already vanquished from the ground,
    And wronged at once your valour and your fame.
    Behold these walls that yet unshaken stand,
    Firm as the rocks on which they rest! These walls
    Bear shameful witness to your weak attempts,
    That boast of nothing Roman but the name.
    What! when the whole world trembles and bows down
    Before the name of Rome, will you alone
    Betray her claims to empire, and eclipse
    Her universal glory here in Spain?
    What an imbecility strange is this!
    Imbecility engendered of sloth,
    Mortal enemy to manliness.
    Seductive Venus, with the hardy Mars
    Have never founded durable unity.
    One follows dainties, th' other pursues the art
    Which straight to damage and fury incites.
    The Cyprian goddess, let her stand aside,—
    Let her son quit our quarters instantly.
    Banish the poison in the martial tents,
    Such as prevails in feasts and surfeitings.
    You well know what alone the walls subverts,
    The battering-ram with its well-ironed point,
    "The great swing and the rudeness of his poise."
    What under foot the battle doth tread down
    But multitudes of soldiery cased in proof,
    Should neither strength nor discretion be found.
    All is prevented, and will guesswork be.
    Squadrons little avail in the foughten field,
    And less in fact are batteries numberless.
    Should all the adjustments military be arranged,
    However small the armament may be,
    You will discern it clear as the noonday
    That victory follows as we all desire.

But should it only to sad weakness lead,
Howe'er abridged, the world will soon detect
That in a moment all goes quite athwart,—
The operative hand and stout breast too.
Shame on you, youths courageous, that you see
To our disgust with full-blown arrogance,
So few of Spain's sons, all environed eke,
Defend the nest of proud Numantia.
Some sixteen years and more are glided by
Since they the war uphold with haughty boast,
And hands ferocious virtually have subdued
Infinite numbers of the Roman host.
You yourselves are vanquished, beaten are
By a low fancy for a gamesome sex,
With Venus and for Bacchus, paramours—
Nor raise your arms to warlike implements.
Shame to ye now, for ye have been ashamed
To see this insignificant Spanish host
Defend itself against the Roman strength,
The greater the surrender, more the offence.
From our camp's centre specially I require
That females all of doubtful lives retire—
For being thus reduced to such a point,
The root is recognised in these women.
For drinking let there be but one vessel;
And beds which one time were a quiet rest,
All impure persons let them be discharged,
And take their rest prostrate upon the earth.
Let no true soldier have any other scent
But what of rosin and strong pitch doth smell,
Nor for a gourmandize of savoury meats,
Apparatus from the kitchen use—
For who in war these delicacies seeks
Will ill know how a stout cuirass to bear.
I wish no delicacy nor fragrance may
Dwell in Numantia while Spaniards are there.
Let not appear, my men, severe, perverse,
The rigorous commandments I impose,
For in time's lapse they will prove salutary,
When this my will tallies with your intent,—
For well I know there will be difficulty
To give to your habits a new impulse;
But should you alter not, firmly will last
The war, which this affront confirmeth more
In amorous chambers, play and dice betwixt.
The troublesome Mars straight finds himself at odds,
Another sort of apparatus seeks
Another way; his standard fresh arms raise,

Each individual fabricates his lot,
A part peculiar fortune does not frame,
A slothful fortune low estate creates,
But diligence, empire, and monarchy.
This being effected I feel sure that you
The Roman name will vindicate at last;
I hold in strict contempt the defended wall
Of these barbarian rebels, born in Spain,
And so I promise you by my right hand,
And swear that if your hands do equalize
The impulse of your souls, my hands shall pay
Profusely and my tongue in praise expand.

[*The* SOLDIERS *observe each other, and make signs reciprocally.* CAIUS MARIUS
responds for all, and thus he speaks:—]

CAIUS MARIUS. If with attentive eyes thou hast observed,
General renowned, in the appearances
Which thy compendious reasons have betrayed,
Those whom thou now around thee entertain'st,
Such shalt thou have seen without colour, disturbed,
And such with it, proofs all-sufficient
Of what do fear and shame unto a man,
Afflicting, troublesome, and importunate.
Shame to see such a reduction
To terms so abject for their fault alone,
So that acknowledging reprehension just
They know not how for faults excuse to find,
Fear for so many errors perpetrated;
And the base sloth which blames them obviously,
Keeps all of them so minded that they would joy
Before they died to find themselves released.
But place and time which yet to them is left
A penitence adequate to show, is cause
That with less force the rigour of such offence
May thus itself wear out.
From this day forth with a more cheerful will,
And quick, the least of these takes care and thinks
To offer to your service positively
His property, honour, and life in sacrifice.
Admit of all these excellent intents
The offer just, my lord, and think well too,
That these brave men are Romans, in whose hearts
Courage and willingness did never fail.
Ye, all of ye, your right hands elevate
In signal that you do approve my vow.
SOLDIERS. All that which thou for us confirmed hast,
To it do we swear.

ALL. Yes, all do swear.
SCIPIO. Relying then on this offer of yours,
    From this day, truly my affection grows.
    Valour and warmth in your breasts growing too,
    And from the old life there is mutation new,
    The wind will not your promises disperse,
    Confirm them with the lance, that mine also
    The very truth may so eventuate, that
    Valour of famous deeds may full proof yield.
SOLDIER. Two of Numantia's sons securely came
    To give thee, Scipio, an embassy.
SCIPIO. What, come they not then, what does them detain?
SOLDIER. They do await full liberty to move.
SCIPIO. If they ambassadors be, detain them now.
SOLDIERS. Ambassadors they are.
SCIPIO. Due entrance give,
    That though the enemy a true breast or false
    Discovers, some advantage may be found,—
    Never did falsehood come enveloped
    With so much truth that no indication is
    Of any the least proof, no opening made
    Whereby malevolence to investigate.
    An audience to a foe assurance is
    Which mostly turns to good rather than ill,
    And in all martial matters experience
    Proof shows in what I say—the test is sure.

[*Enter* TWO NUMANTIAN AMBASSADORS.]

FIRST AMBASSADOR. If, my good lord, thou grateful licence giv'st
    For us to explain the embassy we bring,
    Where we do stand thy sole presence before,
    We come the bent of our mission to state.
SCIPIO. Say why you would that I permission grant?
FIRST AMBASSADOR. With the security which we now have
    To us accorded by your exalted rank
    I will commencement make for what I come.
    Numantia, of whose town I am citizen,
    Renowned General, sends me as envoy
    To the most powerful Roman, Scipio,
    Whom night e'er covered or day witnessed,
    The friendly hand, my lord, to solicit
    In token that contention should break off,
    So joined together, so cruel for long years,
    Causing such mutual damage to both sides.
    Declares it ne'er from law and privileges
    Of Roman senate would disjoin itself.
    Unless th' insufferable outrage and command

Of consul and others did them persecute
They with fierce statutes, hard to be endured,
And with a contracted, covetous condition
Have fastened round our necks a heavy yoke,
That forced we issued from it and from them,
And all the time that hitherto remained
The contest betwixt parties, certain 'tis
That we no general have discovered yet
With whom reciprocal contract we can make.
But now that destiny has willed it so,
To bring our fleet unto a haven meet
The sails of war we quickly gather in
And to capitulation yield ourselves.
But thou wilt not imagine that fear drives
Us to solicit importunely peace,
Since wide experience offers proof enough
Of the firm potency of Numantia.
Valour and virtue is what us do feed,
And us advise that it will be again,
Greater than any we desire or hope,
If for our lord and master we hold thee.
For this great mission is our advent here.
Proffer reply to us as it shall please.

SCIPIO. Of a repentance you give tardy proof,
Your amity yields me no satisfaction;
Exert anew your powerful right hands,—
I wish to witness what my own can do,
And have already set the venture there,—
The glory mine, the want of success yours.
To the disgrace of so many long years
Tis little recompense to beg peace of us;
Pursue the strife, and the mischief renew,
Anew relume the valiant torch of war.

SECOND AMBASSADOR. Ill-founded confidence a thousand deceits
Drags in its train—advert to what thou dost.
My lord, the arrogance thou showedst us
Will stimulate our right hands to new force,
Since thou the peace declin'st, which, with warm zeal,
Has been demanded by our proper selves.
To-day the more our cause with heaven itself
Will better qualified rest; and ere the soil
Thou treadest of Numantia, wilt see
And find in proof how far extends the rage
And indignation of that enemy
Whose object was to be your vassal and friend

SCIPIO. Hast thou aught more to say?

FIRST AMBASSADOR. No; but we have
Aught else to do, since thou, my lord, so will'st—

Not asking now the friendship we proposed,
Which such a correspondence has provoked;
Yet shalt thou see the power which we can bring,
When thou exhibitest the power thou hast
'Tis one thing, truly, to reason of peace.
And another thing to break it by armed fires.
SCIPIO. Thou utterest truth; and hence, to indicate
That if to treat of peace I know how, and to work
In war, I wish not ye as friends to accept,
Nor will I ever be so to your soil.
Hence with this *ultimatum* swift return.
SECOND AMBASSADOR. And with this answer, lord, thou thus conclud'st?
SCIPIO. You have my declaration.
SECOND AMBASSADOR. Up to deeds,
Numantia's breast delights in strife and war.

[*The Ambassadors retire.* QUINTUS FABIUS, *brother of* SCIPIO, *speaks.*]

QUINTUS FABIUS. Our past negligence has been the cause
That makes us now advert to this our lot;
Already is arrived the time, yea, come,
When you our glory and your death may see.
SCIPIO. Vain boastfulness is not allowed to live
In valorous bosoms; th' honourable and strong.
Moderate thy threats, and silent, Fabius, rest,—
Disclosing valour in the battle's rage.
Albeit, I think to act that Numantia
Never may come with hands to ours opposed,
Seeking to vanquish in that mode of fight,
Which most contributes to our vantages,
That will do to abase the liveliness
And sense destroy, which fury's self detains—
To compass them in a deep ditch I think,
And with intolerable hunger melt,
I do not wish that Roman blood shall stain
With its red colour this devoted land.
Sufficient 'tis these Spaniards to subvert,
In a so wide, bloody, and cruel war,
Your good hands exercise now to annihilate,
And hollow out the hard and solid soil,
Covering with dust the friends which are not marked
With deep-dyed blood of fighting enemies;
Let no one be reserved for this office,
Who is pre-eminent in soldier's rank—
Let the decurion as the soldier work,
Nor show himself in aught indifferent.
Myself will handle stout the heavy steel,
And with facility earth's self will break,

And do ye all as I, and ye shall see
Such prowess achieved as all shall satisfy.
QUINTUS FABIUS. Valorous lord, and my own brother too,
    Well in discretion dost thou carry thyself,
    Be set apart all madness recognised,
    Or fear to manifest dotage in your acts,
    Battle continuously 'gainst all bravery,
    However airy of these desperate men.
    Better 'twill be to surround them, as you say,
    And of their valour cut away the roots;
    One may environ quite the city round,
    Except the section which the river bathes.
SCIPIO. Come, let us be off, and quickly bring to effect
    This my new deed—as yet unknown in war,
    And should kind heaven favour indicate,
    Subject unto the Roman senate shall
    All Spain be found, by doubtless victory,
    The haughtiness of that race vanquishing.

SCENE II.

[A female issues crowned with towers, and holds a castle in her hand, which is emblematical of Spain, and says:—]

SPAIN. Lofty, serene, and spacious firmament,
    Thou who enrichest with thy influences,
    That portion of my soul the most fertile,
    And over much more land dost aggrandize—
    Let my so bitter grief compassion move;
    And since thou favouredst the afflicted race,
    Favour me also in my anxiety,
    Who am the solitary unhappy Spain.
    Suffice it sometime since you found me so,
    That all my members strong were burnt by fire,
    And by the sun my entrails did discover
    The obscure kingdom of condemned souls.
    You said to many tyrants and much wealth
    Delivered unto Greeks, Phoenicians, were
    My realms, for thou hast so desired it,
    Or that my wickedness hath it deserved.
    Possible is it that in continuance
    Spain should be slave of foreign nations too?
    And in brief space that I not recognise
    Liberty, although my flags be spread?
    With justest title in me is realized
    The rigour of such heavy fearful pains.
    Since my famous and most valiant sons
    Amidst themselves indifferent become.

Unto their profit ne'er do they concert,
The spirits sprightly in division,
Quite opposite the more they separate,
Where most necessity is predominant
And thus with our discordance do agree,
Barbarians whose boast is covetousness,
To come and all my wealth appropriate,
Cruelty exercising 'gainst me and them—
Numantia, only careless of her blood,
Has dared to draw her shining sword, and strike
For that old liberty she cherished long.
But now, O grief, her time of doom is near,
Her fatal hour approaches, and her life
Is waning to its close; but her bright fame
Shall still survive, and like the Phoenix burst
More glorious from her ashes.
These very recreant Romans, who do seek
To vanquish in a multitude of ways,
Refuse to enter into hostile close
With a few valiant Numantians.
Oh, if your vain attempts should issue forth,
And should your mad chimeras dotage prove,
And should this small Numantian piece of earth,
Secure a profit from its threatened loss.
But woe! the enemy has sought it out,
Not with arms only wisely set against
Its wall of weakness, but with extraordinary
Diligence and ready hands has worked
That a ditch by the border fully trenched
Encompass should the city's sides and plains,
The only part from whence the stream extends,
Itself defends from this blind stratagem,
The shrunken and environed troops stand there,
The sorrowful Numantians at the walls.
They cannot sally forth or be attacked,
And well secure from all assaults remain;
But on observing that they are deprived
The power of exercising their strong arms,
Demand an action, or death with loud cries.
And then the only section whence doth flow
And touch the city, Douro's ample flood,
Is that which aids, and which doth succour bring
To the Numantian prisoner, though small.
Before machine or any turret high
Foundation finds in waters, I would ask
The mighty well-known river in what way
She might assist my people destitute.
Gentle stream, Douro, who with ambient bends

Moistens the greatest portion of my breast,
Thus in thy waters dost always observe
Enclosed sands of gold, sweet Tagus like.
And thus the fugitive independent nymphs,
Where the green meadow and full wood are seen,
Come to your waters with humility,
And to grant favours not avaricious.
So lend, I pray, to my bitter laments
Attentive hearing, or come quick to hear;
And though thou set'st aside awhile content
I do beseech thee in nothing withdraw;
If thou with thy continual increase
Dost not avenge me of these fierce Romans
Opposed, yet some other way I view
For safety to Numantia's children.

[*Enter the* RIVER DOURO *with young men clothed as the* RIVER, *being three streamlets which unite with the* DOURO.]

DOURO. Mother and Spain beloved, awhile mine ears
Have been deep stricken with your sad complaints,
And if detention from quick running forth
Appears, it was for lack of remedy.
The fatal, wretched, and too sorrowful day,
According to disposal of the stars,
Has overta'en Numantia, and I dread
Surely there be no medium to sad grief
With Orvion, Minuesa, and Tera,
Whose copious streams have e'en augmented mine.
My bosom have I filled in such a way
That the accustomed margins are burst through;
But without fear of my rapid career,
As though it were a brook, I see they intend
To do that which thou dost, Spain, ne'er observe
Upon my waters, towers, and trenches too.
But now the revolution, of hard fate,
Touches in fine to the appointed end
Of this loved people of Numantia.
To such a termination is it come,
A consolation yet in event is left,
That never can oblivion's darkest shade
Obscure the sun of your world-wide exploits;
And though the Roman prince extends his sway,
Traversing your soil of fruitfulness,
And there oppresses thee, and eke insults,
With arrogant and ambitious insolence,
A time will come, as well is understood;
The knowledge which Heaven to Proteus has revealed,

That these same Romans may be sore oppressed
By those whom now they in subjection hold.
From nations far remote, I see, will come
People who will inhabit your dear soil,
After they solicit your desire,
And shall on Roman necks a rein impose.
Goths will they be, who, garbed in ornament
Superb, their fame leaving to the full world,
Will into your entrails come to gather themselves,
Giving vitality new to their exploits.
These injuries shall avenge the bloody hand
Of Attila the fierce, in times to come,
Subjecting these same Romans—making them
Obedient to your laws and ordinances,
Opening the porticoes of the Vatican.
Thy children brave, and other strangers too,
Will so do, that to fly may turn his step,
The mighty pilot of the holy ship.
A day will also come when shall be seen
The Spanish knife brandished o'er Roman throats,
And life extended through the benevolence
Of their prince, the great Alban, who will force
The Spanish army to retire, simply
Not from want of valour, but scarcity
Of those who in valour equal the best.
But when more known he has been in renown,
As worker of achievements for both worlds,
He, who remains established generally
As God's viceroy throughout th' extended earth,
To thy kings shall the appellation give,
Which all shall find in unison with zeal.
The Roman Catholics all shall acknowledged be,
Succession worthy of the valiant Goths.
But he who highest shall lift up his hand
To general content and thy honour,
Causing the valour of the Spanish name
To reach by assent of all the greatest place,
A king shall be, and of whose sound intent
My cogitations show me mighty things.
He shall be styled—the very world being his—
The Second Philip, albeit second to none.
Beneath his empire, and so happy rule
There shall be under one crown, firm reduced,
For universal good and thy repose,
Three kingdoms, in disunion until then.
The Lusitanian family so renowned,
Which on a time a rent made in the vests
Of Castile the illustrious, draws the seam

Anew, and to its ancient state unites itself.
What envy and what dread, beloved Spain,
Of thee will nations strange possess themselves!
Whom thou with thy sharp blade of steel wilt dye,
Quite triumphant rendering your flags.
Of a solace in the doleful case
Avail thyself, which thou dost earnestly
Deplore, for what's ordained cannot be marred,—
Numantia's inevitable fate still holds.
SPAIN. Thy reasons have in part comfort supplied,
Most famous Douro, to my quick feelings;
Chiefly because I think there is not hid
Any deceit in these thy prophecies.
DOURO. Well may you, Spain, in this assure thyself,
Although these days have a retarding weight
And now to the God, for me my nymphs await.
SPAIN. May Heaven thy salubrious streams augment!

ACT II.

SCENE I.

INTERLOCUTORS.

[THEOGENES *and* CORABINO *with four other* NUMANTIANS, GOVERNORS
OF NUMANTIA, *and* MARQUINO *a Wizard*; *and a* CORPSE *which rises up.
They sit in Council, and the four anonymous Numantians are styled* FIRST,
SECOND, THIRD, *and* FOURTH.]

THEOGENES. It doth appear to me, most powerful youths,
That in our losses with rigour do influence
Distressful signals and fates contrary
Diminishing our power and our skill.
The Romans hold us here incarcerated,
With cowardly dexterity slaying us.
And in the slaughter dying no vengeance is,
Nor without wings can we escape our fate.
Not only us to kill awake they up,
Those whom so often we have vanquished.
The very Spaniards fall into concert
Our throats with them most ruthlessly to cut,
Heaven will not consent to so vast an ill,—
With machines the light files do they strike,
Which in the destruction of the friend move on,
Favouring the perfidious enemy.
See if you can imagine a remedy
From this misfortune to get clear away,
For this toilsome and protracted siege

Promises only a quick sepulture,
The broad fosse hinders us the means to prove
With arms the fortune of restoration.
Although in stout attempts arms valiant can
Break through impediments howe'er imposed.

CORABINO. Would it might please the sovereign Jupiter,
That our brave youth alone should quickly see,
With all the armament of Roman power,
How our stout arms might fully compass them.
That there to the valour of the Spanish hand,
The selfsame death but a little hindrance were
To open wide a road indubitable,
For the security of Numantia's folk.
For in the straits in which we see ourselves,
We stand encircled like unto deer at bay,
All that is possible in man we do,
To demonstrate souls bold in action.
Our very enemies we by voice invite
To single combat, being weary quite
Of this wide range, that so they might desire
By this way to accomplish a speedy end.
Should this fair remedy have no success,
Or subject be to a medium of desire,
Another road for trial yet remains,
Though it may prove more irksome than I think.
This fosse and wall, both prohibitions,
A passage to the enemy there I see,
Let's break through them in a stout band by night,
Marching for aid to our distressed friends.

FIRST NUMANTIAN. Whether by trench it be, or by the death
A passage must we open for our lives.
Insufferable grief is that of death,
And that we reach when we possess most life.
A remedy to miseries sure is death,
And they go on increasing with our life.
And excellent alone shall that end be
When death in honour us sharply overtakes.

SECOND NUMANTIAN. With what more honour can separation be
Of these our souls from their bodies, than on the arms
Of Romans prompt to hurl them, and in their hurt
The strong right hands to move,—
In the city's forts shall well remain,
He who as a recreant would such proofs evince
I rather would lie dead with my stark limbs
In the closed trench or in the open plain.

THIRD NUMANTIAN. This insupportable hunger macerating,
Surrounding equally and pursuing us,
Induces us to consent to the proposal,

Albeit it hard and temerarious be,
Dying, excuse will give to such affront.
But who to die of hunger desires not,
Let him with me himself hurl into the fosse,
Or make a road for remedy with a sword.

FOURTH NUMANTIAN. Before you move in the experiment
Of this harsh resolution you have ta'en,
It seems but well to me that from the wall
Our fierce opponent be apprised of it,—
Asking in war's law a camp secure
For a Numantian, and a soldier too.
And that the death of one should sentence be
To finish this our ancient difference.
The Romans are of a so haughty race
That quickly they will this alternative choose;
And should acceptance follow, I firmly think
That then our bitter woe has ceased to be.
The brave man Corabino present stands,
Whose valour holds me in persuasion
That he alone against the Romans can
Wrench from their hands the coveted victory.
Then let it be arranged that Marquino,—
For he an augur is of celebrity,
Observe what star, what planet, or what sign
With death us threatened, or end honourable.
And we may find another route which may
Us show, if from this dubious state
So cruel, we who wretched stand oppressed
Victors or vanquished surely shall emerge.
However, first I charge you that you make
A solemn sacrifice to Jupiter,
Of whom we may expect a recompense
Greater far than is our sacrifice.
Quickly may cure itself the profound wound
Of this deep-rooted customary vice.
Perhaps with this will change the dire intent,
Of fate disdainful, and yield us content
To die, should time fail ever to the man
Who desperate would plunge into the grave.
We shall be ever in season and in time
Of a brave soul the end to testify.
But that the time may not evaporate,
See what I have ordered be in unison.
And should it so appear suggest a means
Which may be better, and to all suitable.

MARQUINO. Thy reasons which demonstrate this reason,
Approved is by my will and intent.
Sacrifice and oblations let them make,

And in effect fill bold defiance up.
The opportunity I will not lose
To manifest the potency of my means.
And draw forth from the abyss, centre obscure,
Who may the good or who the ill declare.

THEOGENES. From this point offer I myself, should it
To you seem good, or think my power worth aught
To sally forth from this woe which presents,
If it come by chance aught to effectuate.

CORABINO. More honour doth your rare valour deserve,
Well in your strength may you true confidence,
To difficult and greater things entrust,
To be the greater, the greatest amidst
And since you occupy the principal post
Of honour and valour too, with just cause joined,
I count myself in all inferior,
And wish to be the herald of the account.

FIRST NUMANTIAN. Since I with all the populace do prefer
Myself to do what great Jove pleases most,
Which are sacrifices and orations,
With hearts emended all hither we go.

SECOND NUMANTIAN.—Let us move on, and with quick diligence
Enact as much as we propose to do,
Before of famine the sickness pestiferous
Shall push us all to dire extremity.

THIRD NUMANTIAN. If heaven ratify the sentence passed,
Of what we in this hard case must fulfil,
Revoke it, if by chance doth merit it
The reparation which Numantia offers.

SCENE II.

[*First enter two* NUMANTIAN SOLDIERS, MORANDRO *and* LEONCIO.]

LEONCIO. Morandro, friend, whither goest thou?
And what point towards movest thou thy feet?

MORANDRO. Should I myself not know,
Neither wilt thou know it.

LEONCIO. How do deprive thee of thy usual sense
Thy amorous cogitations!

MORANDRO. Contrariwise after that I feel
To have more weight and reason.

LEONCIO. A proved fact it is
That he who would serve Love,
A heavy weighted reason has for his grief.

MORANDRO. From malice or acuteness,
There is no escape from what you said.

LEONCIO. You understand my wit,

And your simplicity I more understand.
MORANDRO. What, am I simple then in wishing well?
LEONCIO. Yes, if in wishing there no measure be,
    As reason's self requires,
    With a when, a how, a whom.
MORANDRO. Would you rules on love impose?
LEONCIO. Reason may impose them.
MORANDRO. Reasonable will they be,
    But of comeliness not much.
LEONCIO. In the amorous contention
    Reason is hard of recognition.
MORANDRO. Love does not that oppose,
    Though reason sets it aside.
LEONCIO. Contrary to reason is it not,
    That thou being a soldier eminent
    Confess yourself enamoured
    In this straitened necessity?
    At the time when Mars, the Divinity,
    Your impetuosity demands,
    Dost thou entertain thyself with love
    Which into a thousand softnesses divides?
    Your country see consumed,
    With foes environed too,
    While thy memory in perturbation
    Forgets itself in love.
MORANDRO. With rage my breast doth burn,
    To hear you speak without discretion.
    Never by chance did love
    Teach lover cowardice.
    Do I leave my watch-post
    To visit her I love?
    Have I been sleeping in my chamber found,
    When my captain was on his watch?
    Failure any hast thou witnessed in me
    In aught I owe to my duty?
    For any gift or frailty,
    Much less for being loved?
    If nothing of this in me thou hast found out,
    And to me no objection,
    Why givest thou me such blame unmitigated,
    For being in love's trammels?
    And if by conversation,
    Thou seest me distracted,
    Into my bosom thrust thy searching hand
    And thou wilt see if I am reasonable.
    Knowest thou not that for these many years
    I am lost for Lira's sake?
    Knowest thou not the termination

Of my sad woes is come?
For that your father did ordain
To give her me for wife,
And that Lira's predilection
Did with mine accord.
As well thou knowest that did supervene,
In this so sweet conjuncture,
This dreadful, powerful war,
For which my glory ceased.
The wedding was deferred
Until the sad war's close.
For our dear country was not in a state
For festivals or content
See how little hope
Of glory I do hold,
Since our victory lies
All in the enemy's weapon.
By famine subdued
Without all hope of remedy,
Such a wall and trench between,
Few of us, and all surrounded too;
How can I see arise
My airy expectations?
Melancholy and discontent I move,
Just as you see me move.

LEONCIO. Assuage thy breast, Morandro,
Return to the gaiety you owned,
Peradventure by occult paths it is
Our benefit is ordained.
That sovereign Jupiter
Will disclose the way
Whereby the Numantians may
Of the Romans get quite free.
And in sweet calmness and a realized peace,
Thou wilt thy spouse enjoy.
Thou shalt the flames attemper
Of this thy amorous fire;
That to be propitious
To great Jove the thunderer,
To-day Numantia in this sharp crisis
Desires to make sacrifice.
Already come the people and do show
Themselves with incense and the victims too.
O Jupiter, father, Immensity,
Upon our heavy miseries look down.

[*Enter two* NUMANTIANS *clothed as ancient priests and lay hold of the horns, in the midst of both, of a large sheep, crowned with olive and ivy, and other flowers; a boy with a silver font and a towel over his shoulders. Another with a silver jar full of water. Another with one of wine. Another with a plate of silver, wherein is a little incense. Another with fire and wood. Another who lays the covering of a table, on which all is set. And they sally forth in this scene all who were habited as* NUMANTIANS, *and immediately the priest, and one dropping the sheep from his hand says:—]*

FIRST PRIEST. Of a certain grief the certain signals have
    Me on the road a representation given,
    And my white locks in dread have stood erect
SECOND PRIEST. If peradventure I not ill divine,
    Never shall we from this strait emerge,
    To the Numantian people, misery.
FIRST PRIEST. With haste we do fulfil our offices,
    Such as our sorrowful auguries incite.
SECOND PRIEST. Friends, here set down this table, and the wine,
    The incense and the water which you bare,
    Lay them upon it, and retire behind.
    Repent ye of the evil ye have done,
    And that th' oblation greater be, and the first
    Which you should offer unto highest heaven,
    Let it be water pure and a will sincere.
FIRST PRIEST. Kindle not the fire, ye, on the ground,
    For its reception here is a brazier,
    Thus of religious zeal duty demands.
SECOND PRIEST. Give to thy hands and neck ablution due.
FIRST PRIEST. Hereabouts sprinkle water. Doth no fire kindle?
ONE. Can you not find a man, my lords, to light it?
SECOND PRIEST. Oh, Jove, what is this which pretends to do
    Uncertain fate, to our destruction?
    How comes it the fire lights not from the torch?
ONE. It seems already something is alive.
FIRST PRIEST. Depart thee hence! O flame weak and obscure,
    What grief in thee beholding do I receive!
    And dost thou not observe how hasteneth
    The smoke to travel on the western side,
    And that the yellow flame, too ill secured,
    Its points towards the eastern part directs?
    Unlucky signal, sign notorious!
    Damage and evil surely present are.
SECOND PRIEST. Although the Romans bear the victory,
    By our lives lost, to earth must be restored
    In living flames our glory and our death.
FIRST PRIEST. Our duty 'tis with wine then to bedew
    The sacred elemental fire. Give here that wine,
    The incense also which should be consumed.

[*They besprinkle the fire and go round with the wine and then throw incense on the fire.*]

SECOND PRIEST. Of the Numantian people for all good,
    Direct, O Jupiter, the power which will
    Propitious be, opposed to the bitter sign.
FIRST PRIEST. Even as this ardent fire doth burn,
    And as the incense melts into the earth,
    So may our force light on the enemy;
    That on th' eternal soil, Father immense!
    May all thy good, and all thy glory too,
    Wend, as thou canst make it, and I think.
SECOND PRIEST. May bounds within the heaven its power restrain,
    As we now hold this victim in our hands,
    And that which fated is to do, do Heaven!
FIRST PRIEST. The augury doth ill respond; ill we
    Shall offer hope to our people sorrowful,
    To issue from the woes we keenly feel.

[*A noise is made beneath the table with a barrel of stones, and some flying fireworks explode.*]

SECOND PRIEST. Didst thou not hear a noise, friend?
    Didst not see
    A burning ray which shot along in flight?
    A presage true wert thou of this event.
FIRST PRIEST. Troubled I am; trembling stand I with fear.
    Oh, what tokens in the air I ken!
    What prognostics of a bitter end!
    Dost thou not see a squadron, airy and foul,
    Of certain cruel eagles, who contend
    With other birds in martial compassings?
SECOND PRIEST. Their force and fierceness are solely occupied
    The birds surrounding in a heady fight,
    With subtlety and art environing.
FIRST PRIEST. Such emblem do I blame; I cannot praise.
    Imperial eagles surely victors are;
    Quickly wilt thou see Numantia's head.
SECOND PRIEST. Eagles, messengers of mighty ills,
    Divide thyselves! Thy augury I understand;
    Counted with good effect are all time's hours.
FIRST PRIEST. With all, the sacrifice I pretend to make
    Of this now innocent victim, in reserve,
    To appease the face of horror of the god.
    O mighty Pluto! to whom was given the lot
    For habitation the dark region,
    And power e'en to reign in mournful hell,
    Though there thou dwell'st in peace, certain and sure,

That the fair daughter of Ceres consecrate
To thy pure love reciprocates as pure,
That all in which thou an advantage seest
To emanate from sad souls invoking thee,
Collect it thou, as one from thee expects.
Conceal the mouth profound, and eke obscure,
Whence the three cruel sisters do emerge,
On us to afflict the evils which touch us,
And so be light to harm us.

[*The* PRIEST *takes off some skins from the lamb and casts them to the air.*]

Thy intents which may the wind bear off,
E'en as I bathe and do incarnadine
This weapon in this pure blood, with pure soul,
With thought also as pure accompanied.
Thus may the hard soil of Numantia
Be saturated well with Roman gore,
And also serve them for a sepulchre.

[*Here comes forth from the hollow floor a* DEMON *to the waist, who seizes the lamb and places it within, and quick returns to spread and scatter the fire and the entire sacrifices.*]

But from my hands who daringly has snatched
The victim? What is that, most holy gods?
What insane prodigies assault us now?
Have not the wails of this people contrite,
So much afflicted, softened the powers above,
Or sacred Voice of canticles appeased?
SECOND PRIEST. Contrary quite they have been hardened more,
As one may see from indications dire,
Which in opposition meet us.
Our living remedies all mortal are,
All diligence but recognised idleness,
And good externe but ills conglomerated.
ONE OF THE PEOPLE. In fine, the heavens have a sentence pronounced,
As to our end, bitter and miserable;
Its clemency no longer doth avail.
ANOTHER. Let us bewail in lamentable note
Our dire mishap, that late posterity
May speak of this and of our courage too.
Experience absolute let Marquino make
Of all his knowledge, and may he let us know
How much of evil promises our lot
Ail sorrowful, all smiles turning to grief.

[*Exeunt* ALL. MORANDRO *and* LEONCIO *remaining.*]

MORANDRO. Leoncio, how doth it seem to thee?
    Shall my ills find remedy
    With these kindly indications
    Which heaven us offers here?
    Will my ill fortune end
    When only the war ceases?
    Which will be when the all-enclosing earth
    Me for a sepulchre serves.
LEONCIO. Morandro, to the true soldier
    Augury gives him no pain,
    Which sets good fortune in th' enforced soul.
    And these vain apparitions
    Do ne'er disturb the judgment;
    His arm his star is—and his emblem too,
    His valour eke his influence.
    But should you wish to believe
    In this notorious deceit,
    Though there remain, if I deceive me not,
    Experiences greater yet to do,
    Which Marquino shall accomplish
    By his science the most powerful;
    And of our grief the end
    Will fortunate be, or we the ill shall know;
    It seems me that I see him,—
    In what a character strange he doth appear!
MORANDRO. Who with frightful matters entertains
    Himself, no wonder frightful doth become,
    To follow him will it be right?
LEONCIO. It seems right to me
    If by chance there should present
    Aught in which it may him serve.

[*Enter* MARQUINO *in a tight dark buckram suit, a black periwig, feet unshod, and at the wrist hang three small vials full of water, one discoloured and one stained with saffron, the other clear water. In one hand a lance varnished, of ebony, and in the other hand a book.* MILVIO *enters with him, and as they come in,* LEONCIO *and* MORANDRO *stand on one side.*]

MARQUINO. What sayest thou, Milvio, where is the bewailed youth?
MILVIO. Buried in this sepulchre.
MARQUINO. You do not thyself deceive as to the spot.
MILVIO. No. By this stone 'tis surely signalized.
    I left the place wherein the tender youth
    With tender tears was in the sepulchre laid.
MARQUINO. Of what complaint died he?
MILVIO. Of bad nutriment died.
    Hunger and weakness finished up his life,—

A cruel pest which emanated from hell.

MARQUINO. In fine, you say in truth no kind of stroke
    Of vital breath cut off the thread,—no kind
    Of cancer, or fierce homicidal wound?
    This do I tell thee, to my knowledge he
    Did make account, that his constitution was
    Well organized, and in a good physical state.

MILVIO. Three hours it will be since I to him assigned
    The last repose, committed to the grave,
    And that he died of famine I allege.

MARQUINO. Thus far is well, good the coincidence
    Which the propitious signs do offer me,
    From th' obscurest regions to invoke
    The fiercest spirits of malignity,
    Unto my canticle lend attentive ears.
    Of Hades' king, who, in the gloomy realm
    Of souls perverse, dire ministers betwixt,
    Does thee retain to reign o'er lot and chance;
    Fulfil, although 'twere adverse to your taste,
    My ardent wishes,—for on this occasion hard
    I thee invoke, and do not thou delay,
    And mind thou art by me not more oppressed.
    I would the corpse which here has been interred,
    Had the soul back again wherein it lived,
    Albeit the savage Charon hold it fast
    Upon the darkened bank of th' other side.
    E'en though within the three mouths of the fierce
    Cerberus, the corpse concealed lies,
    And punished too. Let it arise and see
    Our world's light, though it quick return to thine.
    And since it has to rise, let it arise
    Informed, to say what end's to our savage war.
    And let this not encumber me,—nothing
    Conceal, nor in doubt leave me, nor confused
    Be the report of this unhappy soul;
    From ambiguity free, and open quite,
    Let it present itself. Say what thou hop'st,—
    Hop'st thou that on which I spoke earnestly?
    Do not reverse the stone, disloyal ye;
    Declare, false ministers, what ye detain.
    How? Have ye not the signals offered me
    That ye do what I say, and this I approve?
    Seek ye your evils in retaining them,
    Or do you enjoy what now I do ordain,
    Effect to give unto the exorcisms
    Which soften your obdurate cruel breasts?
    Go to then, rabble vile, of untruth full,
    Yourselves prepare for a harsh sentiment,

Since you know well my voice is powerful,
Your rage and torment to reduplicate.
Tell me now, traitor husband of the spouse,
That for six months of the year you are content
Without thee she remain like to the moon.[2]
Why to my request standest thou dumb?
This very metal bathed in water clear,
Which never in the May month touches soil,
Shall penetrate this stone, and indicate
The potency of this enforced essay.

[*With the water of the vessel he bathes the blade of the lance, and then strikes the table. Underneath explode fireworks, and the barrel of stones make a rumbling noise.*]

And now, ye rabble, obviously it appears,
Your indications note what fear ye hold.
What are these noises, wicked ones, avaunt,
Although you come, you come by dint of force.
That stone upraise, effeminate as ye are,
And show me quick the body underneath.
What is this? Why delay? Where are ye gone?
Why not my order to the letter obey?
Ye unbelievers, care ye not for threats?
Ye are not in expectation of more threats.
The blackened water of the lake of Styx
Will give you retribution for delay.
Water of the fatal dark-dyed lake
In this same night drawn, both obscure and black,
Which by its potency is to thee joined,
And which no other power annihilates—
Devilish importunity.
Which did the early form of a snake assume,
Thee I conjure, apprise, ask, and command.
Flying you came. Do me obedience yield.

[*He bedews the grave with water, and it opens.*]

O youth, ill-purchased, sally thou forth anon,
Return to see the clear and serene sun;
That place abandon where no hope exists,
Therein to find a comfortable day.
Give me now,—for thou canst, relation whole
Of what in this profound abyss thou hast seen.
I say, for that wherefore thou there wert sent,
And if thou canst, say more if it behoves.

---

[2] Alluding to the waxing and waning of the moon.

[*The* CORPSE *arises in a shroud with the face marked and discoloured like death. It moves on gradually, and is finally dropped on the stage, without hand or foot, until its appointed time.*]

What is this? no response! dost not revive?
Hast thou at any previous time tasted of death?
But with your pain I will make you alive,
Cause you to speak about your favoured lot:
For thou wert one of ours. Do not evade
Speaking with me, and reply,—and look you too
That if thy silent beest, to thy disgrace
I will unloosen thy pent, shrunken tongue.

[*He wets the* CORPSE *with yellow-coloured water, and then lashes it with a whip.*]

Spirits malignant, do ye not approve?
But wait awhile, the charmed fluid shall
Forth issue, which my will can satisfy
However much your perfidy and harm.
Although this flesh converted were to dust,
Being chastised with this magic whip,
A new and light life will it resuscitate
By a sharp vigour though it oppressed be.

[*At this point the* CORPSE *stirs and trembles.*]

Rebellious spirit, to the deposit back
Which only a few short hours thou hast left
THE CORPSE. The violent fury of thy impulse cease,
Marquino. Sad sufficient I have been
In the murky regions of the lower world,
Without your aggravating my luckless hap.
You do yourself deceive if you do think
I satisfaction have to return to this
Sorrowful, sad, short life that now I live,
And which in full haste does abandon me.
Before you cause me a disdainful grief
Another time shall death, of terrors king,
Over my life and soul extend itself.
My enemy a double palm shall grasp,
And such, with others of the obscure band,
Of those who subject are thee to await,—
Let him stand with rage i' th' screw, expecting here
Marquino will finish the information
Of th' end most lamentable, the wicked ill
Which of Numantia I assurance give
To be accomplished by these very hands

Which now are nearest to her—the victory
The Romans will not o'er Numantia bear—
The city brave; nor will she less extend
Triumph or glory to her enemy.
Friends and enemies, both good alike,
Ye do not understand that peace hath its memory,
And rage will nestle in opposed breasts.
The friendly weapon of Numantia
Its homicide will be and its life too.

[*The* CORPSE *throws itself into the grave, and says,*—]

Be quiet now, Marquino, as the Fates
Will not permit me more to speak with thee;
And though my sayings be deceitful held,
The truth of what I say will mount aloft.
MARQUINO. O sorrowful evidence, unpropitious sign!
If this misfortune to the people come—
Friend! ere I this sad tribulation see,
May my life finish in this sepulchre!

[MARQUINO *throws himself into the grave.*]

MORANDRO. Look, Leoncio, if you see—for what
I may speak, that my feelings be not turned
Quite inside out. Already, of all our
Venture, the road is closed—Marquino,
Tell it,—if not, death and the grave.
LEONCIO. These all illusions are,
Fancies and chimeras,
Auguries and witcheries, inventions of hell.
You do not show how that you entertain
Small skill in creating these confusions.
Little regard the dead to the living show.
MILVIO. Never Marquino would effect it—
Such a madness extraordinary!
If were not come our future as present ills.
Of this mishap let us the people apprise,
Which a mortal evil is.
Who will first advance the news to declare?

ACT III.

SCENE I.

[INTERLOCUTORS. SCIPIO, JUGURTHA, CAIUS MARIUS.]

SCIPIO. In reality content I see
    How the adventure to my wish responds.
    And this free, haughty nation I subdue
    Without constraint, and by discretion alone;
    Th' opportunity seen I quickly seize,
    For well I know if it runs, and haste suggests,
    And it should glide away, in affairs of war
    Lost is all credit, and life sacrificed.
    You judge yourselves it a wild folly to be
    To keep your enemies in confinement close—
    And from the Roman spirit a deduction 'tis
    Not to subdue them in th' accustomed mode.
    I know well they will have so said; but I trust
    That those, who practised soldiers may have been,
    Will say 'tis better in account to obtain
    The victory which costs the least of life.
    What glory can more elevated be,
    In martial combats of which I now speak,
    Than, without taking weapon from the place,
    To vanquish and quite subjugate our foe?
    For when the victory is purchased
    By shedding of the blood of our own friends,
    It lessens the gratification which might cause
    Triumph from winning it without such loss.

[*A trumpet sounds from the wall of Numantia.*]

QUINTUS FABIUS. Give ear, my lord, how from Numantia sounds
    The speaking of a trumpet, and I am sure
    That something by it significant is ordained;
    All sally thence the wall has fully stopped.
    Corabino on a battlement seats himself,
    And has a signal of safe conduct made.
    Let us more nearly go.
SCIPIO. Yes, let us advance.
CAIUS MARIUS. Not more—from this point we shall here all learn.

[CORABINO *places himself on the wall with a white flag on the top of his lance.*]

CORABINO. Romans, ah, Roman soldiers, was this voice clear heard of you by chance?
CAIUS MARIUS. If you but lower that flag and gently speak,

Whate'er your reason 'twill be understood.
CORABINO. Announce to the general that th' approach is made
    Unto the trenches, and that an embassy
    To him is directed.
SCIPIO. Tell him straight
    That I am Scipio.
CORABINO. Now hear the rest.
    General, for prudence famed, Numantia asks
    That you consider well that many years
    Between our people and the Roman race
    The savage evils of a war subsist.
    And to effect that no dire increment may
    Aggravate the pestilence of these woes
    Desires, if thou desirest cessation,
    By one brief duel betwixt two opposites,
    One of our soldiers offers himself to fight,
    Environed in a staked palisade,
    With whomsoever of yours you appoint,
    To bring an end to this contention.
    Should fate, however, adverse in trial prove,
    And one should be deprived of his dear life,
    And that one be our champion, let us the land
    Surrender. If it be yours, finish the war.
    And for a guarantee of this compact
    Hostages subject to your will we give.
    I well know into this thou wilt come, being sure
    Of the army which thou entertain'st in charge,
    And knowest that the least in open field
    Will make his lungs perspire, his temples, face,
    Most advantageous to Numantia,
    Thus the advantage and the gain is sure.
    Answer me, lord, if you concur in it,
    That the completion of the act be swift.
SCIPIO. A jest is that thou sayest, laughter, fun,
    Who thinks to do it? a fool indeed were he—
    Of humble supplications use the means,
    If you desire to emancipate your necks
    From proof of rigour and the edge direct
    Of Roman weapons, and our valiant hands.
    The wild beast which in cage is incarcerated,
    Despite its ferocity and its vast strength too,
    May well be tamed by art and subtlety,
    With time sufficient and means of address.
    But he who leaves him free and disengaged
    Would indication give of madness sure.
    Wild beasts are ye, and hence environed are,
    And ye I hold to be subdued by me.
    Numantia shall be mine in your despite

Without the loss of e'en a single man;
And he whom you for strongest ye amidst
Let him break over this entrenched ditch;
And if in this it seems to you I show
My valour e'en to cowardice reduced,
Let the wind dissipate this vengeance now,
And fame resound to whom is conqueror.

[SCIPIO *and his men retire.*]

CORABINO. Hear'st thou no more, O recreant, hid'st thyself?
Dost thee disgust a proposal of equal fight?
This with thy surplus army ill responds,
In this way it will thee badly sustain.
In fine, like as a recreant thou repliest,
Faint-hearted all, ye Romans, base *canaille.*
In superfluity of numbers trust,
And not in brave right hands all high upraised;
Perfidious, effeminate, sans loyalty,
Cruel, turbulent, tyrannical,
Ungrateful, covetous, and meanly born,
Obstinate, ferocious, villainous,
Adulterous, infamous, and too well known
For hands industrious, but rank cowardly too.
What glory will you achieve in murdering us,
By you in this unfortunate lot, fast bound?
Encompassed squadron, or loosened division,
Upon an open country where no power is
To stop the mortal cruel turbulence,
The wide fosse or the wall which do oppose.
Better were it without turning foot,
Or ever keeping sword unexercised,
This your multitudinous brave men,
Found themselves in face with our weak bands.
Yet as you ever are wont in battle's shock
With vantage and dexterity to win,
These propositions founded in valour,
Your knavish plots admit not for a test,
Hares are ye masked in skins of savageness.
Ye magnify and laud your deeds of might,
So that I hope in Jupiter the great
You may be subject to Numantia's laws.

[*He bows down and turns to retire immediately with the* NUMANTIANS, *who made
exit at the beginning of the second act, except* MARQUINO, *who throws himself
into the grave, and* MORANDRO *enters.*]

THEOGENES. Our fate confines us in conditions.
    Sweet friends, and peradventure accident,
    With death itself will finish up our wrongs.
    For our sad woe, for our unluckiness,
    You saw of our sacrifice the sad augury,
    The jaws of the grave Marquino swallowing.
    Our defiance nothing has availed.
    What rests for us to prove, I perceive not
    Save to accelerate our last gloomy end.
    This very night the boldness is evinced
    Of the Numantian high excited breast,
    And let us put in act our last intent.
    The enemies' wall being levelled to the ground,
    Let's sally forth upon the plain to die,
    No life surrendering in confinement base.
    I am convinced that this achievement serves
    Alone the mode of death to change for us,
    Though death itself be its companion.
CORABINO. To this appearance I myself compose,
    Die would I, bursting through the thick-set wall,
    And it demolish by my hand entire.
    Still one thing keeps me in dubiety,
    Should but our women come to understand
    There will be no assurance for the deed.
    When at another time we find ourselves
    Agreed to emerge and leave them, each single
    One trusting to his steed and bold right hand;
    They when the project to them is revealed,
    Importunate, that moment of restraint,
    Deprives us, leaving nothing to effect.
    Then they of the issuing out will us deprive,
    And with facility will so do it,
    If tears demonstrate what they eke have shown.
MORANDRO. To all is patent our intention,
    The women know it, and not one exists
    Who does not bitterly the scheme deplore,
    Yet they declare in good or evil state
    To follow our fortunes or in life or death,
    Though out of season be their company.

[*Here enter* four NUMANTIAN FEMALES *with others, and* LIRA. *The women all
bear figures of children on their arms and in their hands, save* LIRA, *who
carries nothing.*]

Do ye see them who come discourse to hold?
In such embarrassment pray leave them not,
Although of steel, you they can mollify.

The tender children thine all sorrowful
In arms they bear, observe you with what warm
Signals of love they print the last embrace?
THE FIRST FEMALE. Sweet lords, our husbands, if in the wretched ills
Unto this present for Numantia borne,
Which lesser are than those of mortal count,
And in the prosperous deeds already passed,
We ever proved ourselves your wives to be.
As you have shown yourselves husbands to us,
Although in these misfortunes sinister,
Which th' enraged heaven on all doth shower,
Do you now give us brief proofs of that love?
We've been instructed, and it clear appears,
That on the Roman arms to throw yourselves
You do desire, its rigour hindering less
Than hunger which you see encompass us.
From whose weak hands unsavoury I hold
It quite impossible to elude the grasp,
Life abandon fighting would you then,
And leave us all forsaken in despair,
Dishonouring us and being your sacrifice.
Our very necks do offer to the swords.
Let ours be first, which is the best contract,
Rather than we dishonoured be by foes.
I hold it my confirmed intention
That if I can, all in my power I'll do,
To die where'er my husband yields up life.
And this same resolution's—what I wish—
To show that no sad fear of death can e'er
Prevent; to wish in good or bitter lot
My life to sacrifice with him I chose.
ANOTHER NUMANTIAN WOMAN. What think ye, worthy men?
In your minds and fancies do ye revolve
Us to abandon and yourselves absent?
To hazard would you leave,
To Roman arrogance
Numantia's maidens
For a far worse mishap?
And our free children
Would you them in bondage also leave?
Were it not preferable to strangle them
With your own hands?
Do you wish to satisfy the desire
Of Roman covetousness—and that her justice
Triumph o'er our just trophy?
Shall with foreign hands
Our habitations all be hurled down?
And our yet hoped-for matrimonial bonds

Go to rejoice the Romans?
In sallying forth you will enact a wrong,
Mistakes producing numberless.
Why without dogs do you leave the fold,
The shepherd being without?
Would you at the trench go forth?
Take us in the sally with you;
We hold it life to be
At your sides all to perish;
The way to death you'll not hasten, for its yarn
Preserved, makes hunger it continually
To approach.

OTHER WOMEN. Offspring of these sad parents,
What is this? why speak ye not?
And with tears demand
Why your fathers do forsake us all?
Suffices that fell hunger finishes
Its end with woe;
The rigour not awaiting
Of Roman acrimony.
Tell them they were free begotten,
And free too were ye born;
And your dear mothers with affliction broke
In freedom nurtured you.
Tell them that since this lot of ours
Is fallen down so low,
As they did give you being
So now they proffer death.
Of this devoted city, O ye walls!
If you could utterance give, speak now,—
A thousand times reiterate it,
Numantians—"Liberty";
The temples, yea, our very houses e'en
In accord rising up,
Mercy of you demand,
Sons and daughters, yours,
Soften, worthy men,
These breasts of diamonds made,
And show what loving hearts
Numantians do possess.
By the wall subverting
You will not cure an ill so vast,
Quite other, in it will dwell
A nearer evil and not less assured.

LIRA. Although the tender damsels
Repose in your defence
Of the offence the remedy,
And solace to all quarrels.

Leave not such booty rich
To the claws of covetousness.
See how the Romans are
Nought else but famished, sanguinary wolves—
Notorious desperation
Is that which ye would seek,
Where you alone will find
Brief death and glory large.
But higher should emerge
Than I conjecture this same enterprise;
What city in Spain is there
Would wish to grant us favour?
My humble perspicacity adverts
If this irruption obstinately you effect,
Unto the foe vitality you give
And to Numantia death.
Unto your courteous proposition
The Romans will mockings make,
For, tell me, what will effect
Three thousand eighty against?
Should they be open found,
The walls and sans defence,
You would be with offence revenged ill,
And all mercilessly slain.
Greater is that the chance
Of evil which high heaven ordereth—
To sepulture or life, save us or condemn.
THEOGENES. Dry up your humid eyes from grief's excess,
O tender-hearted women, and well know
That we do all your anguish deeply feel,
Which is responsive to our upraised love.
May deep grief now augment, now the burst of woe,
May it diminish for our proper good.
Never in life or death shall we cast you off,
In death or life you faithfully will serve.
We contemplated sallying to the ditch,
Certain therein to die and no escape.
Whether alive or dead no consequence,
If dying we could vengeance realize.
Yet since our plans have been discovered
A downright madness 'tis to venture more.
Beloved sons, wives of our bosoms, too,
Our lives will be this day all yours, and more—
Alone we must observe that th' enemy
Through us no triumph or glory acquires.
The fact will only testimony serve
Our history to eternize and approve.
If all should happen as I do predict

Our memory shall a thousand years endure,
And nothing in Numantia remain
Whereby a profit can be realized.
In the square's centre let a fire be made,
In whose licentious burning flame be thrown,
With quick despatch, all riches we possess,
E'en from the meanest to the choicest ware.
This may you entertain for a sweet joke
When honourable intention doth suggest
That it is indispensable, after there be
Wholly consumed all jewels of great price,
And to support for only one short hour
The hunger which frets and gnaws our inmost bones.
Quickly you'll have to mangle at the time
These wretched Romans here in captivity,
No difference making from the least to the great,
'Mongst all distributing, that with these captives
Shall our festival be celebrated,
By cruelty extraordinary impelled.
Friends, how to you appears it? Stand ye so?

CORABINO. I answer for myself, I'm satisfied.
Let us to execution quickly move,
Of so extravagant yet so honoured deed.

THEOGENES. Of my intention I will state the rest;
When the execution is achieved,
Quick let us all as ministers advance
To kindle flames destructive and so rich.

FIRST WOMAN. From this time forth let us women commence
Our ornaments willingly to surrender up,
Yours to the life ourselves deliver up,
E'en as our true desires have been yielded.

LIRA. Now, then, let us proceed, let's go, let's go—
The trophies all in burning fire consume,
Which might enrich the hands wherein they fall,
Roman covetousness so satisfying.

[*All retire, and at* MORANDRO's *coming out he* (ase á Lira) *seizes* LIRA *by the arm and detains her.*

MORANDRO. Fly not so fast, my Lira, let me enjoy
The happiness which can give me
In death a cheerful life;
Let my eyes gloat
A space upon your beauty,
For so much my misfortune
In my annoyance entertains itself.
O Lira sweet, who sounds emit'st,
In my continued fantasy

With harmony so dulcet
That unto glory all my pains convert.
What detains you? Loiter you thinking
Of my full thought the glory?
LIRA. I think how my content
And thine unto completion do advance.
No homicide shall be
In circle of our earth,
But first grim war itself
Shall cut me off from life.
MORANDRO. What sayest thou, core of my soul?
LIRA. Such oppressive hunger holds,
That of my vital thread
The victory will quickly carry.
What marriage hopest thou from one
Which stands in such extremity?
That thee I do assure, I fear
To die before one hour is fully passed.
My brother yesterday did breathe out life
By hunger fell subdued;
My mother is no more,—
By famine sacrificed;
And if hunger and its strength
Have not o'erborne my health,
It is that youth
Against its rigour is a barrier;
Yet as some days are gone
That no defence I make
'Gainst its attack avail nought my weak powers.
MORANDRO. Dry, Lira, dry those eyes,
Allow these my sorrowful currents fast to flow,
Of this annoyance born.
And though offensive hunger holds thee quite,
Divested of all motion,
Of it thou shalt not die,
Whilst I in life remain.
Myself I offer cheerfully to ascend
The ditch and strong-built wall,
Death challenging, thy precious life to save.
The bread the Roman touches—
Should fear destroy me not—will I
Wrench from his jaws, to lodge it in thy mouth.
With my stout arm a certain road I'll make
For my death and thy life;
For it doth slay me more to see
Thee, lady, in this strait
Something to quell hunger will I bring,
Despite of any Roman—

    And these are hands which would that feat enact.
LIRA. As a lover dost thou converse,
      Morandro; yet it is not just
      That I satisfaction take
      By your sure peril purchased.
      A little will support me,
      Whatsoever robbery thou shalt make;
      Though certain enough it is that you will find
      Your destruction, not my security.
      Your youthfulness enjoy
      In fresh and crescent age. To the city's weal
      Your life is more important far than mine.
      Defend it well thou canst
      Against th' observant foe
      Rather than the powerlessness
      Of this too woeful maid.
      So that, my sweet love, banish now this thought,
      I would not succour crave
      By this your exertion gained;
      And though you might postpone
      My death for e'en a day,
      This very hunger so defiant is,
      That us at last it will annihilate.
MORANDRO. All vain is your labour, Lira,
      To arrest me in my course;
      Where my will and device exist,
      There they invite and draw.
      You in the interval wilt well beseech
      The deities all, that they return me safe,
      With spoils which may relax
      My undoing and your misery.
LIRA. Morandro, sweet friend of mine!
      Go not; for I foreknow
      That this red blood of thine
      Will stain the enemy's sword;
      This day thou wilt do nought
      Morandro, my soul's life!
      Should the sally evil be,
      To return is worse,
      If I desired thy ardour to restrain.
      Heaven's self do I as witness loudly call,
      My hurt suspect, and no profit thereby.
      But shouldst thou, friend beloved,
      This opposition prosecute,
      Carry this armlet for an undoubted pledge
      That me with thee thou bear'st.
MORANDRO. Lira, may Heaven your companion be.
      Away! Leoncio I observe to approach.

LIRA. In thee may be fulfilled all your desires,
    And not one jot of evil.

[LEONCIO *stands listening to all that has passed between his friend* MORANDRO
    and LIRA.]

LEONCIO. Terrible offering is that thou hast made!
    In it, Morandro, it doth obvious show
    There be no cowardice in virtuous love;
    Though from thy virtue and thy valour rare
    More might be hoped. But, nevertheless, I fear
    Unhappy fate will niggard show itself.
    Attentive have I stood to the sad extreme
    In which Lira has told you she is placed.
    Unworthy thy valour such indignity.
    Assurance hast thou made to liberate her
    From this incumbent evil, and thyself
    Precipitate into the Roman arms.
    I yearn thee to accompany my friend,
    And in the honest emprise, so potent too,
    Aid and abet thee with my slender strength.
MORANDRO. O my soul's moiety—venturous amity,
    Which is not severed in a difficulty,
    Nor in prosperous opportunity.
    Enjoy, Leoncio, existence sweet,
    Continue in the city. I do not wish
    To be of thy years mature the murderer.
    Alone I wish to go, alone I hope
    Back to return with meritorious spoils,
    To faith inviolable and to love sincere.
LEONCIO. Since thou, Morandro, well acquainted art
    With my desires, which in evil or good report
    Are measured truly to the taste of thine,
    Shalt know that not death's apprehension
    Shall ever separate me a tittle from thee,
    Nor aught else, if aught be, however strong.
    With thee I am bound to go unitedly.
    I must return—if heaven orders it not,
    In thy defence will I lay stark in death.
MORANDRO. Stop, stop, my friend, in a good omen's hour,
    For if I finish here my cherished life
    In this emprise surcharged with danger's hap,
    You may unto my mother o'erwhelmed with grief,
    In this sad circumstance solace impart,
    And to my spouse so much by me beloved.
LEONCIO. Certain, very agreeable, my friend,
    Thou art in thinking, you defunct, that I
    In such a complacency or repose could be.

Or that I any counsel could supply
To th' o'erwrought mother and the doleful spouse.
In thy decease doth also my death dwell.
In all dubiety do I follow thee,
Look how it is to be, Morandro, friend,
And here remaining see thou nothing say.
MORANDRO. To following me no hindrance can I put,
And in the silence of the night obscure,
Upon the foe we hold to make assault.
With light arms be ye furnished, which, mayhap,
Shall help exactly our lofty design,
And not the coat of mail inwove and stiff.
The good thought with thee carry also to win,
And bear in safety all that appertains
To such provisions as are necessary.
LEONCIO. Let's off—from thy instructions I'll not swerve.

SCENE II.

[TWO NUMANTIANS.]

FIRST NUMANTIAN. Shed, O my brother sweet, shed through thine eyes
Thy very soul, changed to bitter grief.
Let death arrive and sweep away the spoils
Of our existence melancholy, miserable.
SECOND NUMANTIAN. A little longer only will endure
These deep annoyances—then death arrives—
Unseen in its swift flight,
To carry off those who tread Numantia's soil.
Beginnings I recognise swiftly promising
A bitter ending to our well loved-land.
Without regarding this completion,
The adverse ministers of savage war,
Our very selves who in molestation live,
Uneasy all in what doth cast us down,
Irrevocable sentence have pronounced
Of our own death, cruel, yet laudable.
In our large square already there kindled is
A burning deep desiring bonfire's light;
With all our riches as with element fed,
Its flame mounts proudly to the high fourth sphere.
There with a sad accelerated haste,
In a career mortal and timid too,
Do all assist as at some holy rite,
The flames to feed with their materials.
There of the rosy orient, the pearl,
The gold, into a thousand vessels wrought,
The diamond, and ruby excellent,

The purple dye extreme, and rich brocade
Into the centre of the burning gulf,
Where the fire's fury rages, are all cast
Spoils, where with avidity Romans may
Their senses satisfy, and hands occupy.

[*Enter some charged with clothes at one door, and retire by another.*]

Turn all your sights to this sad spectacle,
You will discern with how much haste and zeal
Numantia's populace with all its host
Strives to sustain the insane element.
And not alone with green wood or dry reed,
Nor matter all inconstant to consume,
But with their property so ill-enjoyed,
Desiring ardently it may be burnt.
FIRST NUMANTIAN. If with this act our damage should be closed,
Bear it we might in divine patience;
But woe—what is to do, if no mistake,
'Tis that we die together, sentence dire.
First will the barbarous rigour of hard fate
Show its inclemency in our very throats;
Hangman will it be to our very hands.
Saving the office to perfidious Rome,
They are agreed that no spark shall remain
Of life in woman, child, or worn-out eld;
That hunger, cruel in importunity,
With its fierce rigour is the homicide.
There seest thou one, O brother, doth appear,
Who as you know was truly my beloved
In a time past, such the extreme of love,
And in such depth of grief is she now plunged.

[*Enter a MOTHER with a child in her arms and another by her side.*]

MOTHER. Oh life, most cruel and most hard to bear!
Oh agony, most deep and terrible!
BOY. Mother, will no one me a morsel give
Of bread for all these riches?
MOTHER. No, my son;
No bread nor aught to nourish thee, my child.
BOY. Must I then die of hunger, mother mine.
I ask one morsel only, nothing more.
MOTHER. My child, what pain thou giv'st me!
BOY. Do you not
Wish for it then?
MOTHER. I wish for it, but know not
Where I may seek it.

BOY. Why not buy it, mother?
    If not, I'll buy it for myself, and give
    To the first man I meet e'en all this sum,
    Ay, for one single morsel of dry bread,
    My hunger pains me so!
MOTHER. [*to her infant.*] And thou, poor creature,
    Why cling'st thou to my breast? dost thou not know
    That in my aching breast despair has changed
    The milky stream to blood? Tear off my flesh
    And so content thine hunger, for my arms
    Are weak and can no longer clasp thee to me!
    Son of my soul, with what can I thee sustain?
    E'en of my wasted flesh there scarce remains
    Enough thy craving wants to satisfy.
    Oh hunger, hunger, terrible and fierce,
    With what most cruel pangs thou tak'st my life!
    Oh war, what death dost thou prepare for me!
BOY. My mother, let us hasten to the place
    We seek, for walking seems to make me worse.
MOTHER. My child, the house is near us where at length
    Upon the burning pile thou may'st lay down
    The burden that thou bearest.

ACT IV.

SCENE I.

[*There is a sounding to arms in great haste, and at the noise sally forth* SCIPIO *with* JUGURTHA *and* MARIUS *towards the platform.*]

SCIPIO. What is this noise, my captains? who incites
    Us all to arms in such a season? Is it
    By chance some people without order wild,
    Who come their proper burial to procure?
    O no, it is a mutiny which provokes
    In this conjuncture an appeal to arms;
    Yet so secure am I of the enemy
    That I no more have fear of them than friends.

[QUINTUS FABIUS *advances with a drawn sword.*]

QUINTUS FABIUS. All quiet be the breast, general discreet,
    Thou now th' occasion of this move dost know,
    Which to the cost of your brave men has been
    Containing so much sprightliness and strength.
    A pair of Numantians with haughtiness,
    Whose valour justly due praise may extort,
    Bounding o'er trenches and the wall to boot,

This cruel battle in your camp have raised.
Upon your outer guards assault they made,
Upon a thousand lances hurled themselves,
And with such rage and fury did set on
That they to the camp an open passage made.
Fabricius' very tents they did assail,
And there their courage and vigour displayed
In such a guise, that soldiers six were quick
Upon the points of their lances transpierced.
Not with more swiftness does the burning ray
Pass through the air its flight incalculable,
No, nor the comet in a blaze of light
Itself display in transit through the sky,
As did these two traverse your soldiers' bands.
Dividing them they stained the solid soil
With Roman gore, while forcibly drawing out
Their weapons where they purposed they should go.
Fabricius there remains, his breast transfixed,
Horatius has his capital part in twain
Thoroughly cleft, Olmida's right arm is lost,
And little time is left for him to breathe.
At the same juncture small advantage proves
His nimbleness to brave Estacio,
For his advance the strong Numantian towards,
The way abridged, but to the hour of death.
With lightness unsurpassed in rapid pace
From tent to tent they rush, until they find
A piece of biscuit, which was what they sought
The passage, not the fury, turned them back,
And one of them escaped by aid of flight
A thousand swords the other straight despatched;
Whence I infer that hunger fell has been
That which impelled them to so bold a stroke.
SCIPIO. If being famished and environed round,
They demonstrate excess of hardihood,
What had they done being free and competent
In their first sallies and adventures bold?
Indomitable, vanquished yet shall ye be,
For 'gainst your fury which doth reign within
Our industry is set to overpower,
And mistress is it to war down the proud.

[*Enter* SCIPIO *with his men, and immediately the city sounds to arms, and at the rumour sallies forth* MORANDRO, *wounded and covered with blood, holding a little white basket in his left hand, and a morsel of biscuit, bloodstained, and says,*—]

MORANDRO. Comest thou not, Leoncio announce?
    What is this, my dear friend?
    If thou dost with me refuse to come,
    How can I without thee come?
    Friend, what? Hast thou left thyself?
    Friend, what? Thyself have you left?
    Wert thou not he who me abandoned,
    Or were it I who thee did quite forsake?
    Is it possible that they give now
    Your flesh in pieces minced.
    Evidence confirmed
    What this morsel has cost!
    Is it possible that the wound
    Which left thee of life deprived
    In this same point of time,
    Did not me of life bereave!
    Fell fate did not desire to end me thus,
    To make me to myself more wretched yet,
    And more good to thee give,—
    In fine, the palm thou dost receive,
    Of a most trusty friend,
    Whilst I to exculpate myself to thee
    My soul will quickly yield.
    So quickly too that the sad weariness
    Of death doth me invite, and draws,
    Whilst offering to my Lira sweet
    This bitter, bitter bread.
    Bread wrenched from foes, it has not been earned indeed,
    But with blood bought,
    Of two unfortunate friends.

[LIRA *advances with some clothes, which she bears to the flames, and says,*—]

LIRA. What, what is this which my sad eyes behold?
MORANDRO. That which quickly they will not discern,
    According to the haste they offer me
    To finish my deep woes.
    See'st thou here, my Lira, quite fulfilled
    My word and constancy,
    That thou shouldst never die
    Whilst any life I have.
    And even should I rather say,
    That soon you will behold
    What will your life support,
    Whilst I of life shall fail.
LIRA. What is it you say, beloved Morandro, mine?
MORANDRO. Lira, thou dost hunger clean cut off,

Whilst of the thread of life
Fate wholly me deprives.
But my spilt blood,
Which commingled is with this same bread,
Will give you, my beloved,
A sad, a bitter meal.
See here the morsel which,
Enemies numbering eighty thousand held,
Which cost of a pair of friends
The lives they loved most.
And for that thou art in intelligence,
And how much I do your sweet love deserve.
Now, lady, now I perish.
Leoncio also numbers with the slain.
My sound and equitable will
Receive it with affection,
It is the choicest food,
And which the soul best tastes.
And since in torture and in calm likewise,
My lady eke has been, receive this corse
As you have received the soul.

[*He falls down dead, and* LIRA *folds him in her garment.*]

LIRA. Morandro? Oh my sweetest!
    What dost thou feel? what dost thou entertain?
    How quickly hast thou lost
    Thy wonted loveliness!
    But sad and luckless thou!
    Dead lies my destined spouse.
    O most inexpressible mishap,
    Which in such woe is seen.
    Who did this deed, beloved?
    With valour super-excellent,
    Valiant enamoured one,
    And soldier most unfortunate.
    A sally hast thou made, intended spouse,
    So, to excuse my death,
    Me have you of life despoiled.
    O bread, moistened with gore all spilt for me!
    I hold thee not for bread, but poison rank;
    To my mouth I ne'er will raise it,
    Though it be to sustain my failing strength,
    Save only the blood to kiss which to thee belongs.

[*At this juncture enters a lad, talking in faint accents, who is* LIRA's *brother.*]

BROTHER. Sister Lira, already is deceased
    My father; and my mother stands
    On the confines of death—already will die
    Such death as I experience.
    Famine has killed all.
    Sister mine, hast thou bread?
    O bread, how late you come!
    Of which no morsel yet has passed my lips;
    So closed my throat hath hunger, that were this
    Bread even to water changed, no passage could find.
    Take it, cherished sister, take
    What my anxiety doth more augment;
    I see there will be superfluity
    Of bread when life is passed.

    [*Falls dead.*]

LIRA. Art thou then dead, beloved brother mine?
    Nor breath nor life retain?
    Good is the ill when it doth come
    Contingencies without.
    O fortune, why oppress me
    With contrarieties of affliction?
    Why—why, in one and the same moment too,
    An orphan and a widow hast me left?
    O cruel Roman squadron!
    How held me hast thy sword
    Environed by two corpses,
    A brother and a spouse!
    Towards what shall I my countenance turn,
    In this importunate accident of life?
    If in existence each
    Were pledge of a dear soul;
    Cherished husband! tender brother!
    Ye will I equal in deepest desire;
    For soon I think to see you,
    In regions high or low.
    For the order of expiring,
    Examples both are set to imitate.
    Steel may quickly end—
    And hunger is—my existence.
    To this breast rather will I give outright
    This dagger than this bread.
    Who with solicitude exists,
    For death provision makes.
    What see I? am I a recreant?
    Arm, hast thou disturbed them?

Cherished husband! tender brother!
Expect me. Now I come!

[*Now appears a woman flying, and at her heels a Numantian soldier, dagger in hand in act to murder her.*]

WOMAN. Father eternal! ever-piteous Jove!
    In this disastrous strait still favour me!
SOLDIER. However quick a hasty flight impels,
    My hand relentless on thee deals out death.

[*Enter* A WOMAN *from behind.*]

LIRA. The sharpened iron and the warlike arm
    Against me turn, good soldier; turn it quick.
    Let him live really who delights in life;
    But take from me what sorely doth oppress.
SOLDIER. Since in the senate a decree is passed
    That not a female shall remain in life,
    What acceleration to the breast shall be
    Which in thy beauteous breast may give a wound?
    I, lady, am not so inconsiderate
    T' appreciate such deadly homicide.
    Let other hands and other weapons achieve.
    For nourished was I and born to worship you.
LIRA. This pity which toward me you exercise,
    Valorous son of Mars, to you I swear,
    And to high heaven attestation make,
    That your resolve I hold for cruelty.
    For my friend truly estimate thyself,
    When, with a tribute and spirit secure in act,
    My much-afflicted soul you will transpierce,
    Of life bereaving, with all bitterness.
    For since you pity would extend to me
    In such unparalleled straits, content I am,
    Unto my spouse lamented show it that
    Funeral rites we give; a last contract.
    To my dear brother eke who in repose
    Of death doth lie, deprived of vital air.
    My husband died in furnishing me life—
    Homicide hunger caused my brother's death.
SOLDIER. That to perform what you command is clear,
    On the condition you recount by the way
    Who to thy loved spouse and brother dear
    Brought about the last and sad events.
LIRA. Friend, speech no longer rests within my power.
SOLDIER. Why stand'st thou at extremities? thy feelings what?
    Thy brother now lift up—the lesser charge—

Whilst I in thy spouse do bear a heavier weight.

SCENE II.

[*A woman armed advances with a shield on her left arm, and a small lance in her hand, which signifies* WAR, *dragging with her* INFIRMITY, *leaning on a crutch, her head enveloped in cloths, and in a yellow mask.* HUNGER *sallies forth garbed in a yellow buckram robe, a yellow vizor somewhat faded. These figures become men, and then remove the masks.*]

WAR. Hunger and Infirmity, two executioners
    Of these my terrible and harsh commands,
    Of life and health consumers, and with whom
    No intercession, laws, or prayers avail,
    Now that to you my full intents be known,
    Nothing exists to magnify anew
    What's the extent of my satisfaction.
    But quickly, quickly my behests obey!
    The ever-during strength of Hades' self—
    Whose consequences never futile are—
    Urges me, that from me aid shall come
    To reinforce the military power
    Of very Rome; in time shall they be raised,
    And as these Spaniards shall they be depressed.
    There shall an epoch come when I do change;
    War down the lofty, and th' humble assist;
    For I, that am the powerful War ycleped,
    In vain detested by so many sires,
    Though of me who speaks ill doth sometimes err,
    Being ignorant of the valour of my arm.
    And well I know within this circled orb
    That Spanish valour shall exalted be,
    In that season serene, when there shall reign
    A Charles, a Philip, and a Ferdinand.
INFIRMITY. If Hunger, already our most trusted friend,
    Should not with perseverance execute
    The charge imposed, fierce homicide to be
    To all now living in Numantia,
    By me thy will should be accomplished,
    So that th' advantage will be obvious,
    Easy and profitable which the Romans cull,
    Better than what's in expectation.
    But she, in so far as her power extends,
    Is of such virtue to Numantians,
    That some better effects to hope, she has
    Of the ways and devious paths possessed herself.
    Nevertheless the rigorous lance of rage
    And influence of signals contrary,

Treats them with such bitter violence,
That there's no need of death or suffering.
Fury and rage thy followers ever close,
Have such place ta'en in their excited breasts
That what of Roman visages did consist
Each shall be thirsty for fulness of blood—
Death, fire and rage, her instruments of peace,
In death itself alone contentment know.
And triumph from the men of Rome to wrest,
With their own hand fell suicide commit
HUNGER. Cast round your eyes, and burning they behold
Th' encumbered roofs of the city; hark to the sighs
Which from a thousand piteous breasts leap forth.
Listen to the voice and crying sounds
Of women in their beauty, mangled, whose
Soft limbs in fire and ashes are consumed.
No father, friend, or lover or prayer avail;
So are accustomed the neglected sheep,
Being invaded by the cruel wolf,
To wander here and there quite devious,
In dread of losing their too simple lives.
To children eke with women delicate,
Flying through tremor homicidal swords,
From street to street pass on—O insane fate!
A sure and certain death in vain delayed.
Right through the bosom of the new married bride
The husband passes the steel instrument
The mother against, O when were such things seen!
The very son of piety devoid.
Against the son the maddened parent moves
Raising his arm with rabid clemency,
And bursts th' entrails of his begotten child.
Pitiful, yet all satisfied he stands.
No square is there, no corner, street, or house,
That is not with black gore and death surcharged.
The iron slays, the burning blaze consumes,
While rigour of the fiercest condemns all.
Soon will you see now from the soil is razed
The lofty high erected battlement,
Houses, and shrines, and temples of huge bulk,
Converted into ashes, into dust
Come, you will see on the beloved necks
Of tender children and parents beloved,
Theogenes sharpens, and on them does prove
The homicidal act with his keen sword.
And when he is assured that all are dead,
At nothing estimates his weary life,
Seeking to die in an extravagant way,

To his own people more woe radiating.
WAR. Let us on then—let none be negligent,
    All force upon the deed to concentrate;
    To what I say attend, and careful be
    That none divert thee from my dire intent

SCENE III.

[THEOGENES *comes forth with his two little sons, a daughter, and their mother.*]

THEOGENES. Though a paternal love should me restrain
    From executing the fury of my intent,
    Consider, sons, consider how I am withheld
    By zeal in this my honourable thought.
    Terrible is the grief which does forerun
    The finishing of life with violence;
    And more than mine, since it has pleased fate
    That I should be your executioner.
    Remain ye shall not, children of my soul,
    Slaves, nor shall the Roman mastery
    Snatch from your hands the triumph or the palm.
    Though bravery raises you to subjugate
    A road more level than the plain itself,
    For our liberty does heaven gracious
    Offer us and shows us and counsels,
    But liberty standeth in the gripe of death.
    Nor you, sweet consort, my beloved one,
    Yourself will see in peril, that Roman foes
    Place in your bosom and your gaiety
    Their eyes of vanity, and inordinate hands!
    My sword shall wrest you from this agony,
    And cause that all their vile attempts be vain;
    Albeit their covetousness doth urge them on,
    Their only triumph is in Numantia's dust
    I am, beloved consort, he who first
    Made you to understand that all should die
    Ere we to the insufferable wrong
    Of Roman power should quite be subjected;
    And in the act of death I'll not be last,
    Nor shall my sons be later.
WOMAN. My lord, should we escape by another way,
    Heaven knows only if I should rejoice,
    Because this cannot be as I plain see,
    And my surrender unto death so near,
    Remove the trophy from your very lives,
    And not the perfidious Roman sword, but since
    My fate it is to die, death I desire
    In Diana's consecrated shrine.

There us deposit, my good lord, and swift
Deliver us to the steel, snare, and fire.
THEOGENES. So let it be, let nothing us detain,
Sorrowful fate incites me thus to die.
SON. Mother, why dost thou wail? Whither do we go?
Stop, stop awhile, for very weariness;
Better, my mother, were it that we took
Nourishment, me hunger overpowers.
MOTHER. Come to my arms, child of my life, come, come
Where I may give you death for a repast.

[*They disappear, and enter two boys in flight; one of them is he who projects himself from the tower, styled* VIRIATO, *the other is* SERVIO.]

VIRIATO. Whence would you that we fly, my Servio?
SERVIO. I will go where you please.
VIRIATO. Move on, how weak you are!
Do you command that here we lay down life?
Seest thou not that in pursuit of us
A thousand weapons thirst for our poor lives?
SERVIO. Impossible it is for us to escape
From those who closely follow:
But stay, what think you then to do?
O what means can be left to fit our ends?
VIRIATO. At my father's tower
I contemplate concealment.
SERVIO. Friend, well may you go,
So weak am I and so debilitated
With hunger, that not one step more can I
Give thee, nor follow.
VIRIATO. What, wilt thou not come?
SERVIO. That cannot I.
VIRIATO. If you cannot advance
Here will finish thee
Hunger, sword, and fear;
And I see, for I do dread
That life may slip away,
Or that the sword may slay,
Or in rash fire consume.

[*He goes off, and* THEOGENES *enters with two drawn swords, his hands stained with gore, and as he sees* SERVIO *advance, he flies and goes within.*]

THEOGENES. Blood from my entrails jetting out in streams,
Although thou beest that of my dear sons;
Hand quick directed against thy poor life,
Full of honourable, fell activity.
Fortune conspiring to our proper hurt,

Heaven divested of just piety,
Vouchsafe unto me in this bitter lot
Some honourable near and assured death.
Valiant Numantians, take account, I pray,
That I some Roman am, with perfidy
Instinct, and on my breast avenge your wrong,
And let ensanguined be both hand and sword.

[*He casts the sword from his hand.*]

One of these swords did presentation make
To you, my frenzied fury, my mad grief,
That dying in the heady fight not feels
The rigour of the last sad accident;
And he who would of vital calmness rob
The other, in signal of some benefit,
Let him deliver to fire his luckless corse,
And it a most pious act shall counted be.
Advance, what now detains you? quick, assist,
Of my poor life make here a sacrifice
And that same tenderness which for your friends you boast,
Convert into fierce rage 'gainst enemies.
A NUMANTIAN. Whom, powerful Theogenes, dost invoke?
    What new expedient to meet death devise?
    For you incite us, and do deeply urge
    Us to encounter fell inequalities.
THEOGENES. Valiant Numantian, since that you reduce
    With fears your hardy, brave, enduring strength,
    Accept this sword, and with me kill thyself,
    As if I were an enemy recognised.
    This mode of ending life does gratify me
    In this sad circumstance better than aught.
NUMANTIAN. Me too it gratifies and it satisfies;
    For thus our evil fortune so desires—
    Let's to the square wherein is situate
    The pyre so greedy to consume our bones.
    For who can conquer there, incontinent may
    A victor unto fire consign himself.
THEOGENES. Thy utterance is good, advance, retards
    Itself the time to die as I covet
    Now slays me, steel, now fire annihilates,
    What glory now is ours in this proud death!

SCENE IV.

[SCIPIO, JUGURTHA, QUINTUS FABIUS, CAIUS MARIUS, *and some* ROMAN
SOLDIERS.]

SCIPIO. Should no deception mystify my thoughts,
 Or any fallacious signals interfere,
 From what Numantia displays, the noise,
 The woeful sounds and crackling flames, no doubt
 The barbarous fury of the foe denote.
 Murder converting 'gainst its own bare breast;
 No soldiers now upon the walls appear,
 The wonted sentinels emit no sound,—
 All, all is calm, and silence most profound.
 As if in tranquil and assured peace
 The fierce Numantians in fruition were.
CAIUS MARIUS. Swift shalt thou from this saucy doubt emerge,
 For should you will it, I myself present
 To mount the wall, although I should expose
 Myself to the sad accident which ensues.
 Alone it is to certify if in
 Numantia's walls our enemies remain.
SCIPIO. A scaling-ladder quickly now adjust
 Against the fort, and your promise fulfil.
CAIUS MARIUS. Swift for the ladder run! Ermilius, you
 Go fetch my target, round as the silver moon,
 My helmet too, adorned with various plumes;
 In faith I go either my life to lose,
 Or from the camp entire remove this doubt.
ERMILIUS. See there the round shield, and the helmet too,
 Survey the scaling-ladder Olimpius brings.
CAIUS MARIUS. Commend me unto Jove all-powerful,
 That I may accomplish all I promised.
SCIPIO. The knee raise higher up, my Marius,
 Shrink up thy body, and protect thy head;
 Courage, now, the topmost round attain.
 What seest thou?
CAIUS MARIUS. Holy divinities! what sight is this?
JUGURTHA. At what dost thou so wonder?
CAIUS MARIUS. E'en to see
 A red lake of spilt blood, corses innumerable,
 Expanded widely o'er Numantia's streets.
SCIPIO. Are there none yet alive?
CAIUS MARIUS. I apprehend not.
 At least, no person doth himself present,
 As far as my just sight itself extends.
SCIPIO. Leap into the interior,—all survey.

[CAIUS MARIUS *leaps into the city.*]

Follow him also, friend Jugurtha, do,
We all will follow straight.
JUGURTHA. This enterprise with the office not consists
Which you do hold; assuage your bosom, sir,
And that Marius may return or I
With the reply about what passes in
This haughty city,—fast the ladder hold.
Oh, heavens just, what a sorrowful spectacle,
And horrible to view! event most strange.
Seething blood bathes all the moistened soil,
Dead corpses occupy the squares and streets,
A longing I have to leap in and see all.

[JUGURTHA *leaps into the city, and* QUINTUS FABIUS *speaks.*]

QUINTUS FABIUS. Undoubtedly the fiery Numantians,
By their own barbarous fury mainly urged—
Seeing no remedy to save themselves,
Rather they would their lives surrender up
To the sharp point of their own proper steel,
Than to the victor hand of their foes, held
In every possible execration.
SCIPIO. Were only one alive left 'mongst the dead,
'Twould not deny me a triumph in Rome,
For having subdued this haughty nation.
A mortal enemy to our deathless name,
Stiff in opinion, ready, precipitate,
Every danger and hard circumstance
To meet, which never shall a Roman praise
Who saw the shoulder to the Numantian turned,
Whose valour,—whose dexterity in arms
With reason me constrained to use the means
The fierce indomitably to enclose,
And triumph effect by industry and skill.
For it was not practicable by force alone;
But now meseems that Marius appears.

[CAIUS MARIUS *turns as if to pass through the walls.*]

CAIUS MARIUS. In vain, illustrious general, have been
Our forces occupied in this campaign.
In vain hast thou thyself proved diligent,—
For into smoke and wind converted are
Expectations sure of victory,
By your unwearied industry secured.

The lamentable end and the sad history
Of the unvanquished city Numantia,
Deserve a fame which no time can destroy.
The inmates have by your loss gain acquired,
Wresting the triumph from your receiving hands,
And leaving life with magnanimity,
All our plans vain have eventuated;
Their honoured purpose has been of more avail
Than all the power and subtlety of Rome.
The populace worn out by violent end
Finished the misery of their woeful days,
Extending wide the sad conclusion.
Numantia now is turned into a lake
Of red blood, choked with corpses infinite,
Herself being her own homicide.
From th' overweighted and unequal chain
Of bitter servitude they have escaped
With quick audacity, to fear unknown.
In the square's centre elevated stands
The burning element destined for victims, whose
Bodies and goods yield aliment to the fire.
At the precise time when it I went to see
The furious Theogenes, Numantian,
To finish his existence covetous,
Curses ejecting his bitter token short,
In the flame's centre madly plunged himself,
Fired by extraordinary temerity,
And at the moment of the plunge, cried, Fame,
Occupy here your tongue and eke your eyes
On this exploit, whose virtue loudly sings.
Romans advance, already through the spoils
Of the city melted into dust and smoke.
Its flowers and fruits all into brambles changed,
From hence on foot, with thoughts as free as air,
A large portion have I traversed of this town,
Through streets and passes, indirect crooked ways,
I not a solitary Numantian
Have found who, taken from amongst the quick,
Could information render for what cause,
In what way, and with what auxiliaries
This marvellous distraction did they
Commit, hastening the sad career of death.
SCIPIO. My very bosom was it enrapt by chance
    With barbarous arrogance and foul death replete,
    And empty found of cruelty? Is it by chance
    Unto my nature foreign that I use
    Benignity and clemency to the foe
    Vanquished, as most the victor it becomes?

Ill would you hold it, if indeed were known
   The valour of Numantia in my breast,
   To vanquish and to pardon equally born.
QUINTUS FABIUS. Jugurtha will give you more satisfaction,
   My lord, on that you earnestly would know;
   Behold him now returning full of despatch.

[JUGURTHA *returns by the same wall.*]

JUGURTHA. Most prudent general, futilely you employ
   Here longer your dread force, to th' opposite side
   Turn th' unequalled industry you display.
   Nothing further in Numantia
   Can you engage—all dead, save only one
   Who still is quick, your triumph to adorn.
   There in yon tower, as I plainly see
   Awhile ago, there fixed stood a youth
   Disturbed in visage, yet in manner genteel.
   Were this a proved truth it would suffice
   At Rome to triumph o'er Numantia.
   In this conjuncture most desirable
   Thither let us go and inquiry set,
   How the youth may come to our hands alive,
   A fact to us of importance infinite.

[VIRIATO *speaks from the Tower.*]

Whence come ye, and what seek, O Romans, what?
   If by good luck you would in Numantia try
   To enter, do it you shall, all smoothly too,
   Without obstruction. But my tongue asserts
   That I the badly guarded key of this
   City do hold, where death triumph has found.
SCIPIO. For the keys, my youth, desirous do I wend,
   And more than that you no experience have
   If in my bosom pity holds a sway.
VIRIATO. Thy clemency thou offerest, cruel, late,
   There is none on whom to use it, and I wish
   To suffer the rigour of the penalty.
   What bitter counsel, pitiful to think,
   Of my progenitors and country dear,
   Caused this sad terrible conclusion here?
QUINTUS FABIUS. Tell me, ponderest on this lot abhorred,
   Blind by the frenzy of temerity,
   Thy flourishing age and eke thy tender life?
SCIPIO. Moderate, youth yet in thy puberty, calm
   The innate briskness; thy valour subject
   The rather to my honourable sway.

From this moment I proffer thee my faith,
And pledge my word that thou art of thyself
A master recognised, from capture free.
And with thy jewels and rich ornaments
Live where thou wouldst in all sufficiency,
All which I give to thee if thou desirest,
Thyself to me willingly rendering up.

VIRIATO. All the fury of the united dead,
Of this same people now to dust reduced,
To fly all compacts and conditions too,
Never listening to subjection;
All anger, rancour openly disclosed
Are blended in my breast in unison.
My spirit, a heritage from Numantia,
See if you think this madness to o'erthrow;
Beloved country, people unfortunate,
Ye do not fear nor imagine I am insane,
In doing what I should, being son of thee,
No promises neither me divert, nor fear.
Now the soil fails me, now heaven and fate,
Now to subdue me all the world conspires.
It is impossible I should not pay
The worthy tribute to your known prowess.
Should fear, however, quick concealment urge,
At an approaching and a fearful death,
That enemy with greater boldness shall
Seize me, and with desire your lot t' pursue.
But vile fear passed away, e'en as I can
Boldly and strong will I reparation make,
And the error of my innocent age
Will I repay by dying courageously.
This I assure you, valorous citizens,
That not through me your deep intentions fail,
And that no triumph falls to perfidious Rome,
As if already there were of our ashes none.
With me shall fall their vain attempts, 'gainst me
Now let them lift the red right hand of war.
They sober me with a promise sure of life,
And entertainment kind, an ample door.
Restrain yourselves, O Romans, your courage calm down;
The wall assaulting do not fatigue yourselves,
For were your potency yet greater still,
You, I assure you, will not conquer me.
Already my intent displays itself,
And if there has been the pure and perfect love,
Which I to my so cherished country held,
This fall assures it quick.

[He precipitates himself from the tower.]

SCIPIO. O memorable, unforeseen exploit,
  Worthy an ancient and a valorous soul;
  Not only has Numantia, but Spain
  Acquired in this act glory and wide fame;
  With thee dwells virtue, and strange heroism,
  And my right o'er thee forfeited, is dead.
  Thou with thy fall has truly elevated
  Thy reputation and my power cast down,
  O that yet in existence Numantia were, that thou
  Alone might dwell there, would give me delight.
  Alone hast thou the great advantages culled
  Of this extended fight, illustrious, rare.
  Away then youth, away all boastfulness,
  And the renown which heaven for thee prepares,
  In having vanquished, by your headlong fall,
  Him who in mounting up more fallen rests.
FAME. From nation unto nation my clear voice
  Travels, and in the smooth and dulcet noise
  The soul inspires with an ardent desire
  To eternize an act so elevated.
  Raise, Romans, up the forehead now bent down;
  Elevate now the corse, which able has been
  In this young age to snatch from you the great
  Triumph, which honours with such dignity.
  I who am Fame, the world-wide preacher too,
  Will good care take as far as heaven itself
  To move the passage to th' exalted sphere,
  Giving due force and means to the earth below,
  To publish with a tongue of verity,
  With a just intent, and eke with a hasty flight,
  Numantia's valour sole, unparalleled,
  From Batro unto Tile, from one to th' other pole.
  This unforeseen achievement has given proof
  Of valour which in ages yet to come
  Will signalize the children of stout Spain,
  Heirs worthy the exploits of their bold sires.
  Not the relentless scythe of cruel death,
  Nor course of time, how light soe'er it be,
  Shall hinder me from singing of the brave
  Numantian heroes, steadfast hearts and hands.
  In this sad city do I find alone
  All that a canticle on war may chant,
  And what besides a large material yields
  To occupy infinite ages in full verse.
  Strength unsubdued, valour appreciated,
  Due celebration worthy in sweet rhyme

Or prose to be enshrined; and more than that
My memory doth encharge itself, that it
A happy issue to your history yield.

THE TREATY OF ALGIERS.

PREFACE.

This notice, which might stand excused in respect of *The Voyage to Parnassus* of Miguel de Cervantes, as being a re-impression of a book so well known, exacts also the publication of two poetical pieces equally known, and which we now for the first time print, and translate into another language.

The one is a tragedy and the other a comedy; the former styled *The Siege of Numantia*; the latter, *The Treaty of Algiers*. Of them both mention is made under the identical titles in a dialogue with the poet Pancracio, and in the discourse of the Canon of Toledo with the Curate, Pero Perez, introduced in the Don Quixote, and at the close of the comedy of the Baths of Algiers, printed in the year of grace 1613. These two are in the number of those twenty or thirty comedies which Cervantes wrote about 1582, when he was ransomed from the captivity of Algiers; and of them he states that all had been represented at the Madrid theatres with general satisfaction. Despite, however, of these eulogies, in both are detected certain anomalies which unite them with much which in later time Cervantes himself justly reprehended.

For *The Treaty of Algiers* scarce merits the name of comedy, as being a simple relation, both tragic and comic, of the sufferings of the Christians in the power of infidels, in which portraiture are introduced the blameable customs of one and the other, whose successes are the more credible from the pen of the author. Hence he presents himself as a true Christian. He relates with exactness the various calamities of the captives; the sale of them at the foot (zoco) or the square of Algiers. The danger and facility with which youths turned renegades,—the fixed and venturesome freewill which counselled captives to fly, the brutal castigation which the Moors gave them for it, the martyrdom which in Algiers Father Miguel de Aranda suffered, a nobleman of Valentia, of the order of Montesa, in revenge for a Moor who was burnt alive by the Inquisition of Valencia, who going over into Barbary, openly professed Mahometanism, and following his career as corsair, fell into the hands of that tribunal, whose fate Father Ahedo copiously relates in his History of Algiers.

He omits the relation of all the dishonest acts of the Moors towards the captives of both sexes, availing themselves of witchery and enchantments, under the futile hope of attracting and fixing human will,—a fact of frequency among them, as Ahedo testifies.

Hence Cervantes recounts those loves of Aurelio and Silvia, both in captivity, and taken by Mami Arnaut in a new galley of Malta, styled St. Paul, of whose loss Ahedo also makes mention, attributing the calamity to the fact of Spanish galleys being too heavily built, and this was aggravated by a superfluous amount of cargo, and of our people not having recourse to oars. Now the Moors acted differently, and their boats were better sailers. Izuf and Zara, two principal Moors, bought these slaves. Zara became enamoured of the captive Aurelio, and to induce reciprocity had recourse to the witch Fatima, and not yet satisfied, makes Silvia a party to the love affair. Izuf on his side falls in love with Silvia, and for effect avails himself of the offices of Aurelio.

Albeit in this comedy there is no principal action to which other incidents are subordinate; if any episode could assume its place, it is that complication of affection between master and slaves, whose *dénouement* consists in the King Azan granting to Aurelio and Silvia liberty that they may return to Spain to get two thousand ducats as redemption money, confiding in his words and good faith for the fulfilment of this stipulation.

Now the end of this comedy is the seeing in the Port of Algiers the vessel which bore the price of the redemption, in which came Father Fray Don Juan Gil, whose success was also a true one, for he was the man who redeemed Cervantes.

Neither are the unities of time and place observed. Pedro Alvarez and another fellow-captive travel nights and days pursued by their masters, and Alvarez missing the road, meets a Hon who shows it to him,—which extraordinary good fortune is ascribed to the intercession of the Lady of Montserrat. Then moral personages are introduced.

Necessity and Opportunity pursue Aurelio that he may yield to the importunities of Zara. So in the Numantia this personage is introduced in the form of a maiden, tower-crowned, with information relative to the siege in which Scipio was engaged, and considering that only on the part whence the river bathed the adjacent city, help could be furnished, a doleful supplication for it is made, so that virtually the river Douro, with three youths who represent the streamlets which disembogue on it, pass from the stage. Afterwards, in a long harangue, is prophesied how that the Goths in future, Atila and the Duke of Alba, Don Fernando Alvarez, of Toledo, should make war on Rome, deprive it of all remedy (desaucia), and submerge it in its own waters. It had been easy and more natural to put these discourses into the mouths of actors. However, this invention was so agreeable to Cervantes, that he piqued himself on being the first who introduced these moral personages on the stage with general applause. Still, many years before we see them introduced in the comedy of the Duchess of Rosa, printed for John de Timoneda in the year 1560, by Alonso de Vega, poet and actor, as was also from time to time Lope de Rueda.

About the year 1598 Lope de Vega composed a comedy, styled the Captives of Algiers, the argument of which is similar to that of *The Treaty of Algiers*. Virtually he introduces into it a captive called Saavedra, doubtless intended for Cervantes. At least, the incidents which happened to him in his captivity are identical with those of which we read in *The Treaty of Algiers*, as are the martyrdom of the Cavalier de Montesa, the manners of the King Azan, the complication of the loves of masters and captives, which one may pronounce to be the action of the comedy.

The *dénouement* is almost identical, and is reducible to the fact that Azan grants liberty to the two captive lovers, whose names in Lope are Leonardo and Marcela, with the same condition, that on their return to Spain they should procure the price of their ransom, and remit it to Soliman their master. Amidst other improprieties Lope does not observe unity of time, for according to our supposition the events of the comedy, which happened about 1580, feign that from Algiers one could see the fires in the Castle of Denia, where with sundry kinds of rejoicing Don Francisco de Sandoval y Roxas, afterwards Duke of Lerma, celebrated the union of Philip III. with the Queen Donna Margarita, contracted in the stated year 1598. This conformity of incidents and scenes and even expressions in *The Treaty of Algiers*, being found in the Captives by Lope, shows that some copy of the comedy was before the writer, who plucked the fruits plentifully, although we did not see that facility, liveliness, and discretion which appertains to Lope.

Let us now revert to Cervantes. He reflected many years after he had written *The Treaty of Algiers*, that nevertheless his verses appeared good, and so he composed eight other comedies, and noting that neither the comedians demanded them, nor others appreciated them, sold them to the bookseller Juan de Villaroel, who struck them off in the year 1615.

Amongst them is styled the Bath of Algiers, almost identical with *The Treaty of Algiers*. He preserves therein principally the complication of the loves of masters and captives, the names a little varied—for these illicit affections and oppositions relative to masters and slaves made such an impression on Cervantes, that he not only preserves them in his renovated comedy, but he repeats them in his novel of the Liberal Lover. He introduces anew the love of a daughter and Agi Morato, a rich Algerine Moor, called Zara, who, enamoured of Lope, one of the captives of the bath, or place where slaves were kept open for ransom, held communication with him through the medium of letters appended to a cane, by which same artifice money was also conveyed.

The disentanglement of the plot is equally the liberty of the captives, solicited by the same Lope, who after ransom returns from Spain to Algiers in a bark, in which were all his companions, and also Zara, whom he marries after she had undergone the sacrament of baptism, a fact which not only Cervantes avers for truth, but which is confirmed in Don Quixote.

If in *The Treaty of Algiers* improprieties are obvious, we detect the same in the Baths of Argel. One of the most surprising incidents is the fiction that the Moors saw an Armada of three hundred galleys represented in the clouds struck by sun rays, and they heard the firing and saw the fires. The Janissaries, thinking that the vessel bore Philip II. to subdue the pirates, were so enraged, that in order to have few enemies they made more than twenty captives, and killed more than thirty persons.

An anonymous writer gave a reprint of these eight comedies in 1749, accompanied by an extended prologue, in which he tried to prove that the author composed them to ridicule the comedies of the age, which had erred so much against the rules of wit, and thus he wrote Don Quixote to hurl into contempt all extant books of chivalry.

Finally, the celebrated Abbot Don Xavier Lampillas tried to vindicate Cervantes for this new and singular expedient.

He avers that these eight comedies are not his. That the wickedness of the printers published with his own name and prologue these extravagant productions, analogous to the perverse taste of the commonalty, and suppressing those which really were by Cervantes' hand.

But as the defects of *The Treaty of Algiers* which Cervantes recognises as his own, and which he asserts to have recited with general applause, confirm the irregularities which he caused to be printed, we must infer that Cervantes did not compose his comedies for the end mentioned by the anonymous critic who would find in them more wit and artifice than they contain; hence the judgment of the Abbot Lampillas is not admissible, although engendered of good zeal for the honour of the author of "Don Quixote."

Firstly, for that he admits himself to be the author in his dedication to the Count de Lemos, and in the prologue. Indeed, the style of both compositions will not justify a suspicion that they were from another pen.

Secondly, that it is not within verisimilitude that any one would have the temerity to adopt foreign works in lieu of his own; and had he succeeded it would seem impossible but that a vindication would have ensued, he having survived the publication more than a whole year.

On the contrary, we infer and prove by these comedies the doctrine of Dr. Juan Huarte, alleged by the ingenious D. Vincente de los Rios in the life of Saavedra, that by the application of genius we should examine not only the learning which would equalize each more, but also that which better accommodates itself to the theory and practice of that science. These are indispensable for the different bent of genius.

In Cervantes that observation is notified. No one has succeeded better in composing comedies, and he has possessed the theory in perfection, as so many places in his works testify. And especially in the colloquy between the curate and the Canon of Toledo, as inserted in the first section of "Don Quixote."

By the defects exposed in *The Treaty of Algiers* judgment may be made of the Numantia, but that is much more regular.

The "Treaty" is styled comedy, but it does not realize the ordinary definition of that title. There is not one ludicrous incident or a hint to provoke a smile—it has the characteristic of tragedy throughout.

It is said of Dante that he did not know why he called his poems comedies—a species of satiric epic, full of gloomy wildness of imagination.

This comedy of Algiers may almost rival Dante, and as Cervantes wrote later, and comedies were all explained and defined in his time, he might have assigned another name to the Life in Algiers.

DRAMATIS PERSONAE.

AURELIO.
SEBASTIAN.
SAAVEDRA.
PEDRO ALVAREZ.
FRANCIS, JOHN, *Lads*.
THEIR PARENTS.
SILVIA.
CAPTIVES.
FATIMA, ZARA, *Moors*.
NECESSITY.
OCCASION.
A DEMON.
IZUF, *King of Algiers, a Moor*.
BAYRAN, *Moor*.
ANOTHER MOOR.
A CAPTIVE, *who goes away*.
TWO MERCHANTS.
AN AUCTIONEER.
A LION.

ACT I.

SCENE I.

[AURELIO, FATIMA, ZARA, SAAVEDRA, SEBASTIAN, PEDRO ALVAREZ. *The last three are* CAPTIVES.]

AURELIO. Woeful, sorrowful estate,
   Hard and bitter servitude!
   As the suffering is extensive,
   The good how little and how much abridged!
   O purgatory in life itself!
   Infernal regions planted here on earth,
   Evil inferior to none,
   A strait without an exit.
   Mark of so deep grief,
   Into such and so much sorrow distributed,
   Damage which greatest amongst,
   A greater yet exists,
   Incredible necessity,
   Death, credible and palpable,
   Dealing miserable and intractable
   Woe; visible and invisible both.
   It appertains to know if conscience can
   Discover to be valorous.

Paltry, troublous life!
Of penitence the portrait.
Quiet this torture,
Which in my view confirmed enemy is.
It ne'er will reach unto what I declare,
To the point of what I feel.
Sorrow doth overweight me
In saying, bathed in lamentation,
That my live body is amongst the Moors,
And that my soul is in the power of love.
My anguish is of body and of soul.
The part material, thou seest what it is;
The soul is surrendered up
Unto the amorous chain.
I did once think that love
Could boast no power in slavery; yet in me
Its recent nails demonstrate liveliness.
What, dost in misery seek
Love in captivity?
Whether in life or death, abandon it.
In poverty and wretchedness,
Dost thou not see that severed in twain is the thread
Of this too amorous yarn?
Here with hunger or with thirst
Extended or abridged?
I do believe; for thou hast not desired
In this strait to forget me.
Hast seen my breast how sound,
Though tattered be my garments?
I clearly understand, from this point of time,
That virtue, which within itself is closed,
Both heaven and earth embraces,
And more indeed than I well understand.
One thing would I ask thee, if in this state
A shadow of reason 'midst a thousand shades
Itself should show?
And is so that you were the cause of finishing me.
While you strike continually,
Allow a moment's pause.
I ask not that you spring from out my breast,
For that you cannot do.
I ask that you remain,
And be of use in this sad circumstance.
From the place where you set me,
They did procure my fall.
Who can accomplish what you once attained?
Already approaches Zara with her tale.
O wearisome contention! even day

Itself doth fail me before th' advent of night.
Assist me, Silvia mine,
If you do succour bring,
From the most arduous and unpolished war
I trust to bear the palm.

ZARA. Aurelio!

AURELIO. Lady mine!

ZARA. Shouldst thou hold me for such,
In faith, you would quickly do
What I request, of all contention void.

AURELIO. What thou wilt, that will I;
For, in fine, I am your slave.

ZARA. These words I do commend;
Your acts, however, I vituperate.

AURELIO. What deeds by me have been achieved that they With thy desire accord not?

ZARA. The same which thou doest not,
They me no satisfaction give.

AURELIO. Lady, I stay no longer;
By water quick I go.

ZARA. Other water doth my fire demand,
Which only thou canst bear.
Go not away. Stand still!

AURELIO. There is no wood in the house.

ZARA. Sufficient is there myself to consume.

AURELIO. Myself I love.

ZARA. Entertain no fear.

AURELIO. Let me, dear lady, go;
My lord Izuf will come.

ZARA. Who with so great love remains will not
Do well to let you go.

AURELIO. There is no reason obstinately to oppose.
Lady, let me go.

ZARA. Aurelio, come hither!

AURELIO. Better you retire.

ZARA. Aurelio, thus do you send me away?

AURELIO. Rather I you a favour do,
If with love's compass you do measure it.
Seest thou not that I am a Christian,
In lot and evil fortune?

ZARA. Love maketh all alike:
Give me your hand in token.

FATIMA. Zara, lady mine,
I tell, you that myself have wondered,
Observing what has passed.
Your loftiness and fancy do I see—
A pretty thing assuredly.
Unworthy to be noted,
To be beloved by a Christian,

A so beauteous Moor!
And what brings to a point
Your affection without measurement,
Is seeing you yourself surrender up
To a Christian who is your slave.
To what you wish your gallant corresponds,
Pardon me, you are frail.

ZARA. Whither goest thou?

FATIMA. I well know where.

ZARA. Constant, sweetest friend,
What thou averrest I do not deny.
What shall I do? Love is fire,
And my weak will is wax.
And since the evil I view,
And the end where I shall have to stop,
Impossible it is to oppose
The strength of my desire.
Turn thy tongue and purpose
To fight this rock against,
'Twill be no little glory
This self-conquest to enjoy.

FATIMA. I would in this thee gratify, for you
Can command me to it.
Christian turn to behold me,
My face is none of death's.

AURELIO. Upon me more than death you do impose
By these your blandishments;
Your labour all is vain; leave me in pangs.

FATIMA. Dost not discern how the brave Christian
Retires upon his honour?
He knows no more of love
Than dullest animal of the softest lyre.

AURELIO. How would you that I understood
In this chain aught of love?

ZARA. May this no pain inflict,
Quickly shall we some amendment have,
And both shall be removed.

AURELIO. 'Twill be better to abandon her;
In this retreat I do not wish to pass
From extreme to extreme.

FATIMA. To what extremity wilt thou then pass?

AURELIO. This steel removing from the body,
Into another error shall I fall,
My soul, with greater woe.

FATIMA. Do Christians then have souls?

AURELIO. Yea, so rich and so important too,
Having been ransomed by Divinity.

FATIMA. What—thoughts vain!

For if a soul you have
'Tis of a diamond wrought,
Within the forge of love,
You come out hardened quite.
Aurelio, courage man,
Mind well what I do say,
You do not wish so great a friend to be
Of your so obstinate opinion.
Without liberty you find yourself
Pressed iron chains between,
Poor, naked, weary, full of necessity,
And subject to mischances infinite,
To impalement, buffetings,
Dungeons, and in darkness compassed round.
I promise to you liberty;
Thy irons shall be removed.
In cloth shalt thou be clothed,
Having no fear of stocks to gall thy limbs.
Cuzcuz—white bread for provender.
Poultry in abundance too.
There shall be no lack e'en of curious wines,
If of that liquid you would quaff;
Nothing impossible of you is required,
Labours not excessive,
But quiet and well regulated,
Sweet, sweet as possible.
Avail yourself of this conjuncture now,
Which has been set before you;
Play not the ignorant man, but show
Discretion, most approved.
Look thou at my Lady Zara,
Comprising all due merit.
Look how the sun is obscured
By the clear complexion of the face.
Contemplate her youth,
Her riches, name, and fame,
Unto thy gate see how she safety call.
Ponder well the interest which to thee
Doth in this act revert.
Numberless are they who would put the mouth,
Where she doth set her foot.

AURELIO. Hast thou finished, Fatima?
FATIMA. I have.
AURELIO. Would you that I replied?
FATIMA. So do.
AURELIO. I answer, no.
ZARA. O Allah ! what word is that invades my ears?
AURELIO. I say 'tis not expedient

To ask what you have asked.
Quickly wilt thou recognise
The ill it does comprise.

FATIMA. What ill can come from your request, Lady?

AURELIO. The offence that being of a Moorish race
It complicates me with your Mahomet.

ZARA. Away with Mahomet from me,
No longer now my lord,
Being servant now of love,
Which overpowering quite subdues the soul.
The bosom already casts itself to earth,
And thee to my heaven raises.

AURELIO. Lady, a suspicion I entertain
Which does subvert me quite.

FATIMA. Say, of me suspicion what?

AURELIO. Lady, I no brief means do recognise,
Or circumambulation how to please.
My law receives no order
To do what you enjoin.
Quite opposite, with grave penalties
And threats it interdicts.
Had you been baptized,
And being already wedded, as you are,
'Twould be a thing scarcely excusable
To ask what you require.
This then is my determination,
Rather to die than instrumental be
In doing what you solicit,
So steadfastly I stand in this resolve.

ZARA. Aurelio, is your understanding safe?

AURELIO. It is because I have command of it,
That I to thee so cruel prove myself.

ZARA. Ah cruelty! unfortunate success;
Can it be possible such small effect
Have on thee worked my supplications?

FATIMA. Of a verity, this enemy
Is very sapient, or a very fool.
Ruin bereft of reason, and compass too,
From earth's scum descended.
Think you thus to triumph,
Revelling inordinately.
Futile man, such fantasy
Imagin'st thou in earnest we do speak.
Rather by a lightning stroke shalt die,
Ere day's light shall pass o'er,
With me you have yet to do.
And so, that I inform you,
What he will say who never wished to speak.

Wishing would more avail me;
O Zara, be not discontent,
The remedy leave with me.
On this false Christian,
Tardy repentance will I quick impose.
ZARA. It is not good, you excite yourself for ill.
FATIMA. Nor for good neither.
ZARA. Cease, Aurelio, your assured disdain
FATIMA. This can the false one dare,
Look, lady, at the chamber,
Where, in this aggravated suffering,
Or I my life will cast away
Or thou content shalt be.

[*The* TWO MOORS *retire, and* AURELIO *remains alone.*]

AURELIO. Father of heaven, in whose mighty hand
Of earth and heaven is the government—
Whose potency everywhere is manifest,
In loving, just, and holy laudable zeal—
If that thy light, if that thy hand denies
To rescue me from this chaos, I fear
And eke suspect that as in prison coy,
The body stands, so captive is the soul.
Where art thou, Silvia fair? what destiny,
What insane force of fate implacable,
The course of what so prosperous road hath us,
Reason without and cause, quite sundered?
O star, O lot, O fortune, O signal,
If any of ye has been parent of
So vast perdition, here do I declare
That you a thousand times I execrate—
Die will I for what to the soul relates,
Ere I do that which my mistress requires.
Firm as a rock deep founded do I stand,
Which combats and repels both wind and sea,
Whether my life be much or little, imports
But little—only he who dieth well
Can say that he enjoyed, or long life hath;
Who dieth ill, unmeasured death doth feel.

[AURELIO *retires and* SAAVEDRA *advances, and* PEDRO ALVAREZ, *with*
SEBASTIAN *at the same time.*]

SAAVEDRA. In the brief career I do observe
The hours of time light-footed to advance
'Gainst me with heaven in conspiracy,
Hope doth remain behind, not so desire—

The ill augmenting which environs me.
O hard, iniquitous, star inexorable!
How by the hair hast thou me dragged along,
To that same grief which tramples me quite down!
PEDRO ALVAREZ. Grief, grief is lost in such hard times as these;
But if by my lamentation heaven were
Appeased, why then my tears would current find.
To adverse fortune a cheerful visage should
The generous breast demonstrate; a good soul
Can remedy furnish to whatever ill.
SAAVEDRA. The neck enfeebled to the troublesome
Yoke of slavery in its bitterness,
You see to body and soul is dangerous.
And more to him who does anticipate
Unsavoury death, long time ere he attains
The means of living honestly in the world.
PEDRO ALVAREZ. Should I by hazard your works imitate,
At this conjuncture I should force myself
To be assigned unto hunger's jaws.
I would not aggravate my sufferings,
Entertaining due reflection,
I hold my patroness for a true friend,
She treats me as you see, joyful I walk,
Captive I am, let him say what he will.
SAAVEDRA. Triumph, my brother, this trophy enjoy—
If you in being captive pride yourself,
I know 'tis base, foul, and dishonourable.
PEDRO ALVAREZ. Saavedra, brother mine, if you set up
Yourself to be a preacher, here is no land
From which you may the fruit you wish attain—
Abandon this, and listen to the war
Which the great Philip moves, news certainly,
And in brief space will from you woe expel.
'Tis said a frigate from Biserta came,
This very night here—and comes a captive too,
Who to my expectations life imparts.
Coy destiny hath from him liberty ta'en,
To Barcelona sailing from Malaga,
Mami she captured, corsair insolent;
In his deportment one he seems to be
Of a great quality, and is well trained
In Bellona's hardy exercise.
They say the calculated number which
Has passed of soldiers into Spain, strangers,
Besides two-thirds of ours which have debarked:
The princes, gentlefolks, and cavaliers,
Who to serve Philip willingly did enlist;
Natural born and foreigners are found,

And the demonstration, handsome, gay,
Which his majesty has in Badajoz,
The power of united Christendom.
They say in this, that no one can divine
The purpose of the king, and saying this
The great and little justify themselves.
SAAVEDRA. Heavens, burst' forth, and quickly to us despatch
    A liberator from this our bitter war,
If ye already hold him not on the earth.
When I upon this soil became convinced,
So noted in the world, that in her breast
So great a pirate it conceals, admits,
And closes in, I would not grief restrain;
And in my own despite, in ignorance,
I saw the withered face bedashed with tears.
Presenting to my eyes the open shore,
And mountain high, where Charles the Great observed
His banners waving in the lofty air—
And the wide main no other such force floating,
But moved by envy at his glory, was
Enraged more than ere before it raged.
These things revolving in my memory,
Extorted moisture from my vexed eyes,
At knowledge of disgrace notorious.
But if high heaven should annoyance give,
And 'gainst my luck be not in conspiracy,
And death make off not with my booty too,
When I myself do find in happier state,
Should my lot, or kind favour me assist,
To see myself on bended knee before
Philip the king, my tongue, being almost mute,
I think to move in his royal presence,
Of flattery and untruthfulness devoid,
Saying, Mighty Lord, whose powerful arm subjects
Barbarous nations to an ill-relished yoke,
The dark-born Indians with their tributes all,
Contented vassalage do recognise.
From their concealed corners dragging gold,
Awaken courage in thy royal breast,—
The shame with which a village ill-fortified,
Aspires to heap outrage ever on thee.
The populace is numerous, its strength small—
Naked, ill-armed, and cannot even boast
In its defence, a fort, a wall or rock.
For the Armada's advent each one looks
To his feet to assign the charge and eke the care,
The life which he sustains full to preserve.
Of the prison bitter, scornful, intolerable,

Where fifteen thousand Christians gave up life,
Thou hast the keys of that enclosure vile—
All, all therein, as I, with uplifted hands,
And knees the earth impressing, sobbing loud,
By inhuman torments compassed round about,
Most potent Sire, all standing do beseech
You turn the eyes of mercy upon those
Who supplicate assistance dolefully;
And since now discord has abandoned you,
Which once so sorely vexed you and oppressed,
And concord follows in the peaceful wake,
Effect it so, good king, that accomplishment
With thee may rest, valour and courage eke,
Such as your father in his time commenced.
Only seeing your resolution, will
Due fear infuse into the barbarous rout,
Which I divine their utter loss involves.
Who holds in doubt but that the royal breast
Itself will manifest, on witnessing
The woes which them (the captives) incessantly beset.
But, ah, the humbleness of my genius rude
Betrays itself when vainly I pretend
Address to proffer, though in humility—
Opportunity me justifies—
I would silence adopt—fearing my talk
Offence might give to thee, and they call me
To that same hideous work, which kills me quite.

[SEBASTIAN, A CAPTIVE, *enters.*]

Hast ever the like seen?
Exists a soil so much concord without,
Where mercy even fails,
And cruelty superabounds?
Where extenuation shall we find
For wickedness so fearful?
The innocent pays the debt
For him who is most culpable?
Oh heavens! what is it that I have seen?
A lawless people here
Do entertain a savage taste,
Christ's ministers to slay.
O Spain! beloved country,
Look now at your ill hap,
If thou inflictest just punition,
They take away just life.
PEDRO ALVAREZ. Sebastian, holdest thou it worthy to be,
    Such reasons to advance?

SEBASTIAN. Infinite ills,
    Of good, scantiness.
SAAVEDRA. In being, as thou art, a very slave,
    All anguish is comprised.
SEBASTIAN. A greater suffering
    Is yet reserved for me.
PEDRO ALVAREZ. What can cause
    The pain you stigmatize as so acute?
SEBASTIAN. Of a life which this day ends,
    Ending for ever.
    You know that here in Algiers
    It was well known how in Valencia
    By equitable sentence died,
    From Sargel port, a Moor.
    I said that he inhabited Sargel,
    Although he was from Aragon.
    And in the odour of his nation
    The dog to Barbary passed,
    A corsair did become,
    Ready with such cruel hands
    That he did with blood of Christians
    Satisfy his own.
    In his piratical career he was
    Captured, and being recognised,
    Unto the Inquisition was consigned,
    And 'gainst him was a regular process formed.
    It was averred
    That having the sacrament of baptism,
    A renegade from Christ,
    He did himself transfer to Africa.
    There by his industry and dexterity
    He captive made
    More than six hundred Christians.
    And as were proven full
    Such and so many evils and errors,
    That the Holy Inquisitors
    Condemned him to be burnt.
    The fate of the heretical Moor,
    And the death he suffered,
    Quickly was written
    By the Moors habiting there.
    The sad intelligence known
    By the relatives of the defunct,
    They swore, and concert made
    To give another life unto the fire.
    Quickly they sought a Christian,
    This debt to satisfy.
    And a religious minister they found,

A native of Valencia.
They demanded in hot haste
To execute their plan.
On his bosom they found
A Montese cross,
Which victorious emblem,
If he retained it honourably
On earth, when he should die,
Glorious passport 'twould to heaven be;
For this darkened nation,
Who this symbol on him witnessed,
Thinking Christ himself to annihilate,
Killed him who bore his cross.
They bought him of his master,
Though they were indigent, at this said point,
The money all concentrated,
To alms did consecrate.
Amongst our Christian people, of them God's grace
The afflicted to restore is asked,
And not destroy the sound.
But this unbelieving race among
(Cursed be their place!) the sick to cure
They ask not, but from them their lives they take.
Here in hangman's hands
Have I been witness that God's minister,
Not two between,
But 'midst two thousand thieves a place has found.
The pious priest advanced,
'Midst unjust people set,
His visage withered in humility,
But with alacrity to die for God.
The wrathful multitude is on the watch
To multiply his pains,
Some dealing him a thousand buffetings,
And some his white hairs peel off.
Those hands which unto heaven were consecrate
A thousand times, are now retained fast
By a pair of twisted ropes,
And fastened to his back.
To the yoke of the other cord
The humble neck is raised,
Proof affording to a thousand Moors
What may be drawn therefrom.
On no side does he look
For a friend in recognition;
The mad populace his foe,
Which round him make their beat,
With a damaging volition,

They pain and grief inflict;
And he is deemed a useless, worthless Moor
Who does no outrage offer.
They drag him to the strand,
The innocent victim,
Where with an insolence quite barbarous,
They him to an anchor bind.
Two anchors in one hand did I observe,
With opposite zeal there set,
Of iron one, upon the soil,
The other of faith in Christianity.
One to the other tied;
That of iron is used
To perpetrate a cruel and quick end,
The one of faith to give life after death.
Look then if the zeal is contrary
Of these two in this war.
One rivets to the earth,
The other unto heaven appertains (se ase).
And though such fortune be in currency,
Shocking body and soul,
As if all were fixed in calm,
There is none to disentangle.
Sinless, and to iron confined,
The man of God is found;
His body bound in mortal ties exists,
His spirit free as air.
And his body is compassed round about,
Which nothing but cord binds.
His part immortal,
High heaven's domains doth traverse.
The mob is self-instructed
New cruelty to invent,
In quantity do bear
Fagots knotty and dry.
And a spacious crown
With them they quickly make,
Enveloping therein
The pious, lowly man;
Though comfort none they have
In seeing him expire,
But to torment him more,
Kindle far-off fires.
They do desire, as they who serve up food,
Rather to their office look,
That they do scorch, and not burn up entire
The flesh of that meek lamb.
The smoke ascends the air,

E'en the eyes afflicting,
The flame consumes the spoils
Which barbarous hands retain.
The vestments into wrinkles roll themselves
By dint of ardent heat;
The very fire seems discontent,
Seeking most what's in concealment hid.
Two fires do in rivalry exist,—
One human and quite visible;
The other from the sight removed—that fire
Is of the true love of God.
I know not which to whom the most is due,
Since to both payment is made;
To the body, which is burnt,
Or to the soul, which in effect gives warmth.
Those who stood looking on,
Anger them prevents,
They die by death imposing on the man,
In slaying him do entertain themselves;
Of this very martyrdom in the midst,
The holy sufferer moved not
His tongue a sentiment to communicate,
Whose framework reason was.
Contrariwise they say, and I have seen,
If he utterance made at any time,
In the air the sound up-went,
And heaven echoed the sweet name of Christ.
When in his ultimate agony
The saint did find himself,
Repeatedly he invoked
The Virgin's holy aid.
Now air stirs up the flame,
Itself revolving in such glowing heat,
That, by gradations slow,
The blessed body was reduced to dust.
But when they saw him die,
Stones of weight they cast to accomplish quite
What the consuming element had left.
Oh, holy Stephen, blessed martyr, do thou
Assure me your known zeal,
Who saw the heavens divide,
When thou thy holy spirit rend'rest up.
The corpse upon the shore
Burnt and stoned doth lie,
But the refined soul has taken flight
The empyrean regions towards.
The Moor continues inwardly to rejoice
At the foul deed achieved;

The Turk abideth satisfied,
The Christian still in fear.
I am come to announce to you
What thou hast not been able to witness.
My tears and sighs may you understand.
SAAVEDRA. Sighs, sighs abandon now;
Grief no longer should be shown for those
Who towards heaven have made a certain flight,
But those who here remain.
And though offensive be,
This lot to human view
It finishes with death,
And the commencement is of a new life.
Measure by another standard
Thy anguish; no patience is,
But that the murders of Valencia
In Algiers may be avenged.
There will justice demonstrate herself,
The evil castigating.
Cruelty there shows itself,
Only as much as injustice can shew.
SEBASTIAN. In this bitter complaint
Who will restrain his groans?
Those for faults are punished,
Our dead are from them free.
PEDRO ALVAREZ. Sufficient for us is it captives to be
Without in more confusion being involved;
For if here they the dead cast into fire,
They also scorch the quick.
Valencia doth other means adopt,
Proved renegades to castigate
In public, uncondemned.
May all of poison perish.
Here comes a Moor;
Let us not here appear in union.
Saavedra, go thou there,
I and Sebastian will another way.

ACT II.

[Enter AURELIO *and* IZUF.]

IZUF. Three hundred scudi did I give,
Aurelio, for the damsel,
And these the Turk received, that unto her
Life and soul I rendered.
A small sum, too, if by her beauty weighed.
In distraction did he sell me her,

Observing he had no power,
While she was in his full possession,
No amorous reciprocity to obtain.
I fixed her in the house of a Moor,
Without daring to draw her thence;
And there she is, while there,
My treasure and my property,
With as much glory as love can shower down.
There one sees the goodness which
Is unto cruelty bound,
Greater far than what all earth can show;
And blended without disagreement are
Beauty and honesty.
Promises fail to soften her hard breast;
See me now by tears undone,
Offering only to the turbulent winds
The services which I to her have shown.
She does not recognise her good fortune,
Nor how grief me afflicts,
Sighing gradually.
When I most gentle am,
Her harshness most appears.
I would her to your residence conduct,
Into thy hands deliver her,
My sovereign joy,
Peradventure you can her induce,
A Christian well as she.
From this moment do I promise you,
If to a grateful issue you conduct
My amorous will,
To give you liberty and assured friendship.

AURELIO. In all your wishes,
My lord, I would you please.
Being your slave, and seeing too
The daintiness of women,
Who bring you to this lot.
Of what nation is the damsel,
Involving in such flame her master's heart,
Without looking to his interest?

IZUF. They say she is from Spain.

AURELIO. Her name?

IZUF. Silvia.

AURELIO. Silvia! a certain Silvia came
Where I embarkment made;
And as I see,
She did not there remain.

IZUF. The same is she, and I did purchase her.

AURELIO. If it be she, I can aver

Without untruthfulness that she is fair;
Nor is she so unmannered, so lofty,
Her condition e'en so coy
As make a man to die.
To the house bring her, lord, without delay,
Hold fear in reins,
And you will see if I am capable,
How to my hands and supplications too
The chaste one will strike sail.

IZUF. I go, and while her coming is arranged,
For a present (my contentment being assured)
I will announce unto the renegade
That he be free of chains.

AURELIO. What is it, heaven, what is it I have heard?
Is it my Silvia? Silvia sure it is!
Can it be real? dubious destiny!
That I have seen her who me did surely hold
Quick in death—in death a very life.
This is my Silvia, upon whom I call,
Whom serve, adore,
More than the fertile earth can proffer me.
Gratitude and thanks to heaven I give
That it to both one master has assigned.
To my annoyances a truce,
This evil plight between,
For by an extraordinary chance
My eyes will come to see
In a maid, so singular comeliness.
And if by her master she is rendered up,
'Tis known he saw assuredly
It was impossible to effect escape
From capture, or hurt from wound.
And then such ardent importunities
He in his loves discovers.
If we observe, his griefs
Will him environ quite, and as to mine,
I do proclaim them even deeper still.
But whilst I may take note
Of her loveliness and her carriage,
My discomfort can I soften too.
Until kind heaven dispose
Of both of us according to his ends.

[TWO MERCHANTS *enter*.]

MERCHANT. At last, Aydar, is it in Cerdeña
That you have booty made?
AYDAR. Yes, and of no value particular,

    As in the muster is demonstrated.
MERCHANT. They do allege the Neapolitan
    Gallies did give us chase.
AYDAR. Yes, so they say, but not in earnestness;
    That the freight did us embarrass,
    The thief who goes to steal
    Not to involve himself in the sly snare,
    Should move without embarrassment,
    His purpose flight, and also his ends to reach.
    Christian galleys he knows,
    Or else you should know,
    No feet superfluous or hands can boast.
    The reason is that they may sail
    With heavy freight of merchandise,
    For though six days they move
    No floating bridge will reach.
    We all lightness go,
    As free as fire itself.
    In giving of us chase, quick
    Talk unto the breezes, all ropes out,
    No work below,
    Mainmast and sailyard on the wide gangway.
    And thus make we our course
    The elements against, and without toil;
    But honour there doth hold;
    The Christian in such extremity,
    To seize the oar in such a circumstance
    To him dishonour seems.
    And whilst they there are duly honoured,
    We with dishonour bring our cargo home.
MERCHANT. This honour and this deceit
    Never from the breast do emanate,
    For our superior advantage is
    From its own ill created.
    A boy of tender age
    Of these Sardinians do I wish to buy.
AYDAR. The auctioneer has some
    Whom in the city he disposes of.

    [*Enter the* MOORISH AUCTIONEER, *who sells two* BOYS, *the* MOTHER *and the*
    FATHER.]

AUCTIONEER. Is any here who these two youths would buy?
    The older man is big enough,
    The woman also with encumbrance too,
    I' faith 'twill be a bargain.
    For this one a hundred and two dollars must
    They give. For th' other a hundred twice told.

    But take them away; they shall not
    Pass by here, you dogs.
JUAN. What is this, mother? do these Moors sell us?
MOTHER. Yes, child.
    Their treasures do our miseries augment.
AUCTIONEER. Here, is there any one would purchase now
    The child and mother at once?
MOTHER. Oh, terrible crisis! bitter far than death!
FATHER. Assuage, my dear, your breast,
    For since our God has ordered it,
    That in this state we be,
    Known unto him is this sad ordinance.
MOTHER. I am in tribulation for these boys,
    Not knowing where they will go.
FATHER. O lady mine, let there fulfilment be
    Of what high heaven ordains.
MERCHANT. For this boy, say how much?
AUCTIONEER. Two scudi and fivescore is th' upset price.
MERCHANT. Wilt thou let them go for a hundred and ten?
AUCTIONEER. No. But pass by there.
MERCHANT. Is he in health?
AUCTIONEER. No doubt of it Open your mouth, boy, wide.
MERCHANT. Open; do not fear.
JUAN. Take not this from me, sir,
    'Twill fall out of itself.
MERCHANT. His molar teeth by force he thinks I would draw.
JUAN. Softly, sir, it hurts not;
    Hold, softly, ere I die.
AYDAR. For this other what does any one give?
AUCTIONEER. Two hundred ducats is the lowest price.
AYDAR. How much will they bid?
AUCTIONEER. They ask for him three hundred ducats good.
AYDAR. Wilt thou be docile if I buy thee, boy?
FRANCISCO. Though thou shouldst buy me not,
    Tractable will I be.
AYDAR. Wilt thou so be?
FRANCISCO. That will I be, and in no wise obstinate.
MERCHANT. One hundred and thirty ducats will I give.
AUCTIONEER. The bargain's thine. Out with the money. Come.
MERCHANT. I would transfer them to the dwelling-house.
MOTHER. My heart bursts quite.
MERCHANT. This other, companion, buy,
    Come child, to enjoyment come,
JUAN. Sir, I cannot quit
    My mother to go home with other folk.
MOTHER. Look thou, my son, that thou belongest not Save only to thy purchaser.
JUAN. Oh, mother, hast thou then abandoned me?
MOTHER. Oh, heaven, how cruel, obdurate thou art!

MERCHANT. *Now*, boy, come, follow me.

JUAN. Let us together go, brother.

FRANCISCO. That can I not. It is not possible.
May heaven be with you still.

MOTHER. Oh, my good child, and my delight on earth,
May never God forget thee.

JUAN. Whence do they carry me, and whither thee?
O father! mother! parents both!

MOTHER. Will you that I speak, sir,
A moment to my child?
This brief contentment do accord to me,
Since sorrow with me dwells eternally.

MERCHANT. What would you say to him,
For this assuredly is the last time.

MOTHER. To-night
Is the first time my heart e'er felt such grief.

JUAN. Pray keep me with you, mother, for I know
Not where he would convey me.

MOTHER. Alas, poor child!
Fortune forsook thee at thy birth.
The heavens are overcast, the elements
Are turbid, and the very sea and winds
Are all combined against me.
Thou, my child,
Knowest not the dark misfortune into which
Thou art so easily plunged, but happily
Lackest the power to comprehend thy fate.
What I would crave of thee, my life, since I
Must never more be blessed with seeing thee,
Is that thou never, never wilt forget
To say, as thou wert wont, "Maria, hail!"
For that bright queen of goodness, virtue, grace,
Can loosen all thy bonds and freedom give.

AYDAR. Behold the Christian sly, how she counsels
Her innocent child. You wish then that your child
Should like yourself in error still remain.

JUAN. O mother, mother, may I not remain?
And must the Moors then carry me away?

MOTHER. With thee, my child, they me of my treasure rob.

JUAN. Oh, I am much afraid.

MOTHER. 'Tis I, my child,
Who ought to fear at seeing thee go hence;
Thou wilt forget thy God, thyself, and me.
What else can I expect of thee, forlorn
At such a tender age people among
Full of deceit and all iniquity?

AUCTIONEER. Silence, thou old iniquitous piece of clay, Unless thou wilt
Thy head shouldst pay for what thy tongue hast said.

Will any one bid for the other more,
Who fairer is, with brisker qualities
Than hath his little brother?
AYDAR. Say, for how much will you give him to me?
AUCTIONEER. Have I not said that of ducats of gold
Three hundred is the least figure I take?
AYDAR. Wilt thou two hundred and fifty ducats accept?
AUCTIONEER. All this is dallying with the wind.
AYDAR. The boy's gracefulness has enchanted me,
The offer I accept.
AUCTIONEER. Be ready with the coin and earnest give.
AYDAR. Come, tell me what's your name?
FRANCISCO. Francisco am I called.
AYDAR. Since you have your master changed,
Let Francisco into Maami be turned.
FRANCISCO. No, no, good patron, no,
Still let me Francis for appellative bear.
AYDAR. The stick will make you change
Your appellation and intention too.
FRANCISCO. Since a mad destiny doth separate me
From you, sir, what do you require?
FATHER. My son, that you do live
As a good Christian and an honest man.
MOTHER. Son, no threats,
No pleasures, entertainments,
No stripes, nor sticks,
No covenants, no contrivances,
Nor all the treasures which the earth conceals,
Or e'en the garish sun hath seen,
May move thee to abandon Christ,
Or follow Moorish creed.
FRANCISCO. All this in me, if I am capable,
Will ever manifest be;
O let Jesus aid me, and in my soul
No change of faith through fear or promises.
AUCTIONEER. O how Christian doth the boy appear!
Now you I promise that you raise the arm
And right hand too in such sad circumstance.
These Christian boys at first send forth much wail,
Yet better than older ones to Moors convert.

[*They all withdraw.*]

ACT III.

SCENE I.

[Enter IZUF, SILVIA, ZARA, *and* A MOOR.

IZUF. Silvia, desist from weeping now,
 A truce impose on your solicitude,
 For no slave have I bought you,
 But to be my lady and companion.
 See how I do imagine and believe
 That your great mischance,
 To give you wider range,
 Hath brought this compass round.
 With you fortune in its strictest law
 Makes use of nothing new.
 Slaves into kings have been converted, and
 You more than a monarch are.
 Clear, clear those beauteous orbs
 That they may subjugate all they look upon,
 And when you do their dazzling light withdraw,
 With them may take the spoils of the soul.
 Let not the white veil hide
 This heavenly loveliness, which like pure snow
 Obstructs the rays of heaven.
SILVIA. It is to me so natural,
 Sir, to indulge in mourning and sharp pains,
 That should an interval of cessation come
 I deem it a worse ill.
 Although I be, and will be
 Joyful at your command,
 When so much money you have given for me,
 Knowing not for what,
 Sir, I promise you,
 That in misery and penury
 Riches enough I have,
 If riches in possessing grief consists,
 In that I am so opulent
 A passion do I entertain for this,
 As if 'twere real substance,
 Occasion multiplying realities.
IZUF. O Silvia, you dwell in ignorance
 If you think I love you not,
 By me you wish to be served and treated well;
 The profit I expect;
 Silvia, in the purchase of yourself
 Is your extreme good looks.

And double not the cost
Love improves itself
In showing your brave power,
Making me a slave for a slave maid,
And that slave my slave is.
So satisfied am I
Liberty to lose
That the cruelty I praise
Of this same hard and unaccustomed breast,
And that you may well me understand,
Silvia, 'twere better not me lord to call,
But master or dear friend.

SILVIA. Although a mighty change
Has heaven wrought in my depressed state,
You understand not if it has made me forget
The end of my education.
I know it is an obligation,
In all these things which reasonable are,
That I essay contentment to impart.

IZUF. So gracefully you prattle,
So much vivacity,
That obviously it makes me comprehend
You come of a high birth;
And though I might expect
For thee a ransom high,
To such straits am I brought
That you must ransom me.
But that it plain may be,
You see what in store I have for thee.
Come, Silvia, behind me come,
And thou thy mistress Zara shalt behold.

SILVIA. Let's go, sir, in good time.

IZUF. Silvia, no such a lord am I,
But love and fortune both
Make you my lady dear.

ZARA. Well here arrived Izuf.
Whose is the slave?

IZUF. Mine.

SILVIA. I am thine, my lady.

IZUF. Thine she is, for I have purchased her.

ZARA. Doubtless the purchase is most excellent,
If such a beauty can but honest be.
Tell me now, sir, at what price was she bought?

IZUF. A thousand double ducats did I give.

ZARA. Hopes she to be redeemed?

IZUF. Fame reports her rich.

ZARA. Her name?

IZUF. Silvia is she called.

ZARA. Wedded is she, or a maid?

SILVIA. Married I am, yet in the virgin state.

ZARA. How, how is this? pray, Silvia, now explain.

SILVIA. O lady! thus it is,
 And so my star hath willed it.
 Heaven me has provided with a spouse,
 Not for mine own enjoyment,
 But that I should remain
 A lost one well as he.

IZUF. Where is he?

MOOR. In the Duan, in extreme agony set,
 Ames, Xemi, Zaragá,
 And the Balucos Baxies,
 And the Debaxies all,
 And Daxes are there too.
 All are in council met,
 And it is verified that the Spanish king
 Has great apparatus furnished for the war.
 They say he goes to Portugal.
 But it is feared there's wanting stratagem;
 That Algiers dreads his rage, lest that
 He should it with more ill afflict.
 Many rehearsings is there in a war,
 Of fraud and cunning rife,
 There do the thunders sound,
 There the flash is shot.

IZUF. Let's off, may heaven defend us,
 Subservient making Spain to Mahomet.
 And do you, lady, orders give
 To Silvia what to do.
 And do you, Silvia, to her orders eke
 Freely subject your will.

ZARA. Christian lady, whence art thou?
 Art thou poor or rich?
 Of an exalted lot, or low estate?
 Deny me not an answer.
 I am a woman as yourself,
 Of sympathetic feeling,
 Whose sorrowful misfortunes
 Awake emotions of real tenderness.

SILVIA. O lady, I am from Granada sprung,
 Of a so degraded state,
 As it is evident by purchases,
 I go from hand to hand.
 'Twas said I once was rich, but my fortune
 Converted was to greater poverty,
 And so passed off with time.

ZARA. Hast thou at any time felt love's soft pangs?

SILVIA. In bygone time did me fierce love betray.
ZARA. Wert thou then cherished much?
SILVIA. I was so, and I desired, with a so great
    Advantage, that with difficulty a shroud
    Itself will such exalted faith efface.
ZARA. Wert thou first beloved,
    Or did the passion emanate from thee?
SILVIA. First was I by him beloved,
    I love him, and will love.
ZARA. Is he of youthful years?
SILVIA. A gentleman is he.
ZARA. A Christian too?
SILVIA. Wherefore, Moor?
    Not from decorum does he deviate
    Who bears a Christian name.
ZARA. And is it a sinful thing to love a Moor?
SILVIA. Nothing I know, but 'tis a reproachful thing,
    Unbefitting quite a Christian.
ZARA. Can a Moorish woman a Christian love?
SILVIA. You best can that interpret.
ZARA. Ay, Silvia, how you wrong me!
    And early pity me too.
SILVIA. I, dear lady, and in what lot?
ZARA. Listen to me, and I will a tale unfold.
    By listening emotion shall I stir
    Within you. You must know, O Silvia,
    That time ago there went with a fair wind
    From this port, full of corsairs, vessels twelve,
    With prosperous gales they swept the ocean stream,
    Unto the turn towards Cerdeñas isles.
    There in the holes, turned and turned again,
    And where the sea her flux and reflux makes,
    Themselves they hid, standing on the alert
    For any ship of Genoa or of Spain—
    Or other nation which was not of France.
    Quickly now a powerful breeze sprung up,
    The wind north-west is styled, whose violence
    Say all the mariners so impulsive is,
    That the thick woven sails, and rigging too,
    Of the best vessels, in equipment compact,
    Can offer no resistance, being compelled
    To seek for succour in the nearest port,
    Should its excess e'en that advantage yield.
    The swollen breakers and deep sounding noise
    Of the bold furious wind in bondage held,
    The corsair boats against the headland point,
    The gales them not permitting to attempt
    The furious billows, which on the other side,

Showing their rage, so wearied out a bark
With Christian men, and freight and riches full,
Driving through the inflated element;
Of oars divested, came it of its own will,
Fearing to be submerged in the fierce sea.
But at the termination of three days,
Contending with the stiff sea and tempest,
Descried the land, and that discovery was
A greater grief, greater misfortune too.
For at the isle which bears Saint Peter's name
They came to stop; and where assembled were
The enemies' vessels, all with corsairs full,
Who being of booty avaricious,
Quick sally forth; with warlike ardour urged,
The galley they put to flight; they then attack,
Defended only by desire to save.
A bullet passes in a moment through
The captain's breast, and at the side fell dead
Of the Lusitanian hero, a brave knight,
Who from Valencia drew his origin.
The booty rich, jewels, and captives eke,
Which the Turks found secreted in the hold
Of the unlucky galley, as to me
Recounted it was by a Christian,
Who then his loving liberty lost, taken
Away by one who would surrender himself
To him who overcame him; and this Christian is,
Silvia, I say, this Christian it is he who
Keeps me from being what to Moors is due.
Joy and contentment are beside me quite,
All taste is gone, and what is worse than all,
Of all sensations am I sheer bereft.
My husband purchased him, now in his house,
And though with tears and supplications,
With sighs deep drawn, and tenderness and gifts,
I try to soften his obdurate heart,
And bend it to my own which is like wax,
Whilst his doth show like diamond's hard substance.
Thus, Silvia, my sister, as you said,
That it for a Christian cannot lawful be
In love affairs to bend to Moorish love.
Your reasons do me in offence detain,
And with these selfsame arguments defends
Himself Aurelio, whom the heavens make
So firm a Christian that it kills me quite.
SILVIA. Aurelio did you say was the appellative
    Of that same Christian.
ZARA. *So* is he always styled.

SILVIA. The galley of which you spoke, as I believe,
    Was named San Pablo, late constructed new,
    And of the sacred Maltese faith was known.
    In it was I lost; I imagine too
    That I know this Aurelio; he's a youth
    Of gravity of visage and from Spain.
ZARA. Without a doubt, my Silvia, thou hast divined
    Who is this enemy of my glory? say,
    A cavalier is he or rustic born?
    In his position all doth so appear,
    And his condition hard; the far-famed
    Size of the city, and the mountain's state.
SILVIA. To me like a poor knight he did appear,
    As in the galley he was treated; but
    Of his possessions I am quite ignorant.
ZARA. What to say to you, Silvia, I know not;
    But to such extremities am I come,
    That love him I must, be he who e'er he may.
    I ask you, Silvia, that you try to assuage
    This tiger of Hircania and attract
    With sentiments of affection, that he feel
    The pangs which suffer the slave of the slave.
    Should you accomplish this, my Silvia,
    By the sacred Koran volume swear do I,
    To seek the means whereby with quick despatch,
    To your beloved land you may return.
SILVIA. Lady, leave the charge of that to me,
    And you shall see that which my industry
    To my advantage and your wish shall bring.

ACT IV.

[*Three young* MOORS *and three* CAPTIVES *enter,—some go for water and the others for wood, which are* SAAVEDRA, SEBASTIAN, PEDRO ALVAREZ.]

A YOUNG MOOR. Don Juan comes not, flies not, here he dies.
ANOTHER MOOR. He dies here.
ANOTHER MOOR. He dies here, no flight, yet here he dies.
SAAVEDRA. His brother will come, Don Philip the renowned,
    Who doubtless would have come, had not
    Th' indomitable and stiff erected neck
    Of Lutheran Flanders given such offence,
    All shame without to the crown imperial.
YOUNG MOOR.—No ransom and no flight, Juan comes not.
PEDRO ALVAREZ. Should he peradventure come, surely I know
    Ye all would die, ye infamous of race.
ANOTHER MOOR. Don Juan comes not, flies not, here he dies.
PEDRO ALVAREZ. First shall I see deposited on earth

These mouldering walls, this nest and cave of thieves,
Consumed quite, a punishment their due,
For their continual reckless wickedness.
SAAVEDRA. If we reply we ne'er shall have an end,
Leave them, Pedro Alvarez, friend,
That they may rest, and tell me now in truth
If you on flight do meditate.
PEDRO ALVAREZ. And how?
SAAVEDRA. In what manner?
PEDRO ALVAREZ. By land,
I can no other way or lot pursue.
SAAVEDRA. Such a business do you then undertake?
PEDRO ALVAREZ. What would you that I did, Saavedra mine?
My ancient antecessors all are dead,
And a brother who remains has given up
Himself, has left his goods and furniture;
And yet so covetous is, although he knows
The bitter slavery that I endure,
Would not advance to get me liberty
A single *real* of my patrimony;
When this I do consider, and see I have
A cruel master, as is known to you,
Who doth conclude that I am a Cavalier,
And that no other method is save alms
To realize the money he asks for me,
And the insufferable life I bear
Of hunger, nudity, fatigue, and cold,
I do determine death rather than flight,
To live a life so mean and miserable.
SAAVEDRA. Hast thou a wallet made?
PEDRO ALVAREZ. Yea, I have within
Provision of good biscuit for ten days.
SAAVEDRA. 'Tis seventy good leagues from here to Oran.
And think you only to provide ten pounds?
PEDRO ALVAREZ. No, because a paste I have, 'tis made
Of beans and eggs, with honey blended too,
And right well cooked, which people do aver,
That little ta'en, much sustentation gives.
Should this be insufficient, herbs also
I hope to eat with salt which I bear too.
SAAVEDRA. Have you shoes also?
PEDRO ALVAREZ. Yes, three right strong pairs.
SAAVEDRA. Knowest thou the way?
PEDRO ALVAREZ. I think not quite.
SAAVEDRA. How would you venture then?
PEDRO ALVAREZ. By the sea-shore,
And now as 'tis the vernal part of the year,
The Moors all unto the mountain range

Themselves withdraw the fresh air to inspire.

SAAVEDRA. Do you take any indications
    Whereby to know the wished land of Oran?

PEDRO ALVAREZ. Indeed I do, and know that I have to pass
    Two rivers first; the one of them is styled
    The river of Azafran, which blends itself
    With the other, Hiquina named, yet further off,
    To Mostagan adjacent, on the right
    An elevation is and lofty hill.
    The Gordo ridge is its appellative.
    And from its top discovery is made,
    A mountain front to front, which is the seat
    On which Oran doth raise its well-known head.

SAAVEDRA. Wilt thou travel by night?

PEDRO ALVAREZ. Who would that doubt?

SAAVEDRA. Mountains across, and elevations, depths,
    Dar'st thou to traverse in the obscurity
    Of the enclosed night, without a road
    Or footway which may lead you where you would?
    O liberty, how much art thou beloved!
    Sweet friend, may holy heaven procure
    Success undoubted in this vast labour,
    And now I return and to my toil, the hour
    Is come—Heaven with you be.

PEDRO ALVAREZ. May heaven attend you too.

[A MOORISH LADY *comes in at the side, and others enter.*]

FATIMA. The long-expected moment is arrived,
    The hitherto unseen witchery which demands
    To subjugate the as yet unbridled breast,
    Which otherwise my skill would dominate.
    Throughout the region of the starry sky,
    The car moves on the obscure and cold night,
    And the occasion calls when I shall enact
    Things horrible to tell, fearful, stupendous.
    Golden locks dishevelled in the air,
    Stand quite upright, the body ungirt too.
    The right foot is unshod, the visage turned
    To the ocean, where the sun has made its plunge.
    On the arm this string of stones shall be wrapped round
    Which as impregnated in the eagle's nest
    Was found, and this cord wakens from its sleep
    Its virtue, which my instinct has inspired.
    These five white hairs which eke dissevered were,
    When the moon was at her full, by my right hand.
    In this same form is arranged for certain work,
    All which I trust will easily be achieved;

These heads also of the hawk which were wrenched off,
The serpent in the summer, all useful are
In my design; and e'en these seeds thrown down
Into the earth. This flesh from the forehead torn
Of a tender colt at the precise moment
Of its coming into life, whose virtue excellent
Satisfies wholly my ardent desire,
Enveloped in this herb, whose tooth did touch
The lamb, when from its mother's womb it came.
This, this will make Aurelio to become
That lamb for mildness, humble as I wish,
This figure which of wax is formed, in the name
Of my Aurelio is fabricated,
Shall be with a hard hand and arrow soft
The means of cutting his heart's centre through;
Zara will quickly remain satisfied
As to a will which most disordered is,
And the congealed Christian quick came out,
Burning in amorous fury, living fire.
So ye, O Rhadamanthus, justices,
And Minos too who, by immutable
Laws in th' obscure realms of fear and dread,
Govern the mournful souls of the defunct,
If peradventure the hoarse song has force;
O murmurings of verses exquisite
By them I do conjure you, ask and beg,
That you will soften this same heart of steel.
Rapida, Ronca, Rau, Run, Paris-forme,
Grandura, Desclinfaz, Pasilonte,
Howling, gluttonous, false, disfigured,
Monster pestiferous from the mountain's womb,
Erebus, engenderer of the face,
Shapeless, of every cruel god, immediately
Come to my presence without detention,
Unless you Zoroaster's skill depreciate.

FURY. The power of thy verse not to be opposed,
And thy incorrigible murmurings, have dragged
Me forth thee to obey from oblivion's realms.
But in this dark emprise I see, O Moor,
What weighs me down, for I do understand
That all is but lost time.

FATIMA. And wherefore so?

FURY. To all adjurations now give pause,
And in a moment will I satisfy thee,
If thou dost measure and adjust thyself
To all my proffered counsels and my words.
These preparatives all are vanity;
For a Christian breast which knows to lean itself

On Christ, will little your enchantment heed,
   By many different ways it will be found
   Expedient him for thy friend's love to attract.
FATIMA. What, then, will nought of this labour prevail?
FURY. For nothing has it been done, but listen now,
   That with despatch, and without doublings too,
   You may fulfil in this way your desire.
   In all the lower regions none there be
   A greater torment Christians among,
   Although amongst them many good hearts are,
   And pure intentions, than is the hard
   Necessity which patience 'self drains out,
   This passion proffers no resistance.
   The other is Occasion. Should these two
   Come and with Aurelio hold embrace,
   You quick will see his braveness toppled o'er,
   Converted into softness, and with ease
   Himself abandon unto Cupid's fires.
FATIMA. I ask you then these instruments to send,
   And from this enterprise turn not away.
FURY. With expedition I your behests obey.

[*Enter* AURELIO *and* SILVIA.]

AURELIO. In compensation has kind fortune me
   Given my Silvia for my toils and cares;
   The glory of seeing thee, and this content
   Converts all anguish into merriment
   From this day forth, for Silvia thee I see,
   And my close night into clear day is turned.
SILVIA. Yes, my beloved, I am the fortunate one,
   For I exist your presence to enjoy,
   From being once distrustful as I was.
AURELIO. How has it fared with you, my spouse, in this
   Long absence, in the power of a race
   Of reason, virtue, and conscience devoid?
SILVIA. As hope I have entertained, and do so still,
   In the great Author of things visible,
   And eke invisible, in secure confidence
   As to his goodness, wear I the chaste veil;
   And with his aid in expectation live
   With no suspicion that it shall be stained.
AURELIO. Thou shalt be informed, my spouse, that crafty love,
   Urged by revenge, a dire assault has made
   With fiery rigour and ceaseless impulse
   Upon my mistress' heart, and there has set
   A most incurable wound; enamoured quite
   Of that breast which is thine, me accompanying

Whither I wish to go.
E'en as the female Moor declares to me
And herself flatters to see me alone.

SILVIA. Zara indeed this tale entire has told,
And has solicited me that I should ask
You not to disdain the suit irrevocably.
Still our master, Izuf, passes not
A life less sorrowful, who adores me too,
With a fidelity I must hold sincere.

AURELIO. O poor Moor! O luckless lady Moor!
How thou direct'st in vain to the false winds
Thy futile sighs continuously spent.
Izuf, however, has his intent avowed,
Supplicating me that I thee ask
Alleviation some to his torment
But rather with passionate fury may there come
An arrow which direct my breast may pass,
My soul disjoining from its carnal parts,
That at my cost for his sole benefit
Should such confusion to us both procure,
Though he remain well satisfied with me.

SILVIA. If in this case, Aurelio, 'twere enough
To show to them a changed volition,
And that the ill no further progress make,
I would advance it for a thing assured,
And by this fiction due advantage reap,
Which may not hinder our yet cherished views.
To Zara say that upon my account
You show yourself less hostile, and to the Moor
Hint that your perseverance much avails,
Preserving both this nice decorum, we
Easily may our griefs in interviews melt.

AURELIO. The proposition made is excellent;
What you order shall be done, and then
Inclement fate perhaps may be appeased.
Unto my parents of the breaking off
Betwixt us will I write, and, Silvia, thou
As much may'st write to your kind parents too.
May heaven accord us these rewards. Let us
Unto another time discourse refer.

[*In come* PEDRO ALVAREZ *and* ANOTHER CAPTIVE, *who flies, and* TWO
MOORS *catching him bring him back.*]

PEDRO ALVAREZ. This wide way
A passage through such briars, and mountains across
And the unceasing bellowing of cruel
Brutes impede me so,

That I do fear death must soon finish all.
My very bread is all consumed.
My vesture torn with brambles,
Shoes shattered quite.
O this continual bellowing of beasts,
That scarce can I my feet an inch advance.
Hunger impels me on,
And thirst insufferable torments me sore.
My strength deserts me now;
From this disgrace I do expect
To issue, by delivery of myself
To him who would me seize.
My judgment have I lost,
Nor do I know the right way to Oran;
Nor path nor road
Does proffer me sorrowful fate. What shall I do?
Though paths discovered were, I cannot move.
Virgin all blessed and all-beauteous,
For humanity intermediatrix,
Be thou here my star,
Which on this raging sea my bark may guide,
And from such perils safe diversion make.
Virgin of Montserrat,
Who of these same *sierras* rough
A very heaven dost make,
Rescue I pray thee send;
Draw me from evils out,
'Tis thy achievement aid to the wretch to bring.
These bushes amidst I ask
Me to conceal until the break of day,
For here I hope to die.
Mary, Mary holiest,
In this bitter circumstance
I body and soul deliver to your charge.

[A LION *enters and sits himself by* ALVAREZ. *Then comes the other* CAPTIVE,
who also goes away.]

CAPTIVE. These footsteps are not Moorish, surely not,
A Christian's print they be;
We would the same way take, as I purpose,
Of Arabs the footprints are,
Broad and illy shaped;
Their sandal is more spacious by far,
Ours more hollowed out,
In this the difference consists.
Sure am I that one here doth lie
Concealed, and not far off his course is lost.

The sun rides high,
And my perception is indifferent.
Here would I lie, the nightfall until,
When I turn to follow my road,
For in this section Mostagan must be.
The sun emerges hence,
The north inclines that way,
The strand is not far off,—
O how ill am I at ease!
Saviour, me direct,
Many natives here do pass
Across that level plain.
Could I myself conceal, I not despair
My children, wife, and house again to see.

[*Enter* TWO MOORS.]

MOOR. Zaramix ara furir.

[PEDRO ALVAREZ *remembers himself.*]

PEDRO ALVAREZ. Holy Lord, what is it I behold!
Though lion fierce thou beest,
My heart it makes to leap.
Fulfilled is my desire,
From passion am I free,
But my fortune wills
With its hard extremity
Mydays shall terminate,
And his capacious maw will fully serve
My body for a sepulchre.
Still such mildness rarely is evinced
In a so valiant animal,
Which, despite his savage propensities,
A little occasional clemency shows.
Who knows if heaven affected by my groans
Has sent this lion to point out the way
Which surely I have lost?
Of a verity a miracle 'tis
That doth assurance bring.
In my spirit I feel,
With a force miraculous,
A new and increased courage.
It is a verified tale
That another lion at Goleta took
A captive, who upon the mountain's brow
Had lost his way and fled.
This work is thine, O holy Virgin, thine,

Sprung from thy ministering hand;
For clear and plain it is that any one
Who puts his trust in thee, hopes on,
And never is confounded.
With courage me inspire,
Companion, that I may determine
To follow the path you wish.
Already to me no lion you seem to be,—
A gentle lamb instead.

ACT V.

[PEDRO ALVAREZ *and the* LION.]

PEDRO ALVAREZ. Never less with anguish
Have I travelled a road,
And it meseems,
That from Oran we are not very remote.
Thanks I proffer to thee, O King divine,
Virgin pure! to thee I render thanks;
And, I beseech you, carry to extent
This charity extreme;
For if to me my liberty you give,
I promise ever faithfulness.

[*Enter* OCCASION *and* NECESSITY.]

OCCASION. Necessity, cruel executioner
Of all crimes which for execution wait,
Public Occasion and the secret one,
You see how rewarded and enforced too
Have we been by this cruel infernal thing,
Coming to combat the rock of the breast
Of a Christian fortified, which now rebels,
And more, which fears nor child nor cruel god.
Tis necessary that all attempts you make,
Showing yourself in season and all time,
E'en at repasts of nourishment, and all things
Which unto thought belong.
I, on my part, continually will think
How to present myself before, and the misery
Of my thin hairs will offer for a grasp.
Restrain my flight, that opportunity
May seizure make—occurrence rare
In my too light and swift condition.
NECESSITY. Occasion is sure also something to do.
On my part wonders will I strive to enact,
If they of assistance and favour not fail.

But look you, now, here comes the indomitable,
Do but perceive it, sister, and we strike down
The vain presumption of this Christian man.

[*Enter* AURELIO.]

AURELIO. Wilt not be possible, poor Aurelio,
  From this infamous Moor to defend thyself,
  Who persecutes thee in so many ways?
  Yes, and will come, unless heaven withholds
  The favour which as yet is not denied.
  A thousand crafty methods she does scheme
  Me to ensnare in her wanton intents;
  Now she treats daintily, now vituperates me,
  With hunger and with misery killing me.
NECESSITY. 'Tis certainly great, Aurelio, what you bear.
AURELIO. Necessity, great is that which I pass through.
NECESSITY. Your sandals and your vestments are rent through.
AURELIO. I own my clothes are all in disrepair.
NECESSITY. On a skin sleepest thou, and on the ground.
AURELIO. On the cold ground and on a skin I sleep.
OCCASION. Yet well I know, if thou desirest it,
  You could occasion find to emerge from these
  Woes quick, at little cost, quite unopposed.
AURELIO. This know I well, if I would, that I could find
  Opportunity ready to emerge
  From this evil, at no cost, unopposed
OCCASION. Only love for love reciprocating
  With Zara, or of it indications give.
AURELIO. With only wishing well to my mistress,
  Or feigning so to do, that would suffice.
  How can one feign what one has aversion to?
NECESSITY. Necessity compels you so to do.
AURELIO. Necessity me compels this to enact.
OCCASION. How rich she is for thee, how beauteous too!
AURELIO. How rich and beauteous is my mistress eke 1
NECESSITY. And liberal too, and, what more important is,
  Will more than you ask in superfluity give.
AURELIO. Being liberal, and enamoured too,
  Will give in abundance all I should require.
OCCASION. This is a singular opportunity.
AURELIO. An extraordinary opportunity
  Itself presents, but 'twill not my high blood
  Strain from what is just, to myself due.
OCCASION. Who knows exactly that which you may do?
  A secret frailty, carrying the weight of sin,
  May remedy find and exculpation too.
AURELIO. Who knows exactly that which I may do?

A secret frailty, carrying the weight of sin,
    May exculpation and a near remedy find.
OCCASION. And more! Occasion, secret and concealed,
    A thousand more will offer thee.
AURELIO. Should occasions find me at each step,
    I one alone embrace. Aurelio, soft,
      'Tis not a knightly thought which you revolve,
    Such to your birth and Saviour as is due.
NECESSITY. Mercy in his scheme hath Christ—and had,—
    Who offers pardon for offences done,
    If under swaying laws of necessity.
AURELIO. Well knows providence that here impels
    Absolute necessity, and this goes
    For exculpation in heaven for my crime.
OCCASION. Now is the juncture; now, Aurelio, you
    Can seize occasion by the very hair.
    Look how sweet, how amorous, complaisant,
    The beauteous Moor advances to your will.

[*Enter* ZARA.]

ZARA. Aurelio, art thou alone?
AURELIO. Yes, and accompanied.
ZARA. By whom?
AURELIO. By a deep, loving thought.
ZARA. Of what was it the cause?
AURELIO. Should I thee tell,
    Peradventure you will stigmatize me
    A rigorous, cruel, disenamoured man.
NECESSITY. Exercising force, companion, move.
OCCASION. Is no work necessary? Hear why it stops.
ZARA. Aurelio, follow me; let's to the house.

[*Exit.*]

AURELIO. If I thee follow, lady, it is right
    To be obedient, seeing I am your slave.
NECESSITY. To the earth it goes, Occasion,—the support
    Of the fine Christian already gives way.
OCCASION. Such joint combats have we furnished.
    Into Zara's apartment let us go.
    And then, when enters there Aurelio,
    We will tempt him with renewed assaults.

[NECESSITY *and* OCCASION *retire, and* AURELIO *remains.*]

AURELIO. Aurelio, where dost go? Whither dost move
    Thy wandering step? and thy conductor who?

With so small dread of heaven, darest thou now
Content thyself with futile fantasy?
Opportunities easy and light,
Which wanton blandishment to the heart convey,
Tend to persuade thee and to overwhelm,
Delivering thee to soft, unrighteous love.
Is this the elevated thought of right—
The firm proposal made unto thyself,
To give no offence to God, although you end
In torment the residue of your future days?
Hast thou offence so quickly given? To the winds
Your just and amorous fantasies consigned,
And do you the memory burden with vain thoughts,
Dishonest, trivial, and unholy too?
Away! avaunt! far from me, vain attempts!
All thoughts unchaste be banished from me quite!
The unwise entangler in an insane love
Shall be exterminated for a purer fire.
A Christian sure I am, Christian will live;
And, though conducted to such sorrowful ends,
Gifts, promises, craft, and art beyond compare,
Shall never cause me swerve an inch from God.

[*Enter* FRANCISCO, THE CAPTIVE.]

FRANCISCO. Hast seen Aurelio, my dear brother?
AURELIO. Mean'st thou Juanico?
FRANCISCO. Yes.
AURELIO. Some time ago I saw him.
FRANCISCO. O holy, sovereign Lord!
AURELIO. Some torment dost thou suffer?
FRANCISCO. Yes, a lassitude
    Which pen nor tongue can give expression to.
    You would not further wish to know my care,—
    My brother has his soul to Satan given.
AURELIO. Has he turned renegade for fortune's sake?
FRANCISCO. Renunciation of faith—is that fortune?
    Should he remain, ill luck 'twill be indeed.
    He has promised his word, as I, brother, do hear,
    To turn Turk, and with this he works.
AURELIO. Look, Francisco, at what he aims:
    It is sheer fancy.

[*Enter* JUANICO, *vested as a Turk.*]

FRANCISCO. These clothes have been his death.
    What does he know of Mahomet?
AURELIO. Juan, in the good time thou art avenged.

JUAN. You do not know how now I call myself.
AURELIO. How?
JUAN. Just like my master.
FRANCISCO.—In what way?
JUAN. Soliman.
FRANCISCO. Poison, better 'twere
    To envenom quite that man
    Who changed his name for this.
    What sayest thou, traitor?
JUAN. Well, a very little of this;
    I shall tell it to my master.
    Because I Soliman do call myself
    He threatens me. That's good!
FRANCISCO. Embrace me, brother sweet:
JUAN. Brother since when?
    Let the dog keep off,
    Nor touch me with his hand.
FRANCISCO. Because thou wert in grief converted,
    I am satisfied, my brother.
JUAN. This is a great mistake.
    Is there more taste in being a turbaned Turk?
    Look at this attire,
    The present of my master;
    Another, of brocade I also own,
    Richer and smoother yet.
    How sweet is alcucuz!
    I drink sugar of sherbet.
    And carden, which is sweet;
    Pillau so appetising.
    I shall not toil to appease me with your grief.
    If thou wouldst too turn Turk—
    And certainly you will so do—
    My advice accept: you'll better be.
    But now stay here, for a proved sin it is
    To talk so much with Christians.

[He quits the stage with apparent gravity, yet making jokes.]

AURELIO. Was ever such misfortune on the earth?
    What net has he of hell extended here
    That he may obstruct a Christian's flight to heaven!
FRANCISCO. O tender age, how soon art overcome!
    Being solicited in this Gomorrah foul,
    And combated with entertainment false.
AURELIO. O well indeed are all the arms employed
    In ransoming youths, in whose unguarded breasts
    Faith's not securely founded,
    O if to-day, deficient in charity,

We could inspection make of Christian hearts,
And that they were not so contracted, that
They would from prisons and confinement draw
The Christian captive, more especially
Children who have but predilections weak.
This holy work so excellent in itself,
That in it all works are concentrated
Which, to the body and soul, relation bear.
Him whom you ransom you from peril draw,
The wanderer and forlorn reducing home,
Thou bring'st him from infinitude of ills (zozobras)
From hunger which afflicts continually,
From thirst insufferable, counsels ill,
Which would debar him from the path of truth,
From preparations many, repeated oft,
Which the common enemy employs,
Catching extravagant youth and eke old age.
O sect effeminate of Mahomet
Broad, luxurious, of scruples bereft,
With what facility is th' artless ensnared!
FRANCISCO. Good Aurelio, dost command me aught?
AURELIO. God be thy guide, Francisco, patience hold,
    A blessed powerful hand will surely cure
    The mental frailty of thy brother John.

    [SILVIA *enters*.]

SILVIA. Whither, Aurelio, goest thou, sweetest spouse?
AURELIO. To see thee, Silvia, for thy presence is
    Perfect alleviation to my woes.
SILVIA. So likewise is to me your sight, Aurelio,
    Aurelio dear, for grave ills, remedy.

    [*They embrace and their masters enter.*]

ZARA. Hound, to suffer this before mine eyes.
IZUF. False traitor, slave with slave commit'st thyself!
ZARA. Not so, my lord, Aurelio has no blame,
    Who is but man, no, 'tis that lady hound.
IZUF. The female slave, no lady; but this accursed
    Framer of falsities, a thousand deceits,
    To him be blame for these dishonest acts.
ZARA. Had this licked whelp, this shameless specimen
    Of woman, no occasion given, he had
    Not dared to offer her a close embrace.
AURELIO. Certainly not, ye masters, have arose
    Irregularities from occasions
    Which look like wanton in the proved act;

Silvia I asked that she some earnest would
Give me of a reward, for many days
This boon have I solicited, not for my interest,
And she also had fully persuaded me
That I should do her service, most meet in truth
The better to your house good office to do;
And having mutually concessions made,
Each did enact what most the other pleased.
In signal of contentment us you find
Precisely as you see us, having embraced,
Without a stain to purity of thought.
IZUF. Silvia, is this the truth?
SILVIA. Yea, that it is.
IZUF. Of him what wouldest thou?
SILVIA. Little it thee imports
    To know what of Aurelio I required.
ZARA. Didst thou at last consent?
SILVIA. As I desired.
IZUF. Get thee within—I do believe you too—
    Had I not thee believed, it had been meet
    Your fault to punish with a thousand pains.

[*They go away.*]

Know my lady at this very point
Towards the *Zoco** going, it was told me
How that the king gave orders that Silvia
Should be with Aurelio to his presence brought.
I do conjecture some evil-minded man
And wicked Christian, intimate with both,
Has even now declared unto the king
That these two captives are for ransom meant.
And as the king is not on good terms with me,
For that I the honour and charge would not accept
The walls and trenches to survey again,
Doubtless to cashier me is his wish.
ZARA. The remedy most prominent in my mind
    Is to advise Aurelio not to tell
    The king that he is a Cavalier, but a poor man,
    A soldier going to Italy; that Silvia
    Is his espoused. If the king this rejects
    He will not, let the cost be what it may,
    Surrender them, although the price be high.

---

* A place where a fair is kept.

[*They enter and set a raised seat with four cushions for the king, who sits down, and they enter accompanied by four or five* MOORS, *and then the young renegade* JUANICO *advances.*]

KING. Through anger and through grief I scarce can speak,
    And the occasion of my mad sorrow of mind
    Is that Don Antonio de Toledo has
    Out of my hands escaped.
    The mettlesome Arraces under fear
    That I should capture sure the Christian, has
    Carried him off in haste to Tetuan.
    And has for him seven thousand ducats procured,
    Such an illustrious and rich Cavalier
    For a price so low did ye give, vile *canaille*?
    Who would assist you to a sum like this?
    So large a price did it appear to you
    That you another companion have annexed,
    Who might alone as much have realized.
    Was not Francisco de Valencia
    Able to pay for himself a larger sum?
    In fine the venture favoured him which could be
    Of more avail than all my diligence,
    Assuring more than human knowledge effects.
    Both time and circumstance they knew full well,
    And fled, not daring my presence to meet,
    That if I Don Antonio there had found,
    Fifty thousand ducats he had paid me down;
    Count Alba's brother is he, and nephew
    Of a princess and of a duchess eke,
    And by this one loss, in this way he missed
    Being the general of a bold enterprise.
    Heaven enraged yet shewed itself most kind
    In making him a captive, and yet made haste
    To give him liberty for such an act.
    Desire itself no further could extend,
    But since all remedy is beyond our power,
    We have excuse in further reference.
    Look if any comes to lodge complaint.
MOOR. My lord, here is Izuf the renegade.
KING. Admit him. With intention to appear
    To obey in all respects my due command,
    But though he comes into my presence now,
    What merits he for disobedience?
IZUF. Here without.
KING. What have you asked for them?
IZUF. A thousand ducats.
KING. That will I give for them.
IZUF. It was not expected

From thy valour so much injury.
KING. Do you thus answer me in this?
IZUF. At least
    In part some alleviation to my cares.
    The slave to thee I give, O king, without
    A price. Leave me the maid, for whom I die.
KING. Durst thou so say, O Christian infamous?
    Take him away and the bastinado give
    Until his sides run blood;
    The desire is base and insupportable.
IZUF. Give me the woman slave, then quickly give
    Me death by fire, by steel, by hook or pale.
KING. Get from my sight, and quick effect it too.
IZUF. Am I offensive asking for mine own?

[*Here they bring out* THE CAPTIVE, *who flies; they catch him, and put on a chain.*]

MOOR. Mi zara fuxir.
KING. Whence goest thou, Christian, say?
CAPTIVE. I was trying
    To reach Oran if heaven would so will.
KING. Where wast thou taken?
CAPTIVE. In Almadraba.
KING. Thy master?
CAPTIVE. He is dead, he ought not so
    To have died, since he has left me in the power
    Of a so insolent woman, all beast beyond.
KING. Art thou a Spaniard?
CAPTIVE. I was in Malaga born.
KING. This thou dost demonstrate, being so bold.
    O thou worthless chip (Raxa caud) six hundred strokes
    Administered shall upon the shoulders be,
    Five hundred more upon the body and feet.
CAPTIVE. Without or law or reason such torment
    Hast thou reserved for one who fled away.
KING. Chito, Chifuz, Brequede, Atalde,[3]
    Let him be opened, flayed, and even slain.

[*They put hands on him.*]

I know what is this the race of dogs,
Captives of Spain, who flies?
Spaniards, who cannot these grave errors cure?
Spaniards, who not destroys the thief?
Spaniards, who other crimes commits?
Spaniards, in whose breast heaven influences

[3] Moorish exclamations in Arabic.

A spirit untamable, accelerated,
In preparation ever for good or ill,
One virtue in them duly have I marked down.
They keep their word without prevaricating;
And this my opinion, confirmation true
Two cavaliers from Portugal did give;
Don Francisco has assured me too,
That he who the name Meneses also hath
These same upon his word have been to Spain
Sent on a mission, which they did fulfil
Don Fernando de Ormaza eke
Went on his faith and word, and so has done.
A month before his term was finished,
So much he pays; so I rest satisfied,
Giving them liberty without interest.
I know that they my profit do augment,
That as they go upon their faith full pledged
I ask a treble ransom.
Bayran, come forth and call in immediately
A Christian of Izuf,
Would he obtained in his tranquillity
The means to see if my opinion is truth,
Of loss and gain this is the play.

BAYRAN. Sir, from well doing one may sure await
The reward, and if it fails in this low world
The recompense in heaven expands itself.

[*Enter* AURELIO.]

KING. Christian, I know thee who thou art,
Thy virtue, valour, lot,
And that thy country soon will see thee I know.
Is Silvia thy wife?

AURELIO. She is.

KING. Where were you going when in the treacherous waves
Comfort all you lost?

AURELIO. Please, I will tell you all in very truth.
Of another king and of other prisons too
Was I the slave.
Enamoured of this Silvia at one time
Went I to my own country, and the force
Of this war brought me to the state you find.
In this my end was gained. Thinking to go
To Milan, fate dragged me into this woe
Of slavery excessive which you see.

KING. Lose not thy confidence in this importunate
Life, for well thou knowest fortune is frail.
This moment will I to thee and Silvia

Thy liberty concede, if you agree
To pay my price. A thousand ducats must
I give for you two, and I also require
Two thousand more for you; upon your oaths
This sum advanced both may embark for Spain.

AURELIO. My lord, for so much grace what shall I give?
I promise to remit the sum in a month,
Though it be stolen or of heaven asked.

KING. Prepare yourselves forthwith,
And taking the first vessel bound for Spain,
Your liberty I give.

AURELIO. Heaven and earth do testify how much
Your generosity merits. Take my word
For pledge of ransom. I will lose my life,
But my word shall not fail. This virtue too
In my blood extraction good
Rakes up" and marks.

MOOR. Sir, a vessel appears.

KING. From what quarter?

MOOR. There is a round top on the vessel's mast.

KING. It should be a merchant ship.

MOOR. My lord, the merchandise doth promise good.

KING. Is it then alms for ransom?

MOOR. Certainly 'twill be.

KING. Let's go. Do thou, Aurelio, procure
Thy parting hence, and take thou charge of that
Which to me thou hast sworn.

AURELIO. May heaven augment thy fortune.
Thanks do I offer, heaven's eternal King,
Who, without merit of mine, permission grants,
That by the hand of him I mostly feared
So much good and such glory have accrued.

[*Enter* FRANCISCO, THE CAPTIVE, *and three others.*]

FRANCISCO. Good news, Aurelio dear, there is arrived
A vessel from Spain, as all men do allege
That alms it brings is certain, in which ship
Comes a Trinitarian friar Christian like,
To well-doing a friend, and recognised,
For heretofore upon this soil has he been,
Christians redeeming, and he example gave
Of Christianity and prudence blent.
Friar Don Gil is he styled.

AURELIO. Mark that he be not the Friar George
Of Olivares, and of the order
Of Mercy, who has here before been, one
Of no less virtue than intelligence.

So that since a bishop he is become,
Twenty thousand ducats of his own
Has he dispensed, and for six thousand more
He pledged stands. O breast of purity!
O charity extraordinary!

SAAVEDRA. O happy day! Companions, at the port
The ransom ready stands.
My remedy is sure, money they bring.

SEBASTIAN. No good I entertain, nor any hope,
Nor in my country can help me any one.

ANOTHER. I stoop not to despair.

FRANCISCO. God hath in His hands, brethren, a remedy;
Courage evince. He made us and will not
Let us decline into forgetfulness.
Let us entreat Him as a father; turn,
And to our Lady intercessor true,
His mother and our mother,
By whose holy intercession
Our welfare is assured, our strength and prop,
Our radiation and our remedy.

SAAVEDRA. Turn, virgin, holiest Mary, virgin, turn
The eyes which light and glory to heaven impart,
To those distressed who night and day bewail,
The earth bedewing with their tears of salt;
Succour us, blessed ever virgin pure,
Ere this our mortal and corporeal veil
Rests without soul within the concrete earth,
And be without th' accustomed sepulture.

SEBASTIAN. Virgin all blessed, who by th' eternal Sire
Wert chosen fruit to give to the human race,
Breaking through the door of gloomy hell,
And of the first sin took away the woe,
Revolve thy pitiful and tender face
Towards this deep misery, and to the penalty which
In this our sorrowful calm we here pass through,
For every day the soul in danger stands.

ANOTHER. Virgin, in thee, most sweetest Mary styled,
Betwixt man and his Maker mediatrix,
The sure and certain guide on seas of doubt.
Virgin all other virgins quite before,
In thee, virgin and mother, in thee puts trust
My soul, which thee without, nothing can hope.
With hands beneficent pray drag me out
From that well known as pagan slavery.

AURELIO. Holy Virgin, if I have deserved
Of thy mercy the intensity,
When I would show my depth of gratitude
By so much in the measure do I fail,

Receive my ardent wish which elevated
Above a Christian work such spring shall give
That I may reach, oblivious of this soil,
Th' upraised throne of the empyrean,
By so much do the time and point arrive
To put into effect my warm desire.
To the illustrious audience here joined,
In whom I so much good clearly discern,
If this resemblance is extracted ill
From life in Algiers and its manners foul,
Since my intention has been ingenuous,
In th' author's name humbly I pardon crave.

FINIS.

CPSIA information can be obtained at www.ICGtesting.com
Printed in the USA
BVOW08s1324260516

449681BV00001B/14/P